**His dark blue gaze**
**peering deep into**

"You remind me of someone."

"Hopefully in a good way."

"In an unexpected way." He rose and started toward her.

The ship shuddered again. He stumbled. She put an arm about his waist and attempted to ignore the sudden pulse of awareness that traveled up her arm. Men like him were never attracted to women like her. They had their pick of women and always chose the golden ones, not the mice, according to her old nurse. She had yet to see this disproved.

"Time to jump, Karn."

He gripped the side of the boat and retreated a step. "Maybe I should wait. Take off the trunks first."

"You don't like jumping?"

"Never fancied heights." A crooked smile played on his full lips, and his eyes assessed her form. "Tell you what—give me a kiss, Maer of the sea, and then I will."

Giving in to impulse, she angled her face, intending to brush his cheek with her lips, but he turned his head slightly and their mouths met.

The briefest of touches, but a jolt rocketed through Maer, making her knees tremble. It was as if it had gone beyond the mild flirtation and he could see all the way down to the hidden parts of her soul.

## Author Note

One of my favorite sagas, *Halfdan Eysteinsson*, inspired this story. In the saga that is probably as close to a modern romance as the Icelandic sagas get, Princess Ingigerd of Lagoda Town changes places with her namesake after her father's death and has many adventures but eventually has a happy ending. Rereading the saga recently, I wondered what could have really happened and if I could set a story on Islay, as it is one of my favorite places to visit. The result is *Secret Princess for the Warrior*, which is indeed partly set on Islay. The bay where the whiskey distillery Bunnahabhain sits was very much on my mind when I wrote this. Hopefully, you will enjoy the story of Karn and Maer as much as I enjoyed writing it.

As ever, thank you for reading my stories. If you'd like to get in touch, I love getting comments from readers and can be reached at michelle@michellestyles.co.uk or through my publisher or Facebook or X @michellelstyles.

# SECRET PRINCESS FOR THE WARRIOR

## MICHELLE STYLES

HISTORICAL

# Harlequin®
## HISTORICAL

ISBN-13: 978-1-335-54007-2

Secret Princess for the Warrior

Recycling programs for this product may not exist in your area.

Harlequin Enterprises ULC
22 Adelaide St. West, 41st Floor
Toronto, Ontario M5H 4E3, Canada
www.Harlequin.com

Printed in U.S.A.

Born and raised near San Francisco, California, **Michelle Styles** currently lives near Hadrian's Wall with her husband and a menagerie of pets in an Edwardian bungalow with a large and somewhat overgrown garden. An avid reader, she became hooked on historical romances after discovering Georgette Heyer, Anya Seton and Victoria Holt. Her website is michellestyles.co.uk and she's on X and Facebook.

### Books by Michelle Styles

### Harlequin Historical

*Taming His Viking Woman*
*Summer of the Viking*
*Sold to the Viking Warrior*
*The Warrior's Viking Bride*
*Sent as the Viking's Bride*
*A Viking Heir to Bind Them*
*Tempted by Her Forbidden Warrior*

### *Vows and Vikings*

*A Deal with Her Rebel Viking*
*Betrothed to the Enemy Viking*
*To Wed a Viking Warrior*

### *Sons of Sigurd*

*Conveniently Wed to the Viking*

Visit the Author Profile page
at Harlequin.com for more titles.

In loving memory of my mother-in-law,
Mary Cecilia Styles (1935–2024)

# Prologue

October 836, Royal Hall of Agthir
(Modern-day southwestern Norway)

Ingebord, the only child of the current king, hugged her knees to her chest and tried to ignore the sharp elbow in her side and the sounds of muffled sobs emanating from the girl hiding beside her as well as the more distant sounds of axes hitting wood, loud war cries and the frightened screams of women.

She screwed up her eyes. Her father had lost, just like her mother the queen predicted. Now all Agthir was going to face the dire consequences. Ingebord wasn't entirely sure what her mother meant, but she suspected it would be uncomfortable.

A lone howl made Ingebord stiffen.

'Oh, my stars,' she whispered. 'Tippi is out there, crying. I can't leave her. I simply must rescue her. I promised my papa to always look after her.'

Five months ago, she'd given her father her solemn vow that at nine, she was old enough to look after a puppy and train her properly. Tippi had been outside, investigating a leaf when Ingebord's nurse bundled her and her sobbing companion into the dark and airless recess behind her mother's bed. Now Tippi was in grave danger. Inge-bord knew it was her sworn duty to rescue that dog. Her mother would agree if she knew. Ingebord was certain of it.

She started to creep towards the entrance on her hands and knees.

'Ingebord, you must stay here. You know what Helga ordered,' her companion Svanna said, grabbing Ingebord's upper arm. Svanna was the orphaned daughter of one of her mother's closest friends, and therefore they were sup-posed to be special friends as well. At Maer's instigation, they had sealed the friendship with blood only a few short weeks ago 'You will get us both in trouble.'

Ingebord rolled her eyes. Svanna was too frightened to scream, and Helga was off tending the wounded. It was why Ingebord was stuck here with Svanna rather than waiting in the main hall like she'd told her mother she would do. 'My mother loves Tippi as well. She'd want me to do the right thing. Tippi is my special charge. I will return before Helga gets back. Promise. No one will ever know.'

Svanna made a disapproving noise in the back of her throat which resembled the sort Ingebord's mother often made. 'You are going to get us in trouble.'

Ingebord scrunched her nose. 'You can come if you want. Tippi likes you.'

Svanna shook her head, in a movement reminiscent of Ingebord's mother. There were times when Ingebord thought her mother would have preferred to have golden-haired Svanna as her daughter rather the mouse-haired girl she had. Helga, who was Svanna's distant relation, had commented several times on the matter.

'Your mother—' Svanna whispered as Tippi's howl rose again.

'You are my mother's pet. Always doing what she wants.

But this is about what my dog needs,' Ingebord said, knowing what was coming next. She didn't have time for a lecture from her companion and supposedly best friend for their entire lives. She had a terrified dog to save.

Svanna flinched as if she had slapped her. 'I want to do what is right. You should as well. And your mother... Well, I don't have one.'

Instant remorse passed through Ingebord. She patted Svanna's hand. 'I'm sorry. My tongue runs away with itself. Mother always says that.'

'The lady queen wants her daughter, her only child, to be safe.'

Another howl swiftly followed by a whimper. Tippi was moving closer. Ingebord crouched, getting ready to spring out.

'Tippi needs me, Svanna. She really does. You'll see. You will feel braver with her here with us.'

'Maybe,' Svanna admitted, hugging her knees into her chest.

'I'll be straight back. Promise.'

Svanna gave a hesitant nod. 'Go quickly if you must.'

Ingebord tumbled out of the hiding place with a distinct thump. The autumn sunshine blinded her after the darkness of the hidey-hole. Even though she could hear the distant shouts of the battle, the hall appeared unnaturally still when she tiptoed in. Spindle whorls lay where they'd been dropped. And the iron bowl of pottage bubbled above the dying fire.

Another of Tippi's whimpers made her stiffen. She turned to see a young warrior, crouching down trying to retrieve the dog from under a stool.

'Keep away. She is not your dog,' Ingebord said, kicking him in the right shin. 'Get out of here while you can.'

The warrior, who was probably only a few years older than she was, jumped back. A lock of blond hair fell over his deep blue eyes. He pushed it away with impatient fingers. 'Who are you?'

'Ingebord, the king's daughter, and that is my dog.' She snapped her fingers, and Tippi rushed forwards, evading the warrior. 'Now, go.'

'Your king is dead.'

'You had best take care no one finds you here,' she said, putting on her fiercest face. 'The tide of battle may yet turn.'

He looked like he might say more, but sounds of heavy footsteps caused him to scamper away.

Ingebord buried her nose into Tippi's soft fur, and the dog licked her face. 'We need to go, sweetie. I've got to keep you safe. And he lied. My father will return. He always wins. He promised.'

The little dog squirmed and wriggled, but Ingebord kept tight hold of her and started to make her way back to where Svanna hid.

'What are you doing here, Ingebord?' her mother's annoyed voice rang in her ears. Her mother often seemed irritated with her these days. Ingebord tried hard, but she failed to please her, unlike the way Svanna did. Svanna always managed to make her mother smile.

'Tippi was stuck,' Ingebord said, holding up the squirming puppy.

'Ingebord, why are you never where you are supposed to be?' her father's helmsman Halfr asked, coming to stand beside her mother. He sported fresh bruising on his face, and his eyes appeared tired.

Ingebord blinked rapidly, trying not to cry and dishonour her father. 'But I promised Papa I'd always look after her. She required my assistance.'

'Required your assistance?' Her mother pinched the bridge of her nose. 'The gods help me. Your notions, Ingebord, are sent to try me.'

'It is all right, my lady,' Halfr said with a nod. 'Easier this way.'

'Easier for whom?' her mother asked.

'For everyone.' Halfr hunkered down so that his face was level with Ingebord's. His tunic was torn and seemed to have several blood stains. Ingebord took a step backwards, clutching Tippi to her chest.

'You trust me, don't you, Ingebord? Your papa trusted me.'

He reached out and stroked Tippi's ears. 'Tippi trusts me.'

Ingebord loosened her grip on Tippi and gave a hesitant nod. Halfr always had a treat for Tippi. 'Uncle Halfr, will you take me to my papa?'

The two grown-ups exchanged a look.

'You know what we discussed, my lady. Our only hope, her only hope,' Halfr said. 'Agthir's future.'

Her mother held out her arms. 'Give the dog to me, Ingebord. You must go with Halfr. I will look after her for you until…until you return. It is what your papa wants.'

Both adults' faces were resolute and determined. Ingebord wished her father was there but decided that crossing her mother on this was a poor idea. She placed a kiss on Tippi's nose. The dog licked her hand as if she knew Ingebord was required elsewhere. 'I won't be long, Tippi. Promise I'll return. It's just that little dogs can get lost on battlefields.'

Her mother's throat worked up and down, but no sound came out.

'And Svanna?' Ingebord said, remembering her promise

to her friend. 'Her mama is dead, and she never knew her papa. She is in our special hiding place. Should I fetch her?'

'The time to go is now, my lady.'

Ingebord fancied a tear gleamed in her mother's eye. 'Yes, yes, I will look after her. Best as I can. But you keep with Halfr the Bold, now.'

The battle cries crept closer, and the sound of axes splintering wood echoed in Ingebord's ears. Her mother wrapped her in a fierce embrace before she tore Tippi from Ingebord's arms.

'Ingebord, you do exactly what Halfr says. You go where he says. You answer to the name he gives you. Can you do this for me? For your dear dead papa?'

Ingebord wrapped her arms about her middle and tried not to stare at the squirming dog. Questions circled around her brain. That young warrior had told the truth? Her father was dead? How could that be? She'd seen him yesterday evening, so full of life, so certain that it was a little storm and her mother worried about nothing.

'Mother? Is my father...' Somehow the word stuck in her throat. 'Will I see Papa again?'

'My lady, we must go if I am to have any hope of saving the child.'

'Ingebord, give me your solemn word.' Her mother balanced Tippi in her arms. 'On Tippi's life, obey Halfr.'

Tears streamed down Ingebord's face. 'I will, Mother. I promise.'

Her mother touched her neck where she wore the amber globe pendant that she'd acquired last name day, the one which matched her eyes. 'As we discussed, then, Halfr. You know what to look for should any claim to come in my name...if the worst should happen.'

With that her mother and Tippi were gone. Halfr threw

Ingebord over his shoulder. 'I will look after you, Inge-bord, but none of your tricks. Keep quiet, hang on, and do as I say.'

She griped Halfr's tunic tight as he started to run.

'I promise,' she whispered.

# Chapter One

*Ten years later, September 846,*
*off the coast of Jura (part of the collapsing Dal Riada con-*
*federacy, in modern Inner Hebrides, Scotland, a waterway*
*officially classified as unnavigable by the Royal Navy)*

Instead of blowing itself out after a short fierce spate as
the other squalls had done in recent days, this storm with
its cold lashing rain and fierce winds only increased in intensity as the ship rounded the tip of Jura. The waves began
to wash over the prow of the boat as the boat suddenly appeared to have developed a mind of its own, being pulled
along by some great invisible force and not responding to
Karn Thorfison's hand on the tiller.

Karn tried to concentrate on navigating correctly, rather
than not just reacting and going over in his mind about what
had led him to this dire predicament, but the memories refused to be silenced.

Three warring seasons ago, life had taught him the folly
of acting on impulse when his dearest friend and mentor
had been killed trying to protect him from his own foolish
errors. With his dying breaths, the old warrior had pressed
Karn's late mother's lucky pendant into Karn's hand, telling him to become worthy of it. Filled with remorse, Karn

had striven to become truly skilled, a warrior worthy of his late friend and indeed one who his father, the king of Agthir, and his late mother, a noted warrior in her own right, would have been proud of. However, his father refused to acknowledge that effort or indeed the steps he'd undertaken to ensure the kingdom's safety.

After his father made several coded remarks about Karn's frivolity and lack of purpose during a feast to honour his father's current chief advisor, the one whom Karn considered all mouth and no sword, Karn decided to confront his father in the morning and ask what more he needed to do. However, right before the skald began his father's saga, the one which told of Halfr the wicked magician and the golden-haired princess who caused Thorfi to spare her mother, the advisor remarked loudly that Prince Karn required a woman like the current queen's daughter as his wife to ensure the wisdom and caution necessary to rule Agthir.

His father had clapped his hands. 'What a splendid idea. Prince Karn and Ingebord must marry as soon as it can be arranged. It will do my old bones good to know that the next king of Agthir has such a sensible consort.'

'Never will I marry the queen's daughter, Father!' Karn shouted, trying to control the white-hot anger coursing in his veins. 'Go ahead, declare me a *dauthamathr* or a wolf's head to be slaughtered on sight.' He took a breath. 'I've lost count on the number of times you have threatened me with it over some misdemeanour. Why will you not admit that I am a worthy warrior in my own right?'

His men began to chant his name and the many victories they'd won in the last two warring seasons, victories his father liked to take credit for.

Karn stood, shoulders back, thumbs hooked in his belt,

waiting for his father to mumble something placatory and back down like he had done in the past, when the chanting died down.

One whispered conference with his advisor later and with a contorted face, Karn's father screamed out, 'Not only you are a *dauthamathr* who no longer has any claim to the title *prince* but all of those who follow you and their families, if they are found within my borders by sunrise!'

His father stomped away, leaning heavily on his advisor's arm.

In the shocked silence, Karn silently vowed that even if his father currently thought little of him, one day the older man would be forced to admit his grave error.

'Prince—I mean Lord Karn, we must go. We will require many ships if we are to remove our families before the sun rises,' his helmsman said, grabbing his arm and shaking him.

The import of what had happened seeped in. His men had played no part in the final quarrel except to protest that he was capable.

'I never thought my father would issue that decree!' He drew his sword and raised it above his head. 'Return, Father! Face me and explain why my men and their families deserve a traitor's death?'

The silence echoed, telling him that he'd inadvertently condemned to death people whose only crime was to believe in him. The knowledge that he'd had shown that he was unworthy, just like his father's advisor had predicted, penetrated the red mist of his temper, and he lowered his sword.

'A way to ensure their safety exists,' the queen of Agthir, his father's current wife said, beckoning him to come and stand beside her and her gold-haired daughter at the high table. Both faces were white-lipped and pinched as if neither could quite believe what had just happened.

'I won't marry your daughter.'

'Why do you think so little of me and my daughter? Shall we speak, or will you see the blood of your men's families spilt?'

Shrugging off his helmsman's restraining hand, he'd gone to her, even though he didn't fully trust her. He bowed low. 'My lady, I meant no disrespect to you or your daughter, but we would not suit. Not now. Not ever. She is like an annoying sister to me.'

'If you will do me this one favour, I will see that your men's families survive. I will bring them under my protection until Jultide,' she said with that cool smile of hers as she placed a pendant she'd been wearing in his hand. 'Find Halfr the Bold under whatever rock he currently hides and convince him to return with the object which he stole.'

'How will I know if he gives me the correct item?'

'Halfr will return what he took once he sees this,' the queen confidently predicted holding out the amber sphere pendant. 'He may be reluctant, but use your considerable powers of persuasion and he will come.'

Karn eyed the pendant cautiously. 'Why are you willing to do this?'

'I've always hated the unnecessary shedding of lives. Will you accept my terms, or will you continue to be pigheaded?'

'How easy will it be for you to escape with that many people?' her daughter asked in her sing-song voice. 'Think, Karny, for one single solitary time.'

He glanced at his men's tense faces and knew he had little choice but to trust these two women, even if he loathed Ingebord's new nickname for him.

Thus, to save the families' lives, he'd given his word that he would find this former helmsman of the queen's first husband, one Halfr Hammdrson, and retrieve the object he'd stolen from her.

She'd kept her word about providing a ship, an old hulk, away from prying eyes, sending her daughter to see them off while she attempted to usher the families to safety.

'One itsy-bitsy clue, Karny, from me—go west and make certain the half-moon shines in Halfr's face before you ask him anything.' She glanced over her shoulder. 'Hurry! The sun begins to rise, and they are coming. Go now or die on this shore.'

She scampered off, before he could ask what her so-called clue meant. But he, too, spied the advisor's men massing. He leapt aboard the barely seaworthy ship and shouted for his men to put their backs into it as the first arrows rained down.

His men required no further urging, moving faster than he'd ever seen them do to launch that boat.

'The hardest part is over,' he declared when they reached the open sea, trying to improve morale after the brief fight. 'How easy can it be for a notorious man like Halfr to hide?'

How wrong he'd been. The quest was far more difficult than he'd imagined, with days and then weeks slipping past. Halfr had become a ghost legend and a whispered rumour from years past. Karn kept heading ever westwards until he reached Dubh Linn.

Two nights ago, an elderly man well into his cups confided that he'd seen Halfr casting his runes on the far side of Islay. It was enough for Karn, and he'd readied the boat for the journey, discounting the jokes about the fabled whirlpool which guarded Halfr.

A loud crack shook the boat from bow to stern, bringing him back to the present.

'Lord Karn!' one of his men screamed. 'What should we do? The mast is nearly split in two. And that roaring noise sounds like we are about to enter the jaws of Hell.'

'We will get through, men!' Karn tightened his jaw and braced his legs against the bench in front of him. He knew in his heart the truth: if the longship went any closer to tumult, they would be swept in and unlikely to emerge.

'How?'

'Brace the mast. Row like Fenrir the Wolf slobbers at our heels,' he yelled, gesturing to the nearest man to help him move the tiller.

Despite their combined strength, the tiller barely budged. The whirlpool was not just a tale told to frighten the gullible but real.

Ignoring the clenching panic in his stomach, he redoubled his efforts, all the muscles and sinews in his arms straining. Suddenly the tiller moved. He and his helmsman exchanged relieved glances.

Rather than responding instantly, the longship moved sluggishly.

'Same again.'

The ship shuddered. He knew the rudder had broken. They were not going to be able to turn away from the whirlpool.

The boat started to move towards the centre of maelstrom. He had visions of circling around and around, never escaping. One option remained: rowing with all their might on the starboard to break free of the current. Up and over.

'Put your back into the starboard oars if you wish to see tomorrow,' he shouted above the storm and hoped his hunch was the correct one. 'We go over the waves and skirt around the other side. We will prevail.'

'But—' one of his men cried, his face becoming creased with sheer terror.

'Don't think, do. Over the waves like a duck, not into the current.'

The wind whipped the words from his mouth, rendering them next to useless, but the man appeared to take comfort in them and redoubled his efforts. All his men did. Despite everything they had endured in the last few weeks, they retained a misplaced belief in his skill and that he'd see them right like he'd done more than a dozen times before. And he now couldn't explain to these loyal men that they were wrong to believe in him so earnestly and that this time failure was a near certainty.

He slammed his hand down, knocking the rudder sideways, and the boat began to do what he wished.

He straightened, hardly daring to believe it: a slim chance for escape existed.

'Keep putting your backs in, lads,' he called. 'We will beat the whirlpool yet.'

His men chanted his name, pulling in unison.

A heavy blow glanced his temple. He blinked five times and wiped the blood from the side of his face. The mast had gone, but they were clear of the whirlpool. His luck held.

'We make landfall where we can on Islay. We will find Halfr the Bold,' he shouted, pulling harder on his oar. 'We will recover that which the queen lost. We will complete the quest. We will give your families life and a better future.'

Maer, formerly Ingebord of Agthir, stood outside the small hall where she now lived with her adopted uncle on Islay and breathed deeply, enjoying the peace and the warm sun which came after last night's dreadful storm. The sunlight twinkled on the protected inlet and lit up the heather-covered paps of Jura just across the strait.

The day promised to be a good one or rather one without adventure or misfortune. Even after four years of living on this peaceful island and a little over a decade since she left Agthir burning behind her, Maer never took that calm for granted. Since her uncle, the former Halfr Hammdrson, cut the arm ring from her father's corpse and then carried it and her to the fishing boat, she had spent most of the decade living in terror and fear.

At first, she'd never been completely sure if her uncle would carry out his threat to abandon her at the nearest port if she continued to cry, but she'd learned if she kept quiet, didn't ask too many questions and worked hard at perfecting her fighting skills, he kept her with him, rather than depositing her with some horrible woman who beat her like he did the first time. To be fair to her uncle, once he'd discovered what the woman had done to Maer, he ensured her punishment.

'Quite the storm last night,' said one of the Gaels who farmed the fields on the far side of the harbour interrupting her morning thoughts. 'My wife barely slept a wink. She sent me over here to ensure your well-being, seeing how your uncle is away on business. You always have a place at our table, she says.'

Maer gave a little smile. Sweet of them. She knew his wife hoped she'd make a match with their eldest son, but Maer had no interest in him or spending a lifetime milking cows and tending sheep. Instead, she hoped the lad would actively court the farmer's daughter from the next valley over who sighed after him, his green eyes and his strong shoulders.

The sour taste of her failed romance with a Northern warrior as they travelled from Constantinople remained in her mouth. She'd thought he was the one and had exchanged stolen kisses with him, despite her uncle's comments about his lack of steadfastness. The man who promised to adore her for always had abandoned her for an Irish king's daughter just as her uncle had predicted. Thankfully she had not completely melted in his arms and given him her body like he'd urged.

'I will bear that in mind.'

'A ship perished,' another said, pointing towards bits of wood and rope that lined the high-water mark.

'May St Columba preserve their souls.'

'If we see anyone in trouble, we assist them. Enemies can become friends with the right sort of persuasion,' Maer said, scanning the horizon for any ship which might be in trouble. All the little rituals to ensure survival. She'd come a long way from the little girl who wanted to save her puppy, instead of listening to grown-ups. 'I gave my promise to my uncle. Sanctuary to seafarers in trouble regardless of where they come from, even the Black Pool. *A life debt owed can save your life in times of trouble* is not a meaningless saying but something I know for the absolute truth.'

'I sleep easier when I know your uncle's sword arm is here,' the first farmer said. 'We've had no trouble from the Black Pool once the rumours of it reached the right ears.'

Despite his age and now snow-white hair, her uncle remained a formidable warrior, able to dispatch the twelve bands of assassins King Thorfi had sent after him in the first three years of their travels.

Thieves were up to five men, a band was up to twenty and anything larger was an army, her uncle had said, cleaning his sword after the last band had tried and failed to kill him. Maer predicted that it would add to his legend, and he'd laughed. Taking his good mood as a sign, she'd wondered out loud if King Thorfi suspected that she had escaped.

'Why would he, when your mother swore that golden-haired friend of yours was her one and true daughter?'

Her uncle wiped away the single tear which slipped down her cheek and told her in his gentlest voice that she was safe, which was what her mother desired. Maer nodded and pretended to believe him, even if her mother's betrayal gnawed at her insides, particularly at night.

Sometimes she dreamt of returning in triumph, a warrior in her own right with her father's arm ring, the traditional symbol of Agthir's royal house, the one her uncle kept hidden away in a trunk, gleaming in the sunshine on her right arm. Other nights, she dreamt about creeping in and freeing her mother and Svanna from a dreadful fate, while her mother clasped her to her bosom and proclaimed she'd made a dreadful error of judgement.

Always she'd wake to the same reality: a small bed, abandoned and unloved by everyone except for her adopted uncle. But it didn't stop her dreaming.

'When will your uncle return, Maer?'

'He needed to confer with the kings of Islay about the danger from the Northmen,' she said, keeping her tone measured. 'He thinks they are too complacent, too willing to fight amongst themselves. The Northmen from Black Pool say they want to trade, but they conduct raids where a king appears weak or a country divided. The Northern way rarely varies. Protection through strength.'

'The kings prefer to fight themselves and forget about the ordinary man's troubles,' the farmer said with a sigh.

The other men nodded in agreement.

Maer kept her face impassive. Even if the kings failed to care, she understood the threat from the North. As a child both in Agthir and on the journey to Constantinople, she'd witnessed what could happen when power-hungry kings were denied. 'Even still, I wonder which North dragonship was unfortunate enough to cause this flotsam.'

'Is that a boat on the rocks?' the first farmer said pointing to a shape just before the horizon. 'Or has one of the ships your uncle sank risen in the storm? I don't understand why someone would want to narrow the harbour in the first place, but that is probably why I am a farmer, and your uncle is the one consorting with kings.'

Maer shaded her eyes. The outline of a hull, stuck on one of the large rocks which guarded the harbour, was just visible in the slight morning haze. Just after they had arrived, her uncle had various broken boats sunk between the rocks, dramatically narrowing the harbour and ensuring the harbour was harder to attack—a trick he claimed would have saved her father from Thorfi's warriors. But those ships would not rise after a storm, even as fierce a storm as the last one was.

'From the looks of it, the rocks have claimed another ship,' the second farmer said.

'Break out the boats,' she cried racing to the shore. 'We may yet find people alive.'

The largest coracle was launched in a matter of heartbeats. Willow-framed with leather-covered hulls, coracles appeared far flimsier than the dragonships of her childhood, but they were perfect for the tricky waters in and around Jura and Islay. Lighter and nimbler, they rode over the waves, rather than ploughing through them.

'Hold on, we are coming,' she called in Gaelic, straining to hear any sign of life.

Faint cries in a Northern tongue came from the stricken vessel which appeared to be wedged tight between the larger of the two rocks which stood at the entrance to the natural harbour. *Dragon's teeth* her uncle had called them when they first arrived here and predicted that they would prove a blessing if the Northmen ever attempted to raid the settlement.

As the coracle neared the stricken vessel, Maer clearly saw it was a dragonship, one used by Northmen for long-distance raiding, rather than a simple merchant's vessel used for trading.

Her stomach flip-flopped. The stylised roaring-dragon pattern on the prow reminded her of the ships King Thorfi had used when he invaded her father's kingdom. She wished she could see the sail to be certain, but the mast appeared to have vanished. She silently prayed to any god, angel or saint who might be listening that she was wrong and that these warriors had no designs on her uncle. Over the years following her uncle dispatching the last of the assassins, she learned to listen quietly for any rumours about Agthir, hoping to glean something which meant her mother missed her. It never came.

'Enemies to friends,' she muttered, pushing all thoughts of her mother away. 'Enemies to friends. And breathe. Never allow them to smell your fear.'

When her uncle first taught her this in the fishing boat with Agthir's coastline disappearing behind them, she asked her uncle if that meant friends could become enemies, but he'd told her not to dwell on the possibility and focus on providing friendship. She wanted to keep that advice in the forefront of her actions as she directed her first rescue operation without him. These men were *in* danger and not *a* danger, as her uncle would say. It made all the difference, and her giving in to fears best left to nighttime dreams would not alter that simple fact.

'What should we do, my lady?' One of the farmers stuck a finger in the air, testing the wind.

'We follow my uncle's instructions. We rescue them,' Maer replied. 'Few Northern warriors fail to honour life debts.'

'Please help us,' a man called out in Norse and then re-peated the phrase in heavily accented Gaelic. 'Our ship is wedged fast. We come in peace. Can you tow us off the rock so that we might be on our way?'

'Not only stuck but hulled beneath the waterline. You stay onboard and you will drown when the tide next rises.' She held up her hands to show how big the hole was. 'You must abandon ship. We are here to help.'

'My men can't swim, but they will fight all who seek to board this ship.'

'We come to save lives, not take them,' Maer replied, keeping tight hold of her temper. Just because some might rob or plunder wrecks, it didn't mean everyone did. 'If I just come aboard and see your injuries, will that suit?'

'Then, the gods do listen after a fashion,' the man with a deep gash on his forehead called. 'My men first. They are a long way from home.'

'Yes, the North lands are far from here,' she said. 'But ships do travel there. I am sure you can find passage on one in due course. I am coming aboard now.'

She hastily vaulted onto the vessel while the others held the coracle next to the ship. The crew of seven Northmen appeared to be in varying states of injury. A band, not an army. Three had complicated injuries. One had received a head wound while the remaining three appeared to be suffering from a range of cuts and bruises. The one with the head wound was clearly the leader. The fineness of his cloak and the amount of gold he wore proclaimed it. A faint smile played on his full lips as if he knew she stared at him for a little bit longer than she should. Maer hastily averted her eyes.

'Why are you here?' She winced, hating the breathlessness of her voice.

'We mean no harm,' the leader said, bowing his golden-haired head. 'Our boat floundered in the storm after we managed to get clear of the great whirlpool. The rudder and mast were destroyed.'

'Floundered?' Maer stared at him in astonishment. What sort of person risked a boat like this on the Great Whirlpool in a storm? What sort of person lived to tell the tale? He had to be bending the truth. 'A lucky escape. The three Nourns of fate have decreed your life threads are longer.'

'The Nourns had nothing to do with it,' one of the other men said. 'Lord Karn, here, navigated around the whirlpool, forcing it to spit us out. Karn the Lucky he must now be called.'

Maer blinked. 'Impossible.'

'Nothing is impossible to Lord Karn. The gods favour him. Born on a lucky day.'

'The Nourns have an odd sense of humour,' the leader, Lord Karn, said giving his men a stern look which appeared to subdue them. 'I'm uncertain how we managed to get away from its clutches. Nothing to do with my being born on a lucky day, and no skald will be singing after a feast about it.' He frowned and then gave a smile which was more like a grimace. 'We came in peace and have no wish to bring harm to this place wherever this is. Will it be possible to tow us off the rocks now? My ship must be saved.'

'Do you understand what *hulled under the waterline*

means? Off this rock, the boat sinks. It will go no farther,'
Maer said, gently as she could. It was obvious the man had
taken a blow to the head and suffered from unclear thinking. She could remember when it had happened to her uncle
after the fourth would-be assassin and how he'd raved for a
week. But finally, he'd held out his hand and said how glad
he was that she'd stayed with him.

'There must be a way to save this ship.' He put his hands
to his head. 'I've a promise to keep.'

'A promise like that is not one which is worth taking
the spit to give. You can look after a ship well, but the sea
decides which ships it claims.'

Lord Karn cursed softly. 'The need remains. The promise must be kept before Jul begins. Innocent lives depend
on us finding the man we seek.'

'A long way from Agthir to here,' she said, making her
voice brisk and matter-of-fact, rather than giving in to the
panic which clawed her throat. The leader couldn't be seeking her uncle, not after all this time. 'You will owe us a life
debt once this is done. Even the men from Agthir do not
attack those they owe life debts to.'

His deep as a summer's midnight in the North blue
eyes became narrow slits. 'How do you know we are from
Agthir?'

'Agthir's devices are very distinctive,' she said attempting a reasonable tone, even though her heart thudded in
her ears, making it difficult to think. For many years, her
uncle had made her recite the sort of devices and patterns
on the sails the men of Agthir used so that she would not
be caught unawares. 'My uncle had business dealings there
many years ago.'

His dark gaze bored into her soul. 'But not too recently,
I think.'

'Why?' she asked clasping a hand to the back of her neck.

'This ship has not been used for many years. A decade most likely.' The other men on the boat murmured in agreement. He motioned for them to be quiet. 'Happenstance we came across it in our time of need. A gift from the queen, you might say.'

'Funny sort of a gift.' Maer forced her voice to sound light while inwardly she kicked herself. Old devices, devices only someone who had been away a long time might know. And the queen, her mother, had provided it. Why after all these years?

His lips curved upwards. 'When one requires a ship, one seldom asks too many questions. Is there something about this ship that your uncle mentioned?'

Maer's stomach knotted, tighter than it had in years. The truth needed to stay hidden deep down inside her. She couldn't risk blurting it out to a stranger, particularly not one like Karn who was intimately connected to Agthir and the man who wanted her dead. 'You would have to ask him, but he retired from being a merchant a few years back. It must be over a decade since he was in Agthir.'

His long lashes fluttered shut. 'I would like to meet your uncle. Does he wait on the shore?'

The words were said a half-slur.

'Away at present. No idea when he'll return. Probably after you are safely on your way.' She hated the way the sweat poured from her. How to lie by telling a version of the truth? 'Before, however, we get you to safety.'

His eyes snapped open. 'My men before me. Always. First on. Last off.'

'Let's take the worst off first. I will stay here and tend to the wounded.' She gestured to her men to start the operation. 'You are with friends, Lord Karn. You can leave your men in safety.'

'You are very forthright about my injuries, my lady, but I will be the last one off.'

'Part of my charm,' she said, with a gritted-tooth smile. *Ladylike* was nothing she'd been able to achieve. She never had been able to be ladylike. Her mother used to sigh about it and say how she wished Maer was more like Svanna—deft at needlework, docile and demure. Maer had tried but she had never quite managed the knack of being deft, docile and demure. Luckily her uncle failed to care, claiming being a lady was overrated. 'Although few would say it as a compliment.'

'From me, a compliment of the highest order, if you will accept it with one of your smiles.' His warm voice slid over her like soft fur, the sort of voice a man uses when he flirts.

She pointedly ignored him and concentrated on ensuring the safe transfer of the wounded. Flirtations seldom ended well in her experience.

The pair who were most severely injured went into the coracle without too much trouble, but there was no more space. Maer pushed the craft off and told them to hurry as the tide was starting to come in and the wind was beginning to build, pushing her gown against her meagre curves.

His full lips turned upwards at the sight. It bothered her that she noticed their curve, how long his lashes were, and the spun gold with a hint of red which was his hair. Far too handsome to be a warrior of repute, she thought. Battle-hardened warriors like her uncle always were a web of interconnecting scars. He was most likely the spoilt son of some warlord, given everything on a plate, never having to work hard for anything, gliding through life rather than fighting for every toehold like she and her uncle did. Not a man she should admire.

'The lovely rescuer waits with us. No need to fear that we will be left stranded, then.'

She frowned. The term *lovely* failed to apply to her. She had the hair of a mouse and a sharp nose, and her figure was far too angular. *Lovely* described women like the Irish princess with deep chestnut hair, emerald eyes and dark red lips, or her mother who had raven-black hair and unblemished translucent pearl skin, or Svanna who now bore Maer's old name of Ingebord. That Ingebord looked the very essence of a king's daughter with clear blue eyes, golden hair and a smile which always charmed. Rumour said that Svanna's smile stayed King Thorfi's sword, allowing both Svanna and her mother to live.

Her uncle always cautioned against too much faith in rumours as they only told part of the truth, but she suspected that one to be true as she'd heard it enough times in the now-popular saga about Thorfi and his rise to become king.

'Where did you travel from?' she asked to get the conversation onto safe shoals and away from memories which haunted her dreams even ten years after the events.

His eyes slid away from her. 'Does where I'm from matter as much as where I am going? The past should remain in the unlamented past.'

Someone with secrets, then. Secrets she suspected she needed to discover to keep her uncle and her safe. 'Where were you going in such a hurry, then?'

He gave a smile which seemed designed to take in all her form. A true flirt, the sort who steal unwary women's hearts and give nothing in return. Her uncle's warning about such men after her heartbreak echoed in her brain.

'Tell me your name first. Your full name.' His smooth voice rippled over her skin again.

'Maer. My father died years ago, and so you have no need of his name. I suspect I'm one of the few who remember him,' she said, swallowing hard and trying to bid the off-balance feeling to go. She wasn't sure if it was the design on the prow or the way his eyes appeared to bore deep into her soul which had unsettled her more.

'Maer in my country means *the woman who comes from the sea*. Appropriate for one such as you.'

He obviously was trying to ingratiate himself with comments a foolish woman might take to heart. Maer breathed deeply, and some measure of calm returned.

'I live with my uncle in this place.' She gestured to the harbour behind her and willed the men in the coracle to hurry. The water was already lapping at the board below the hole.

'Does your uncle have a name?'

'Sigmund Sigmundson,' Maer said giving the name her uncle currently used. The name Halfr Hammdrson, Halfr the Bold as her parents used to call him, had not crossed her lips since they left the smouldering ruins of Agthir behind.

His brow furrowed as if he'd heard the name before. However, as her uncle explained to her when he chose it, it was a common enough name.

'Sigmund Sigmundson from Agthir? I wonder if we have any friends in common.'

Sweat pooled at the base of Maer's neck. She hadn't said anything untoward. 'News from the North, even from Agthir, always interests him.'

A small stretching of the truth and the leaving out of important information, but as far as explanations went, it was close enough to the truth to serve for now. It wasn't as if he required an explanation about how they escaped from the warriors who hunted them and how the new king of Agthir would not sleep easily if he knew his old rival's actual heir lived and breathed freely instead of residing in his hall as his current queen's daughter.

'Karn is my name,' he said into the silence. 'As my father no longer wishes to claim me as I refuse to bend to his latest whims, I no longer have any claim on him.'

Karn. The prince of Agthir? King Thorfi's son with the warrior woman her uncle held in such regard? He had often invoked her name, particularly when Maer said that she couldn't do something because she was a girl. Her uncle would also say that it was a tragedy for both countries when she died because the fragile alliance fell apart and ultimately led to her father's ill-conceived invasion to reclaim land.

Her nerves jangled afresh, but she forced her breathing to steady. There were many Karns in this world, even if he had seemed interested when she mentioned Agthir. Acting like a scared rabbit served no one. Wasn't that what her uncle kept telling her? The night terrors of her childhood were just that: ghosts who vanished when the sun rose.

'Keeping the past in the past is fine by me as long as you do not seek to bring any harm to this place,' she said.

He closed his eyes. His lashes made dark smudges against the paleness of his skin. 'No, I don't seek to bring any harm. I wish to fulfil my quest and then live the remainder of my life in peace—a free man tending his garden.'

A feeble laugh escaped her lips. He sounded like she had back in Dubh Linn when she'd been certain her life was over because that warrior had married the perfect Irish princess and all of his honeyed words about loving her until the end of time were meaningless. 'Don't we all?'

His hand caught her sleeve. 'What war have you seen, Maer?'

She removed the fingers one by one. He didn't need to know about the battles she'd witnessed or the number of warriors' eyes she'd closed in the years since she left Agthir. 'Allow me to attend to your men instead of speaking about a past which has no meaning.'

His dark blue gaze examined her face. 'We speak again, Maer.'

Rather than thinking on Karn's mysterious quest or the way his smile appeared especially designed for her, Maer made herself busy tending to the wounds of the others and trying not to notice that Karn's eyes appeared to follow her. Finally, after she finished binding the wounds, she glanced back. He had closed his eyes and appeared to be asleep in the morning sun.

Guessing his insistence on remaining on the ship until all his men were rescued would be unaltered, she let him sleep and helped the others off the stricken ship. She watched the boat land and then start to head back for the final journey.

The ship shifted and shuddered under her feet, ending the conversation. The tide had turned, and the ship with it.

The water started lapping higher, and she knew the ship wouldn't last, but she made sure the ropes were fastened to the rocks so if it did float off, they could possibly salvage something.

'Time to go, Karn,' she said. She shook his shoulder when the Northman didn't move or answer her. 'The tide is coming in.'

His eyes blinked open, and he glanced about him as if he wasn't quite sure where he was. 'Go where?'

'To my uncle's hall. You and your men can heal in safety.'

He raised a hand to his head. 'Safe? My men?'

'They will not thank me if I allow you to perish.' She crossed her arms. 'Once you are on shore, we will try to salvage what we can at low tide.'

His searching stare caught and held hers, peering deep into her soul.

'You remind me of someone.'

'Hopefully in a good way.'

'In an unexpected way.' He rose and started towards her.

The ship shuddered again. He stumbled. She put an arm about his waist and attempted to ignore the sudden pulse of awareness which travelled up her arm. Men like him were never attracted to women like her. They had their pick of women and always chose the golden ones and not the mice, according to her old nurse. She had yet to see this disproven.

'Time to jump, Karn.'

He gripped the side of the boat and retreated a step. 'Maybe I should wait. Take off the trunks first.'

'You don't like jumping?'

'Never fancied heights.' A crooked smile played on his full lips, and his eyes assessed her form. 'Tell you what. Give me a kiss, Maer of the sea, and then I will.'

Giving into impulse she angled her face, intending to brush his cheek with her lips, but he turned his head slightly, and their mouths met.

The briefest of touches, but a jolt rocketed through Maer, making her knees tremble. It was as if it had gone beyond the mild flirtation, and he could see all the way down to the hidden parts of her soul.

'Given because I can't be bothered to argue.' She put her hand firmly on his chest and pushed. 'Now, jump. Boat, not sea.'

He did as she commanded and landed on the coracle,

making it rock. He then looked up at her with mocking eyes. 'Are you coming?'

The ship shifted violently in the incoming tide, and she tumbled into the ice-cold sea. Her men unceremoniously hauled her into the coracle. She lay there like a beached whale, displaying far more leg than was strictly proper. She rapidly sat up and smoothed her skirts down.

'The kiss was for luck?' he enquired softly, bringing his hand to her cheek after the coracle started moving swiftly to shore. 'Mine or yours?'

'The coracle is headed for the shore,' she replied and made a show of wringing out her braid.

His hand dropped down to his side. 'No answer.'

'The only way to get you off that ship,' she said and injected a note of exasperation in her voice. Her heart racing had everything to do with the ducking in cold water and nothing to do with his mouth moving over hers. 'Saved your life. One day, be sure to thank me.'

He put a hand on her shoulder. 'Thank you. From the bottom of my heart for the rescue and the kiss.'

'I would have done the same for any,' she said, knowing her words were a loose version of the truth.

# Chapter Two

The afternoon sunlight filtered into the barn which had seen more prosperous days. The combined scent of old straw and even older sheep filled Karn's nostrils, a welcome change from the salty tang of the sea and the terror of nearly having his ship sucked into the whirlpool. But it also meant his quest had hit another hurdle. He'd lost almost everything including that most precious commodity, time. Jul was another day closer.

Karn rested his aching head against his knees and tried to think of something other than the mysterious Maer's mouth and the way it had felt so right against his. The kiss had been a throwaway request, something to ease his tension at having to jump into the sea. He'd expected her to refuse with a deep blush. And when she hadn't, he took advantage of her slight hesitation. He had wanted to deepen that kiss in a way he had not done for a long time. It bothered him that he kept turning it over in his mind, rather than concentrating on the more important problem of fulfilling his quest in the time Queen Astrid had stipulated. She and Ingebord had both warned of consequences if he failed to return before the start of Jul.

Each day of delay meant the prospect of failure loomed larger. He knew that, and his men must have guessed it.

But he wanted to do right by them and to fulfil his promise to the queen and ensure their families' safety. Giving up simply because the task appeared impossible was alien to his nature. His mother had never done that and neither, while she lived, had his father.

Light filtered into the hut from the open door, highlighting Maer and her nut-brown hair, slender curves and her long fingers. Something about the way she moved commanded his attention. He studied the sweep of her long neck and tried to figure out where he knew her from. *Nowhere* was the logical answer, but that air of familiarity intrigued him.

'Treat her with respect,' he called out when one of his men appeared to grab her wrist. He dampened down the sudden surge of jealousy. Maer did not belong to him, he reminded himself.

'I'm perfectly capable of using my voice if someone irritates me,' she said, putting a hand on her hip. 'Your man objected to the salve the good father sent. Can you please tell them that we want their wounds to heal and not fester?'

Karn glared at the man who meekly held out his arm, wincing as he did it. 'If one of my men fails to give you the respect required, I will ensure he is properly disciplined. All assistance is to be gratefully received, men. We owe Maer a life debt.'

She rolled her eyes. 'We're not aboard your ship.'

Karn glanced at each of his men in turn. 'But they remain members of my felag. Abusing hospitality offends the gods. I try to avoid it.'

'This from King Thorfi's only child?' she asked softly.

Karn rested his head on his hands and tried not think of his late mentor gazing sorrowfully down at the mess Karn had made of his life. 'My parentage plays no part in my future. My mother is long dead, and my father has disowned me.'

Her knuckles shone white against the bowl she carried. 'Then, you don't deny it.'

'My father may have declared me a *dauthamathr*, a wolf's head, Maer, not because I abused another's hospitality but because I refused to bend to his will. He sent men to the shore intent on killing me and my men. We fought and escaped,' he said. 'Do you wish to do his pleasure and have me and my men killed after spending so much time rescuing us?'

Her white teeth caught her bottom lip. 'Your father seeks to kill too many people.'

He wanted to ask her why she knew this—Was it only rumours, or did she have specific knowledge, say, from her uncle?—but he didn't want to spook her. He knew in his gut that her uncle, the one who was away on mysterious business, was the key to completing his quest. If he wasn't Halfr, he suspected the man knew Halfr the Bold's hiding place. All exiled men from Agthir bonded together. 'I'd not disagree. He was a good king before my mother died, but recently he seeks to kill shadows and ghosts.'

'I see.'

Karn knew he was not ready to explain about the queen's scared face when she witnessed his father's foaming rage at the final feast. He liked Ingebord, but he'd sooner poke his eyes out with a knife than be married to that cold fish. He knew Queen Astrid had been enormously successful in managing his father throughout the years they'd been married, keeping his rages under control. At first, he'd been wary of her, but she'd slowly won his trust, telling him stories about his mother's prowess as a warrior, how she managed to subdue various jaarls who sought her lands before she finally married Thori, and how Astrid had considered her a role model as they'd been fostered together.

In the half-light of the barn, Karn suspected Queen Astrid had abandoned her famous pragmatism for fantasy, but he knew in his heart that he wanted to believe in that fantasy, find this Halfr where so many had failed and return what she lost, regain his self-respect and finally his father's admiration in the process.

*Go west and make certain the half-moon shines in Halfr's face before you ask him anything.* Even now weeks later, Karn still could not puzzle out on how seeing the man in moonlight would make a difference, and he had no idea what Ingebord wanted beyond keeping her mother safe.

'Will you offer us hospitality despite the wolf's head decree, despite the fact my father might have sent men to do his bidding?' he asked, pushing aside the puzzle Ingebord had delighted in handing him and concentrating on the woman before him. 'I feel compelled to warn you of the dangers, my lady.'

'My uncle and I have no reason to fear King Thorfi or his men.' Her knuckles loosened on the bowl, and a slight bravado laced her voice. 'If I might continue without unnecessary comments, your men will heal quicker.'

He waved his hand and settled back against the clean pallet. The pouch he wore about his neck settled against his chest.

He heaved a sigh of relief. The queen's token, a sphere of amber wrapped in gold and silver filigree which could be worn as a pendant, the one thing he had to prove that he came in her name, rested alongside his late mother's pendant, a near identical one except with amethyst instead of amber. It matched his memory of her eyes. His mentor had given it to him before he breathed his last, saying that he should think of it as a lucky charm. And so it had proved.

'When will your uncle return?' he asked, fingering the pendant and willing the luck to be there once again.

Maer arched a brow. 'Speaking impedes healing.'

He bared his teeth in the approximation of a smile and watched how the mysterious Maer moved amongst the men, talking to them quietly and giving them draughts to drink.

'As all appears satisfactory, I will leave you,' Maer said with a faint tremor in her voice and walked out of the barn before he could think up another way to question her about her uncle and his connection to the Agthir exiles, most especially Halfr. Coincidence? More than likely. His quarry travelled alone. Always. The queen had mentioned that Halfr had little love for Thorfi, something to do with Karn's mother from before his parents married.

The ache in his head increased, making it difficult to think. He pressed his hands against his eyes and willed his mind to move away from his father's mistakes and back to what he could control: finding a way to complete his quest in time.

'I will unwrap your secret, Maer, somehow,' he muttered. 'But I also will honour my life debt and ensure you're kept from danger.'

Maer leant back against the church wall and allowed the bowl to slip from her nerveless fingers, crashing against the stone floor. Her legs had barely carried her out of the barn.

She'd never expected Karn to confirm her wild guess about his parentage. She had to hang on to the fact that Karn was a declared wolf's head and had no reason to do his father's bidding. He wasn't one of the assassins, and her mother could even have sent him. She dismissed the idea as silly. Her mother had not sent any word ever.

His arrival was a coincidence, nothing more, but she needed to figure out a way to have him leave before her uncle returned. Ten heartbeats of panic and then positive action was what her uncle had taught her. Time and again it had saved their lives.

'Enemies can become friends,' she muttered, stooping to pick up the bowl. 'Life debts matter.'

'Maer, have you seen a ghost?' The young priest caught her arm. 'You have gone pale. Allow someone else to take over the nursing duties. Those Northmen are monsters.'

'Your hands are full, Father,' she answered and pushed the panic back down into a dark corner of her brain. 'I am no fainting flower. I can attend to those warriors' needs better than other people as I speak their language fluently. I'm from the North, after all.'

'We must do all in our power to hurry them along,' the priest said, his cheeks becoming florid. 'That is what I wanted to say.'

'There I agree with you. Heal their bodies and they will depart in peace, owing us a debt that they will struggle to repay.'

'When your uncle returns, what will he say if you allow yourself to get into a state?'

Maer concentrated on the bowl. All sorts of questions buzzed in her brain, including what would her uncle do, but her brain kept circling back to what men from Agthir, even if they were wolf's head, were doing in these waters? Agthir traded to the lucrative east, not with the Northmen from Dubh Linn in Eire.

'My uncle will applaud my actions. A Northern warrior would sooner die than dishonour a life debt.'

The priest's face cleared. 'Be careful, Maer. Their leader openly flirted with you during the rescue. My bishop warned how weak a woman's flesh can be.'

Maer's throat closed. She knew he meant well, but he and the rest of the people who lived here had no idea about her parentage or who her uncle had once been. 'Thank you for the warning, Father.'

He patted her shoulder. 'You're a good woman, Maer. You need to find a husband who will look after you properly, not some warrior who steals a kiss in full view of others.'

Maer pretended to cock her head. She knew the dangers of believing in any sort of flirtation, perhaps better than the priest did. That kiss had been a one-off, never to be repeated. 'I believe my duties are calling me, Father.'

The next afternoon, Karn shifted his weight so that his shoulder wasn't jammed up tight against the wall. A full day had passed, and he was still no closer to figuring out if he could act on his hunch that the missing uncle somehow held the key to his completing his quest if Maer pushed him and his men to go before her mysterious uncle returned.

'Are you certain you don't want some weak ale this morning?' Maer asked, coming to stand in front of him, her full lips curved upward.

Karn tried not to think about how sweet her mouth had tasted or how she had populated his confused dreams.

In one, he mixed up her and the queen. The queen's little dog, Tippi, had been in the same dream and that mysterious girl who'd kicked his shins, claiming to be the queen's daughter and whom Astrid swore only existed in his fevered imagination. He hoped that it did not signify anything, as he had liked that little dog, but he'd never encountered the little girl with the saucy mouth again. No, his head had obviously taken a far harder knock from the mast than he first considered if his dreams were becoming that confused.

With nothing to do but think, what he did realise this morning was that his father's advisor, Drengr, began the quarrel with a curled lip, goading him to ask his father what he truly thought of Karn's skills.

'Some weak ale, Lord Karn?' Maer asked, looking at him with her perfectly arched brows drawn together.

He took the bowl from her, being careful not to brush her fingers. 'My remaining men, the severely injured ones who came off first, may I see them? Or are we being held prisoners here?'

'You and your men are guests here. I simply request that you keep the rules of hospitality.'

'But shouldn't we be housed together?' he asked, trying to think around the pain.

'Your men are being well-tended, but the church hospital is tiny. Luckily the priest has some small experience in repairing heads and setting broken limbs.' She piously lowered her head. 'A useful skill being able to repair broken bodies and broken souls. When he says they may receive visitors, I will take you to them.'

'Do you follow the Christian path, then?' He forced a smile. 'Forgive me, but you speak the Northern tongue so well. One would almost think you were from the North, perhaps somewhere near my old country.'

Her smile lit up her entire countenance, making her stunningly alive. He was reminded of his earlier brief taste of her mouth and knew her cool exterior hid a fire.

'I attend church,' she said. 'Good for my soul, my uncle says. Our priest is an excellent healer, as you'll soon witness. Far better than I ever could hope to be.'

He nodded briefly and dragged his mind away from the gutter. The woman had saved his life. 'I give thanks to whichever being had us saved.'

His men were safe and healing, but his ship would take weeks to repair, if such a thing was even possible. His quest to find Halfr had reached yet another delay. Sometimes the gods twittered at him. And at others, they roared with laughter. Karn the Lucky? Karn the Irresponsible. But he'd learn from his latest mistake, just as he'd learned from past ones. He would honour his late mentor's shade and make right his mistakes. He'd learned to clean up his own messes.

He noticed her watching him with intent eyes. 'What do you require, then, Karn? Why were you out on the sea in a storm? Why did you brave the whirlpool?'

For a heartbeat he wondered if he should confide in her about his quest and why it was important, but then the more sensible part of him exerted control. *Trust too quickly, and you end up dead.*

'Does your uncle object to strangers?' he asked instead.

'Why should he?' she replied with a frown. 'Hospitality towards strangers in need is something which always brings blessings. A motto he has taught me to live by and which keeps us safe.'

'Have you lived with your uncle long?'

Her knuckles shone white against the dark brown of the bowl she carried. 'Ten years since my fa—since my parents died. Any reason for these questions? I thought the past didn't interest you.'

Karn lifted a shoulder. Maer was trying to hide something, something to do with Agthir. The question was how to get her to reveal it without revealing his promise to Astrid. 'What can I say? Trying to make idle conversation. Saves discussing other things.'

Her tongue wet her lips as if she, too, was thinking about the kiss. 'Make conversation about something else.'

He leant forward, looping his hand about his knees. 'Shall we speak of the kiss we shared? My mind keeps turning it over and over. Does yours?'

'Now you tease me.' She smiled. 'A fleeting moment signifying nothing.'

'Nothing? I must try harder next time.'

'I'm not some green maid, blushing in front of a warrior. My priest has already warned me about your intentions because I am a good woman, but I knew already. Once my uncle told me, "Never trust a flirting warrior." On the boat from Constantinople to Dubh Linn, I learned he spoke the truth.'

He focused on the rafters rather than her mouth, but his mood lifted. She wasn't immune. A pleasurable way to winkle out her secrets existed. 'Flirtation or something more? We won't know until we try. When, proud Maer, shall we try again? Name the time, and I will be there.'

She ducked her head, but her cheeks flamed scarlet. 'Perhaps you are right—it is easier to speak of my uncle. He was a trader of fur and amber before we settled here.'

'Is your uncle from Agthir like you?' he asked softly, pretending to transfer his gaze back to the blackened rafters but really watching her from underneath his lashes.

She retreated several steps. Her hand clutched her slender throat. 'How do you know I am from Agthir? And I have already told you, Sigmund Sigmundson is my uncle. My father—my parents perished a decade ago. It is why he looks after me. He was none too pleased when it first happened. He sought to settle in the east, but the circumstances became too difficult, so we travelled west.'

Karn stroked his chin, trying to think around the ache

in his head. Ten years would be right for Halfr. The battle for Agthir had been his first battle. And Astrid said that the girl had not existed. 'Your accent reminds me of the people from there.'

She bowed her head and pretended a sudden interest in the rushes. 'The prow was a shock, that is all. After all this time. After what we had been through…when your father invaded.'

'Will my being from Agthir be a shock to your uncle?' He reached into the pouch and fingered the queen's pendant again, the proof he had to give Halfr along with her message so that the helmsman would know he spoke on the queen's behalf.

*Halfr will return what he took once he sees this,* Astrid had confidently predicted when she handed the amber sphere pendant to him. It had surprised him how closely the piece resembled the one which his late mentor said had brought his mother such luck in battle. Identical except for the colour of the stone.

'A shock to Uncle Sigmund?' Maer asked with what sounded like a forced laugh. 'He paid all his debts and left. No enemies, just didn't want to be ruled by your father.'

'But never a warrior? I find that hard to believe.'

'He was a fur and amber merchant before we settled here. He only wishes to live in peace.' She retreated several steps. 'I have other obligations to attend to, Lord Karn.'

'Would you have rescued us if you had known about my parentage?' Karn asked in a quiet voice. 'Am I to be forever condemned because of an accident of birth?'

Her feet skittered to a halt.

'I accept your words that you travel in peace. We will speak no more of King Thorfi or speculate on what he did to my uncle or my parents.' She looped a strand of hair about her ear, but Karn noticed a slight tremble in her fingers. 'The past is behind us through mutual agreement, unless that was some sort of ruse.'

'Thorfi's days are numbered, Lady Maer. His age and many injuries creep upon him no longer softly but with clunking feet,' one of Karn's men who had no more than superficial cuts and bruises called out.

'Despite everything the queen and her women have done, his many wounds refuse to heal properly,' another shouted. 'He can't stand that his son is now a far better warrior than he will ever be.'

The rest of the men beat their fists against the rushes in the hut. Karn inwardly rolled his eyes. He knew the mistakes he'd made which led them here.

Maer put her hand to her throat. 'How…how do you know this? The last I heard was his grip on Agthir was tighter than ever.'

Every sinew in his body became alert. Maer cared about what happened in Agthir. He heard it in her voice.

'Trust us. We were there,' another of his men called out before he could make a sign warning them to keep quiet: his father's health should be a private matter.

'Drengr seeks to advance by marrying the queen's daughter at Jul, but first he must get rid of Karn. So he planted the idea in Thorfi's brain, knowing Karn would refuse Ingebord's hand or any portion of her.'

'She is the frost maiden, after all. Her icy glance causes men to wither.'

Karn glared at the speakers who gave unrepentant shrugs.

'Better Maer knows, Karn,' another one said quietly. 'Maybe then she will understand who our quarrel is with. Your father would never have done it if he'd been in his right mind, instead of under some curse. Never would have any time for Drengr or that bootlicker Beorn who is always bad-mouthing you.'

Karn inwardly sighed and hoped the news about his father's affliction would not spook Halfr into running again, if he somehow learned it from Maer or her uncle. However, since his father's concussion during last warring season, he'd behaved more erratically than usual, leaning on Drengr and even excluding the queen. Their own quarrels had increased, but he always thought his father loved him and had no desire for his death.

'Yes,' he confirmed. 'The reputed price on our heads is a high one. We're dead men in Agthir. Drengr's men attacked us as we left, claiming to act on my father's order of all wolf's heads to be killed at sunrise, even though Queen Astrid predicted my father would soon come to regret his actions and would spare the women and children. She swore that she would ensure their safety, and I do believe her.'

'King Thorfi's temper is terrible,' one of his men called, drowning out Maer's swift intake of breath. 'He is ever likely to send someone after us.'

'Please, you are speculating,' Karn said, forcing his best smile. 'In time my father will remember that I'm his son and that my men are only guilty of loyalty to their leader, a quality he has always praised.'

No slight smile from Maer, merely a severe frown and a paling of her cheeks. 'Thorfi and the other petty kings of the North hold no sway here. And I care not who the queen's daughter might marry. Makes no difference to my life.'

'That's the spirit!' his men called out.

She inclined her head acknowledging the compliment, but her fingers plucking at her gown showed her agitation. 'We are aligned with the Gaels and fight to keep these waterways clear. The Northmen from the Black Pool are learning that they are no longer able to prey with impunity. I dare say we can face a band of warriors from Agthir if they come with evil intent.'

'You have difficulties with the Northmen from the Dubh Linn?' Karn asked, intrigued. He needed a solid reason to stay, or she'd have him and his men gone before her uncle returned. And he required that mysterious man's memory.

She examined her hands. 'My uncle fears that an invasion of some sort will become inevitable. They will need to control the straight between Islay and Jura. The whirlpool is far too dangerous for most of the year. And trade between Dubh Linn and the North increases with each passing season.'

'You will need sell-swords to defend you.'

'My uncle has everything in hand.'

He held back the remark about Halfr and his legendary sword. Whatever the man had taken, it was not a sword with magical properties. Such things only existed in skalds' tales.

Karn bowed his head. 'As I found to my cost, circumstances can alter in a breath. For as long as we are here, my lady, we will fight for you. Find us the weapons. See if we can salvage any from the ship. Let us prove our worth until your uncle returns.'

His men stamped their feet in agreement. Several called out what a beautiful rescuer she was.

Maer's cheeks coloured prettily. 'Such flattery.'

'Allow me to think differently. You are our beautiful rescuer.' He reached behind her ear and pretended to retrieve a gold ring. 'You see gold drips from you.'

She made no move to take it. 'A cheap and unworthy trick.'

'Your quick thinking saved all our lives.' He placed the ring in her palm and curled her fingers around it. 'Take it as a token.'

She deposited it back in his hand. 'There are other calls on my time, but I will have a think about the weapons.'

She rushed out of the hut. Karn collapsed back against the straw and returned the ring to his pouch. She'd refused his offering. Unexpected.

'What was that about, Karn?' his helmsman asked him. 'How long are we staying here?'

He looped his hands about his knees. 'We leave when the time is right. No man left behind. You were loyal to me, and therefore I am loyal to you.'

'But Jul approaches. Why not go back and do as your father bade? Take Ingebord as your wife. She is biddable enough.'

Karn concentrated on where Maer had stood, with her chin lifted high. His body thrummed at the thought of un-wrapping her. He would not take a wife to secure the crown, particularly not one like Ingebord who chilled him to the bone. 'Provided Queen Astrid keeps her end of the bargain, it is nothing which need concern us.'

# Chapter Three

What had she been thinking? Maer's blood pounded so loudly in her ears that she stopped beside the pigsty and put her hands on her knees. She'd entered that barn to tell Karn that he and his men must leave, and she'd ended up agreeing that they could help defend this hamlet until her uncle returned.

'Are you all right, Maer?' one of the farmhands asked. 'Are our visitors behaving appropriately? Or shall we sort them out? Me and the lads are always up for a scrap.'

'Thus far, no problems.' She stood up straight and adjusted the folds of her gown. The people on this island had no reason to know about her quarrel with Agthir or her anger with her mother's betrayal. 'They've offered to guard us until my uncle returns.'

'We won't hold with anyone behaving inappropriately towards you. Your uncle will have my guts for fish line. The good father mentioned it.'

'The good father would be better tending to the injured than worrying about me. I can look after myself.'

'How long do you think they will stay?'

'Several are injured. Let's allow them to heal. How can they depart without getting their boat off the rocks?'

The lad's eyes widened. 'Do you think it can be repaired?

It seems well and truly stuck. Still there on this morning tide.'

Maer worried her bottom lip. What if King Thorfi sent men after his wayward son despite what the queen—her estranged mother had said? Her mother had once promised to send for her as well, and she knew how that had worked out. First the assassins searching for her uncle and then nothing for over five years. But never for her. It was as if she had never existed.

That boat could serve as a beacon if Thorfi sent a band after his errant son. She needed to get it off those rocks… even if they had to use several coracles.

'A way may exist,' she said, putting her hands on top of her head. 'Let me think on it.'

'That is what I like to hear,' Karn called out from the doorway.

'You are not supposed to be here, bothering Maer,' the lad said, jabbing his forefinger at Karn. 'Me and my mates—'

'The lady failed to give a direct order.' Karn held out his hands and shrugged. The sunlight shone on his red-gold hair and highlighted the well-toned muscles of his arms. He looked the part of the warrior who all the foolish maids sighed for, but he was a king's son. She attempted to re-member the whispers she'd heard of him over the years. Indulged. Pampered. Reckless but certainly lucky. He had survived the whirlpool and had earned his men's devotion.

'He fails to frighten me,' Maer said in an undertone to the lad, indicating he should go. She raised her chin and called out to Karn. 'We should speak, Lord Karn. I may have need of your men after all.'

'We're here, my lady, me and my mates, to do what needs doing,' the lad whispered. 'Just say the word.'

She hated to think of the mismatch between simple farmers, even ones roughly trained by her uncle, and well-trained warriors. 'They are sworn to me now on account of the life debt, but you know how touchy Northmen can be. Let everyone know.'

The lad touched his hand to his forelock and ran off.

Maer waited until he had disappeared around a corner. She strode over to where Karn stood with a faint smile playing on his lips as if he thought she'd made an excuse so they could be alone together.

She hated that her heart had done a little jump at the deepening of his eyes. Practical reasons existed about why showing her attraction was a bad idea. Her uncle had drummed them into her head after she'd made a fool of herself over that warrior.

'Lord Karn, do you have some concern which you could not speak of in front of your men?' she asked, making her voice sound stern and efficient. 'You should be conserving your strength.'

Karn's lips turned up in an amused smile. 'You refused my ring. I wanted to know why.'

'No need for payment. Insulting to be offered it.' She crossed her arms over her breasts and tapped her foot. 'What do you really want? No need for sweet talk. I'm no frivolous maiden in the feasting hall.'

His bluer than midnight eyes sparkled with hidden lights. She had no doubt that many women in the feasting hall sighed after him. 'Should we surrender our weapons? All we have is our eating knives. The rest remains on the ship which remains stuck fast on that rock. You heard the youth—stuck fast and not about to sink. You had me jump for no good reason.'

Maer glanced out to where the boat remained stuck but visible. 'Too dangerous with the current tide.'

'Recover our trunks, our weapons and shields. We can then truly defend you should the worst happen.'

She screwed up her nose, trying to imagine what her uncle would say. But Karn was right: the weapons would be of far more use on shore. 'My men know how to use the coracles. You will sink them.'

'They are willing to learn. We hate being idle, my lady.'

'But it will be quicker if I arrange it for a slack tide.' She tapped a finger against her mouth. 'However, I dare say the women could use a good laugh. The assistant swine herder can teach you to use a coracle.'

'We exist to amuse.'

'Amuse, but refrain from antagonising. The locals fear the Northmen. I will act as interpreter, understand.'

He bowed. 'We can be of more use to you with our weapons than not. And I would be grateful for any lessons, my lady interpreter.'

'You have given your word that you are peaceful. I must trust your honour will demand you keep it, despite everything.'

His eyes darkened. 'I'm unaccustomed to having my honour questioned.'

'Yet your father saw fit to make you a wolf's head.'

'My father's quarrel had nothing to do with my honour, merely my refusal to do as he dictated.' He shook his head. 'In exchange for her help, the queen set me a task to complete by Jul or the crown will go to another.'

Maer put her hand to her throat and willed her heart to stop pounding. He had no idea about the deception. Her mother had not sent him looking for her. 'I thought you were his only child.'

'The lucky man who wins fair Ingebord's hand will inherit the kingdom at my father's demise—his words.' He put his hands on his head. The bruising showed clearly on his cheek but somehow it made her insides ache. 'I fear for Agthir. I've grown to love it and its people. I blundered into Drengr's trap and caused my men to get caught as well, but I will get them out. I will find a way.'

'The most obvious way is to marry the queen's daughter.' Maer laced her voice with heavy irony. 'Surely, she is not as awful as all that. You can always divorce.'

He laughed, a great belly laugh, which unaccountably cheered Maer up. 'Ingebord and her sing-song voice is a fate I'd wish on no man. The only thing we've in common is our love for her little dog, Tippi.' He sobered. 'Afterwards she confided that she didn't desire this either. I will not take an unwilling wife and certainly not one I consider an annoying sister.'

Maer wrapped her arms about her middle. Tippi survived. She wondered if the little dog even remembered her. 'How noble.'

She tried to hold back the questions bubbling up in her throat. There were so many things she wanted to know, but asking was far too risky. Her only hope was that he might allow a few more nuggets of information to fall before he left.

His laugh sounded bitter to her ears. 'My father was once a great warrior who strode the battlefield as competently as Thor. The skalds sing about how he won my mother's regard, capturing her heart.'

'The rumours have even reached these islands.' She swallowed hard and hated that she had this irrational hope that her mother had finally sent word. But would she really use the king's disgraced son as her messenger? Such thoughts belonged in skalds' tales and in the dreams of maidens who had never been kissed, not in her practical thoughts.

His fingers curled about her hand, warming her straight down to her toes. 'I will not put you in danger after you risked your life for mine.'

'The rescue was easy. The recovery good now...'

'The fact remains.' He raised their joined hands to his mouth. 'I'm grateful.'

Maer hated how a curl of heat started in her middle. She knew her uncle would tell her that, despite everything, she should look on this man as the enemy who could destroy their world. She also silently hoped that her adopted relative would find a reason to remain away and knew that was wrong of her. She allowed her fingers to rest in his for a few heartbeats more than she should have and then gently tugged. His warm hand slipped away.

'My uncle will know where you can best find a ship for the next part of your voyage,' she said and hoped he couldn't hear the slight breathlessness in her voice.

His lips curved upwards, and the back of her neck prickled. He'd guessed about her attraction.

'I pray he'll arrive soon, then. We're anxious to be on our way. After we get our swords and have provided amusement in our coracle lessons, of course.'

The words were brusque but gently said. She swallowed the bubble of disappointment. She'd read the situation wrong. Just because he was not enthralled with Svanna, it was wrong to hope that he might be attracted to her. Allowing her desire to cloud her judgement had led to that Northern warrior discovering her uncle's plans about getting a place with the Irish high king and using them to further his aim of marrying that king's daughter.

'Then, I will do what I can to ensure your belongings are brought off that ship.' She tilted her head to one side. 'Easier to be a sell-sword if you have a sword to sell.'

He caught her hand once again and raised it to his lips. His mouth made a warm imprint on her palm. 'You are good for me, my lady. My hope has been restored.'

Maer pulled her hand away and resisted the urge to cradle it against her cheek. 'The tide waits for no one.'

She felt the speculation in his eyes as she strode away. She tried to tell herself that he was far more experienced around women than she was with men and that her uncle would say he was the sort who used women. Karn Thorfison was not for her, she told her heart, and hated how her heart kept whispering *Liar.*

Karn regarded the growing pile of iron-bound trunks and shields with a mixture of disbelief and relief. Maer had accomplished everything she'd promised and more. Ever since they'd spoken yesterday afternoon about retrieving things from his ship, she appeared to be a whirlwind of activity, barely stopping to rest. All his men who were able, including himself, had been given a lesson in coracle rowing, much to the amusement of the onlookers, but they all had eventually managed it. Far harder than he'd considered.

Between strokes, he watched Maer, telling himself that he was watching how her hands were placed on the oars. Important for gaining the skill. Except he knew he watched her for other reasons which had nothing to do with his men or the quest and everything to do the tilt of her head, the way her brown hair escaped from the couvre-chef in ringlets and how the stroke of the oar pulled her gown against her breasts, revealing their curve.

He wanted to explore this sensation of knowing her from

somewhere, but he suspected it was caused by the bump on his head. Astrid and Ingebord never mentioned Halfr travelling with a relation, just the bloody half-moon shining on Halfr's face.

'Nearly there,' Maer said, getting out of the overladened coracle. 'Finally. You failed to travel light.'

Her tawny-brown hair lay in ringlets about her face. The state of her gown showed she had not merely supervised but had taken an active role in retrieving the trunks and other items.

'My men are unaccustomed to idle hands,' he said. 'They showed they can row this morning.'

Maer put her hand in the small of her back and stretched, pushing her breasts forward. Karn tried not to think about the thrusting mounds. 'My men know what they are doing and don't have time to waste on beginners. They had enough amusement earlier.'

'Allow us to move everything up to the barn.'

'Something hidden in the trunks? Are you keeping secrets from me, Karn?'

'Only the ones I need to.' He smiled at her. 'Confide in me first.'

'What sort of secrets?' Her lashes swept down over her eyes. 'Like I am really Queen Astrid's daughter? Or some other nonsense?'

All the merriment drained away. He narrowed his gaze, searching for the mockery.

'I know who Astrid's daughter is,' he bit out. 'Sarcasm doesn't become you, Maer. What sort of fool do you take me for?'

Her laughter held a bitter note like he'd disappointed her. 'I don't think you are a fool, Karn.'

He blinked twice. Queen Astrid's daughter, indeed.

What game was she playing? He could hear Ingebord's sing-song voice mocking him asking in what way wasn't she the queen's daughter the first time they met, and he questioned the queen about the girl who had taken Tippi.

'I merely want to ensure all trunks make it ashore,' he said, steering the subject on to safer waters.

'I checked the ship three times and seem to recall that you dislike jumping from any height.'

'I enjoyed our kiss. You did as well. Admit it.'

She bowed her head and pretended an interest in one of the iron-bound trunks.

'I don't react well to teasing, Karn,' she whispered to the first trunk.

He pressed his lips together and wondered who had made her wary and if he'd lived. 'As it is destined not to be, we shall have to leave it to the imagination. Luckily, I have a good imagination.'

Her head came up at that. 'You do?'

He put his hand under her chin and raised her eyes to meet his. Her tongue flickered out, wetting her lips. He forced his hand to let go instead of drawing her into him.

'A very good one.'

She stepped away from him. 'Then, I suggest you use it and allow the rest of us to get on with our work.'

He started laughing and noticed the hidden passion in her eyes. One day, he silently promised, one day, she'd consent to a kiss, but for now, he enjoyed the pursuit.

She tried to be stern, but her blue-green eyes sparkled like light dancing on the water.

'I have been put properly in my place by a very beautiful lady.' He waited, his breath unaccountably catching in his throat.

'Something wrong with your eyesight if you think I am a beauty. Addled from that blow on the head, I suspect.'

'Beauty is always in the eye of the beholder.' He bowed and retrieved a tiny daisy from behind her ear. He was quietly thankful that he'd picked the flower earlier. 'You see, this flower agrees with me.'

'I'm not sure how you do it,' she said allowing him to tuck the flower behind her ear. 'Magical.'

'Magic is easy if you know the trick.'

He leant down and picked up his sword which lay atop a pile, feeling the comforting weight of it in his hand. His favourite shield had made it as well and his trunk which contained the bulk of his gold. 'Makes me feel whole again, just holding it. Thank you.'

'I hate to see waste,' she said in a low growl. 'As you rightly pointed out, these weapons and shields are far too valuable to be left to the sea.'

Karn struggled to keep a straight face.

'What do you find amusing about this?' she asked, picking up one of the trunks.

'I'm thinking how few women in Agthir would be as decisive as you. The queen, maybe, but most are content to allow the men to do things like that.'

'You mean like Lady Ingebord,' one of his men called out. 'She rarely lifts a finger to anything practical. Purely decorative, that one. All la-di-da woven braids for her many gowns and bows for that dog of hers.'

The colour drained from Maer's face, and she set the trunk down heavily, narrowly missing his foot. 'The queen of Agthir? I'm nothing like her.'

'How do you know?' he asked.

'I do.' She narrowed her eyes. 'Please refrain from giving such compliments in the future. Keep them for the giggling girls in the feasting hall.'

'Not in my nature,' he called after her retreating back. 'Giving praise where it is due is important to me.'

She stopped and turned. 'False praise is worse than no praise.'

'My quarrel was with my father, not the queen or even her daughter.' He tilted his head to one side. Even the flower in her hair seemed to glower at him. He'd spoken the truth. He and Astrid were friends after a fashion, not close as the queen kept her emotions on a tight leash, but she had encouraged him to perfect his skills as a leader, a leader like his mother who had valued peace more than she loved war. Once Astrid confided that she thought his mother would not have allowed events to spiral into the war which had torn apart both their countries.

She drew her top lip down over her teeth. 'We agreed not to speak of Agthir and its inhabitants. They have no bearing here. You bring them up at every opportunity.'

He rubbed the back of his neck trying to understand her change of mood. 'You joked about being Queen Astrid's daughter.'

She shook her head. 'Forget it.'

'Why?'

'Do you consider the rules only apply to others, Lord Karn?' she said, lifting her chin.

He was prepared to swear that the iciness of her intonation was precisely like Astrid's when she discovered him locked in an embrace with some unsuited skirt in his younger years. He dismissed the notion as fanciful. Astrid only had one daughter—the irritating Ingebord who so idolised her mother that they dressed alike.

He had to stop grasping at wisps of straw. Maer had

nothing to do with the queen. The blow to his head had affected his reasoning.

'Will the ship last for much longer?' he asked, shading his eyes against the glare on the water and willed cold logic to return. 'It strikes me that it could serve as a beacon, indicating to any passing ship that this harbour exists.'

'Why? Are you going to be like the assistant swine herder and swear you saw a dragonship bristling with shields on the early morning tide?' She gave a light laugh. 'I swear that lad has some fanciful notions. As you can see, no attack from the North today.'

'Is it unusual to see dragonships travelling up and down this straight?' he asked, keeping his voice casual. Internally he decided to set a watch for any ship which Drengr might send. Maer and her uncle might know older watercraft, but did they know the latest ones?

Maer shrugged. 'From time to time. It is why my uncle is away, but the lad likes the thrill of it all. It is because he has never been in a battle that he longs for one.'

'Have you ever been in a battle?'

'Enough for this lifetime.' She indicated the trunks. 'Have your men carry them back to your quarters. My other duties call me. The kitchen's roof needs patching if you need something to occupy yourself.'

'I wondered if you could patch the hole on the hull while it was on the rocks? And then float it off on a high tide?' Karn said thinking aloud.

'To what purpose? You wouldn't be able to get any wooden patch to hold for long.'

'There might be a way of properly repairing the ship's hull if we can get it ashore.'

She tilted her head to one side. 'Doubtful. Maybe you should try one of the markets farther along the strait to see if you could find passage to Black Pool, now that you and your men are well-recovered. Easier to find a proper ship that way. I could spare a few coracles for ferrying purposes.'

Worse and worse. He appeared to have talked himself into a quick trip elsewhere. He gritted his teeth. If ever there was a time to trust his instincts, this was one. She wasn't indifferent to him. She wanted him to remain.

'Trying is always better than being idle,' he said, adopting his most seductive voice. 'Before my men and I set off for somewhere which might have passage to either the Dubh Linn or the North.'

She raised a brow.

'Unless there is some reason why you wish us to depart,' he added. 'Something to do with the place which must not be discussed.'

'Are you always this obstinate?'

'Stubbornness is one of my endearing qualities,' he said looking directly into her eyes and willing her to give in.

The corners of her mouth twitched. His day suddenly became brighter.

'No reason at all,' Maer replied smoothly. 'I simply wanted to help you get wherever it was you were going as quickly as possible. Who precisely are you seeking? You have never said.'

'I appreciate the offer.' He put a hand under her elbow, and she did not pull away. The day literally brightened immeasurably as at that instant the sun came out from behind the clouds, throwing the beach into high relief. Instinct worked. 'I do want to meet this uncle of yours and express how much we appreciate the hospitality.'

She abruptly pulled away and examined the ground. The clouds covered the sun again. 'He will be interested to meet you, should you still be here.'

He gave a half shrug to show indifference but watched her intently. A strand of her dark brown hair curled about her jaw. His fingers itched to push it away, but too many people watched them.

'That boat holds a place in my heart. Simple as that,' he said, giving a half truth.

'But it could take a long time. I thought you were in a hurry to get wherever you wanted to go, once my uncle returns.'

'My men and I are not expecting to simply accept charity. We can assist about your farm, make good the repairs. It will give those who are injured a chance to recover. I dislike leaving any man behind.'

Again, a truth, but not the full one—something Astrid had taught him, about how a wise ruler holds the entire truth to their chest.

She tilted her head to one side and appeared to consider the matter for a long time. Karn forced the words begging her to consider back down his throat. He'd found in negotiations that it was best to allow the other party a chance to speak before jumping in.

'Very well,' she said with her full lips curving upwards. 'We will try to free your ship if I can figure out a way to create a patch which might hold, but I'm not making any promises.'

His shoulders suddenly seemed lighter, and he could breathe again. He could fulfil his promise. He wanted to grab her by the waist and swing her round and round, but he forced his hands to stay by his side. He was aware of how much her eyes sparkled, like sunlight on a summer's sea. 'What?'

'You appear so happy.'

'I'm grateful, my lady.'

'Your gratitude is acknowledged,' she said in a voice which rivalled Astrid's for its cool calmness. However, he glimpsed the barely suppressed twinkle in her eye and instinctively understood that she was teasing him, perhaps even flirting.

He lifted a brow. 'Only *acknowledged*? Somehow, I'd hoped for better than that. I will have to try again with more extravagant gestures.'

He reached out and spun her around several times before setting her down. Her slender waist felt right, between his hands. 'There. Gratitude demonstrated.'

She retreated several steps. 'No need for that.'

He watched her from hooded eyes. 'But I suspect there is. I wouldn't want my men to consider me remiss, my solemn-voiced lady.'

Her hand plucked at her sleeve. 'Stop making light of me, or I shall rescind the offer.'

Giving in to impulse, he caught her hand and raised it to his lips. Her palm tasted sweet like a piece of stolen honeycomb. He let it go and stepped away from her before he drew her into his arms again.

There were many practical reasons why kissing her thoroughly and properly like his body longed to do was precisely the wrong idea, starting with jeopardising his mission and ending with trespassing on hospitality. He needed to hang on to those reasons rather than thinking about her scent, the slenderness of her waist or the changing colour of her eyes with her mood.

'Only because it is deserved,' he said and knew the words were inadequate. He had not felt this awkward and unpractised since he was a beardless boy, unbloodied in battle and unused to the intricacies of courtship.

She withdrew her hand after having allowed it to linger for a fraction too long. The fact made his heart feel lighter.

He knew his smile became a little too broad.

'When I have figured out a scheme for refloating the ship, I will let you know,' she said. 'In the meantime, the barns need cleaning.'

She walked away with her skirt gently swaying. Karn noted with a frown that several of his men were watching as well. He wanted to tell them to keep their eyes to themselves and show her some respect. The stab of possessiveness unnerved him. Unlike only a few months ago when he was his father's acknowledged heir, he currently had little to offer her besides his sword arm, and he prayed that he would never have to use it in her defence.

'What are you staring at?' he asked his men who watched him with open mouths. 'You heard the lady. She wants the barns repaired. We might as well muck out the stables. We earn our keep while we lodge here.'

'What if her uncle is the man you seek? What if he refuses you? What if what you seek harms our Lady Maer?' his helmsman asked after the barn was thoroughly cleaned and they were washing in a stream a little way from the compound. 'What then? Which will you choose—our families who remain in Agthir or the Lady Maer?'

Ignoring the question which had haunted his early-morning thinking, Karn splashed his face with the clear-tasting water. 'Nothing has altered. Why would it?'

The man gulped. 'I've a bad feeling about this, Lord Karn.'

'We wait, we watch, and we act decisively when we have to,' Karn said, starting to dry his face, pretending a nonchalance. The truth was he didn't know. He hoped he would not have to make that choice. There could be an innocent explanation to the puzzle. 'Our duty is clear. Your families hang in the balance.'

'Do you think we could bring our families somewhere like this? Away from the poison which is Agthir?'

Karn looked towards where the peaceful farm stood. A curl of smoke billowed out of the main hall, showing that the meal preparation was well underway. A world away from what Agthir had become in recent months with the accusations of disloyalty and Drengr's constant searches for traitors who threatened the crown, a practice his father encouraged. Once Karn had dreamt of bringing such peace and prosperity to Agthir, but now he knew that dream, unless he managed to find Halfr and retrieve that which he stole, was beyond him.

What was worse was that he knew deep down living here was a habit that he could acquire, and that frightened him. 'I cross bridges when I come to them.'

Maer tied off the last bit of wool and rocked back on her feet. Her latest effort was nearly complete. Weaving helped her to think. It was hard to believe that when she was little she used to hide away and refuse to do it. Svanna had been the opposite, eagerly drinking in the lessons and showing Maer's mother the intricate braided ribbons that she used to weave in double-quick time. All Maer could normally show was a tangle of threads with a mismatched pattern. Now, a decade later, she took pleasure in creating complicated patterns which reflected the natural world. She might not be the quickest weaver, but in it she found a certain peace.

The act of passing the shuttle back and forth cleared her mind and enabled her to think on the day's problems. Often, she found a solution by the time she had finished.

She pressed her hands into her eyes. Once her uncle returned, she'd confess about her brief lapse in confessing to be Astrid's daughter and how Karn had thankfully taken it for a bad joke, but she realised her mistake the instant the words had left her mouth.

She yanked, the thread broke, and the shuttle went bouncing across the floor. She swore. Loudly.

'Hopefully it is not anything my men have done.' Karn appeared in the doorway as if she had conjured him.

His hair shone slightly and curled gently about his face. A warm curl started in the depths of her belly, and she knew she was staring at him. She wet her lips. He lifted a brow.

'My own annoyance at not being able to come up with a solution to refloating the boat,' she said reaching for the errant shuttle. He was there first, and their fingers collided. She quickly drew back, and the shuttle tumbled to the ground again. 'My impatience got the better of me.'

'I'm grateful that you are even considering it. Beyond making the boat even lighter, I can't think of a way to patch that hole.'

'It wouldn't be patched for long. Just long enough to get it ashore.' A memory of when she was little and her father arranged for a longship to be refloated filled her. She had just had the gift of her puppy, and they had gone to the harbour to watch. Her father always liked making things with his hands and trying to find solutions to intractable problems.

He had placed specially hewn overlapping planks over the hole, lashed them down and had proved to her mother that the boat could be repaired. Her mother pointed out that it would have taken less time to build a new boat. Her father had simply laughed, kissed her and told her that she was far too practical.

Now she had to wonder whether, if she took the waterproof leather off one of the coracles and used that as a patch, they could get the boat to shore? Would it hold long enough for that? Once ashore, the correct size plank needed to repair the boat could be obtained. And it would cease to be a beacon to any passing raider.

'You've thought of something,' he said in a low voice. The glow from the embers made hidden lights in his eyes dance. 'But you are afraid to share for fear of being dismissed. Don't worry. I want to hear your ideas.'

'How can you tell?'

'Your eyes lit up for a heartbeat.' He tilted his head to one side. 'Whoever dismissed you, Maer, did you an injustice.'

'Does the lighting up of eyes mean a useful scheme?' she asked.

'For some women. I learned early on to notice my stepmother's eyes before approaching her with a request for help.'

Maer froze. His stepmother. Her mother. He'd dismissed the truth as a joke. And she'd always favoured her father's side. Her mother used to laugh and called her the little changeling. Sometimes, Svanna had whispered that she should be the daughter as she was the fair-haired one.

In the end, Svanna had her wish. It was on the tip of her tongue to ask what the queen's daughter was like, but she swallowed hard and counted to ten. She wanted to hug every greedy nugget to her soul and then compare with her memories. She wanted…

She picked up the shuttle, retied the thread and regained control of her thoughts. 'We need to concentrate on the matter at hand, rather than discussing my eyes or my moods.'

'There was just something about the way you looked

which put me in mind of her. I've great admiration for her.' He gave a lopsided smile, one which warmed her straight down to her toes. She tried to tell herself that she was playing with fire, basking in that smile, wanting it to be for her and her alone, but a large part of her refused to care. 'What else do you need to make your idea succeed?'

'We need more men with strong backs. The boat will be wedged tight, even if it is lighter.' Maer wrinkled her nose. 'Forget it. It was an idea.'

'My men can row, Maer. They proved it this morning. They can follow directions as well. Have a Gael calling time in each coracle. We will get this done.'

She ducked her head. His quiet assurance shamed her doubt. 'We will attempt it tomorrow. High tide will be about noon.'

'Splendid.'

The warmth of his smile made her tingle down to the tips of her toes. It seemed like she had been trapped in ice for a very long time and was slowly being thawed.

'Anything else?' Maer asked, belatedly aware that standing staring at him in this darkened room made her insides ache to be held.

He started and raised a brow, curling his lips into a half smile. 'Must there be?'

She tore her gaze from his and gestured towards the loom. 'My weaving remains undone.'

'Maer...' He reached out and touched his palm to her cheek.

'Don't,' she whispered. 'You will be leaving. Best to keep it at friendship and no further.'

He smoothed her hair from her forehead. 'Until tomorrow, then. Sweet dreams, my new-found friend.'

After he left, she stared at the loom for a long time with an aching emptiness, knowing that her dreams would be filled with a forbidden warrior from the North holding her tight.

# Chapter Four

'Pull a little harder to the right,' Karn shouted, trying to ensure his voice carried across the water to all the boats. 'Put your back into it, men!'

'Wait!' Maer's strident voice carried across the water from where she stood on his dragonship.

'What? Why? We are ready.'

'Row with all of your might when I give the signal and not before!' Maer called back. 'The final ropes need to be secured or all our efforts will be wasted.'

Karn waved his hand to show he understood. He sat with an upraised hand while Maer tested the ropes a final time, moving with a confident assurance which seemed to give everyone heart. Finally smiling broadly and back in her coracle, she gave the signal, and the operation began.

Karn knew he pulled harder on his oar not only because he wanted his ship clear but also he wanted the scheme to succeed for her sake. The thought scared him. Maer's happiness was none of his business.

He mistimed the next stroke and caused the coracle to wobble. The other men in the boat glared at him, and he redoubled his efforts.

The ship creaked and groaned but slowly and with a

great sucking sound as the rocks gave up their prey, it began to move.

'Steady, now,' Karn called out. His men responded working in time with the Gaels.

Maer's satisfied smile, which transformed her face from pretty to take-your-breath-away, told him everything he needed to know about the outcome: his boat had floated clear of the rocks and did not immediately sink.

'Increase the stroke speed,' she called out. 'I've no idea how long that patch will last.'

'Row like Fenrir the Wolf is snapping at your heels,' Karn called.

All the men put their backs into it. And the boat began to move, sluggishly at first but with definite purpose. And although it was riding lower in the water than he'd like, he began to hope.

'Your idea worked, Maer,' he called out. 'You have saved my ship. From the bottom of my heart, thank you.'

She flashed a smile at him. With her eyes alight and a faint sheen glowing on her skin from the exertion, Maer was utterly desirable. He longed to take her into his arms and unwrap her complex layers. A means towards an end, but he no longer knew precisely what that end was.

'Thank me when we get to shore and not before,' she called back with a laugh.

All her men shouted her name, and he joined in. Her cheeks flamed a bright hue, and she ducked her head.

'No need for that,' she called back. 'What are friends for?'

He silently promised himself that he would discover a way to be alone with her and demonstrate his gratitude. She had single-handedly managed to turn his life around, saving him. And he suspected that she was not as indifferent to him as she appeared. A little voice reminded him that he should be concentrating on finding Halfr, but he paid no attention to it. Finding Halfr would come once he met the mysterious uncle and had his ship repaired. Until then, he intended to enjoy exploring this attraction.

'I disagree, every need. Without you, where would we be?' he called back. 'Stop being modest.'

'Practical, not modest. Still too many things to go wrong. Thank me when the boat is repaired.'

'Accepting praise is not a weakness, Maer.'

'I will try to remember that. Old habits die hard.'

He concentrated on the next stroke and visualised hurting whoever had caused Maer such pain and doubt.

Maer released the breath she'd been holding. After hard rowing, they were able to drag the boat to shallow waters where the hole was just above the waterline. Definitely taking on water, and listing to one side, but the ship was now out of eyesight of any passing ship. How hard could it be to repair it?

Her uncle would surely allow Karn and his men to do that, rather than insisting that they travel to the nearest market to find a ship to return them to the Black Pool the instant he returned. Selfishly she wanted Karn to stay for as long as possible. And she knew it was not a good thing to be selfish. She had to think about what was best for her and her uncle instead of thinking about how wonderful it felt to be appreciated.

'All yours now, Karn. My part of the job is complete,' she said, clambering out of the coracle and into the swell. The cold water made her breath catch and drove all her conflicting thoughts away. 'Your men can beach this boat without any further assistance.'

Karn's broad smile grew until he looked like a little boy who'd been given the biggest treat. The sheen on his face and forearms showed that he'd worked as hard as anyone. Harder than most. She ran her tongue over her suddenly dry lips. The sheen enhanced his muscles rather than detracting from them.

'Repairing the hull is simple enough, given some good, hard wood. I look forward to showing you why this boat is worth saving. My helmsman serves as one of Agthir's best boat builders in the winter months.'

'Your helmsman?' Maer glanced over towards the man with the filed teeth inlaid with gold. She'd never have considered him a boat builder, but it was clear from the way he was running his hands over the craft that he did have some affinity with it. 'A boat builder?'

'We can't all be useless sons of a king like me.' His eyes danced to show he was making a joke at his own expense. And expected her to protest that he was far from useless.

She pressed her lips together. He might be making a joke, but she could see the seriousness lurking behind his eyes. She'd been wrong to think of him as some spoilt king's son when they first met. He was someone who liked to lead from the front, and that was a quality which was impossible to teach. 'True enough.'

His mouth drooped. 'True?'

'If you're willing to think yourself useless, then who am I to dissuade you?' She put a hand on his arm, feeling the warm muscle ripple under the pads of her fingers. 'Even if I am sure your men who know you better than I do will argue differently. You should respect their opinion instead of trying to undermine it.'

His brows knit. 'What are you saying?'

'Don't do yourself down even in jest. It serves little purpose and disrespects the men who follow you.' She inclined her head. And forced her hand to drop by her side. 'Something my father told me once. Just like he told me that a true leader leads from the front and refuses to cower behind women's skirts.'

Her voice hitched. Her father shouted that at her mother during their last quarrel. He had gone and done that, instead of sending her mother who had been fostered with Thorfi's late wife as young girls to negotiate like her mother demanded.

'Did your father fall in battle?'

'I believe he now resides in Valhall for he followed the North path instead of the Christian one,' she said pressing her hands against her gown. She needed to be careful or she'd be confessing everything. And this time, he might not see the truth as a joke to be laughed off.

His hand squeezed her shoulder, a tiny intimate touch, which sent a pulse of heat through her. She focused on the water with its small waves lapping the shore and tried to remember why he must always ultimately be her enemy, but the reasons kept slipping away.

'Full of good ideas and helpful advice. What more could a man ask for?' His low voice sent a further pulse of heat through her.

'I suspect there are a few things,' she said, clutching at the shield sarcasm afforded her.

'Why must you always be dismissive of compliments?'

'Is stating the truth being dismissive?' Her voice was too high and reedy for her liking. She started to move ashore, but he caught her arm. His warm fingers seemed to sear through the fabric, and the heat radiated throughout her body. 'We are standing in the surf. Can the compliments and expressions of gratitude wait until a more opportune time?'

'Stay. Watch us beach the boat. We will show you how the North does things.'

'Something tells me that I have seen this before.'

'You might learn something new.'

'What—how *not* to do it?'

'Never took you for a coward, Maer.' He turned from her, laughing as if he suspected her words were being used to deflect.

Rather than going up to the hall as she had intended, she lingered. Several of the women sighed over the way his wet tunic moulded against his well-muscled back. Maer crossed her arms and pointedly rolled her eyes to show she was immune, but she watched with avid interest.

'According to my helmsman, eminently repairable,' Karn said to her after the boat had been beached. 'Ten days, no more than that.'

'The sort of thing I like to hear,' she said, forcing her lips to turn up. 'A guest's intended date of departure.'

He placed a hand on the small of her back. 'We owe you another debt which I shall struggle to repay.'

Her breath caught in her throat. She examined her hands rather than looking into his eyes. Even though her mouth ached and all she had to do was to sway slightly towards him, she knew kissing Karn out here in the open would be folly in the extreme. She cleared her throat and moved away from him.

'Needed to be done. Couldn't have the assistant swine herder being fearful of dragonships. He is jumpy enough as it is. Earlier this morning he shouted a tale about Northmen camping in two harbours over. Foolish nonsense. Up there with his tales of ghosts and sprites.'

She forced her lips to turn upwards again to show that she wasn't afraid.

'You are certain that the herder is telling tales?'

'I've lost track of the number of tales he's told. My uncle says that he likes to have an excuse to go to the kitchens and get a scrap of pastry. He means well but always likes spicing up a dull day.'

He screwed up his eyes. 'I never thought we'd get her off the rocks in one piece. There was a time I'd thought none of us would.'

'Important to save strangers and send them on their way as friends,' she said and moistened her dry-as-dust lips.

Far too easy to tumble into his soul-searching stare and confess more than she should. Her hands itched to smooth that lock of red-gold hair from his temple. She took a step backwards, and his hand fell to his side.

'I hope we are more than strangers.' A dimple went in and out of his cheek. 'After all, you do call me Karn.'

She knew her cheeks flamed at that. 'Strangers who have become friends, then.'

His gaze seemed to point straight at her mouth. She instinctively wet her lips again. 'What I like to hear.'

'There are things I have neglected in the herb garden. My uncle will return soon.'

'Has he been gone longer than you expected?'

Maer shrugged thoughtfully. She refused to think about harm coming to her uncle. 'Slightly longer, but you know what it is like with negotiations. All the kings want their say.'

His hand caught a strand of her hair and pushed it back from her face. 'I can tell you are worried even if you try to hide it. From what you say, he is a capable man. I am sure he will return. I can't wait to meet him.'

'You have been studying me?'

'Is that odd? You are an intriguing woman, Maer.'

'*Intriguing.* How to damn with faint praise,' Maer said firmly and hoped her voice didn't sound too breathless. He was going to kiss her, properly and thoroughly this time. Everyone would see, and a large part of her refused to care.

Karn put a hand on the side of her face. 'You are running away?'

'Only cowards run,' she whispered, wetting her parched lips. 'What do you recommend?'

'Maer, what is going on here?' a loud male voice boomed. 'Why is this ship from Agthir on our shore? Maer, why are *you* here on the shore instead of in the far field where the assistant swine herder said you were when I met him on the road?'

'I never planned to be in the far field today.' Maer pressed her hands together and stepped away from Karn. She silently blessed the herder for getting it wrong and sending her uncle on a wild-goose chase. 'You should know better than to trust his words.'

Her uncle harrumphed. But she was pleased to see him. When she was little, the sight of his face with his half-moon scar had always signalled that all remained well. Even today her neck muscles relaxed, when she spotted it. 'Who is this man you appear to be standing so close to? The women are gossiping about it, like a gaggle of clucking hens.'

Maer hastily retreated several steps. Her uncle's return had saved her from doing something incredibly stupid like thoroughly hugging—or, worse, kissing—Karn with everybody watching. Which would have been an error of colossal proportions, particularly if the older man had witnessed it. 'My uncle has returned, Lord Karn. Isn't that lovely, particularly as you were starting to become concerned for his well-being?'

'You have done nothing wrong. Nothing to warrant malicious gossip,' Karn said quietly. His fingers curled about hers, and he took a step forward like he was prepared to be a shield.

She tugged, and he let go.

'I remain fully capable of handling my uncle,' she said in an undertone, putting her hand on her hip. 'My uncle's standing orders are to save any in trouble on the sea. He always is in a grumpy mood when he returns.'

'I apologise. I misread the situation.'

His voice was far more remote than he'd used before. Almost as if he sensed that with her uncle back, their growing friendship had altered. Her heart sank. It was going to be a missed opportunity, and to her surprise, she'd wanted something more.

'Next time, remember you seldom feature in my dreams.' She fluffed out her skirts and straightened her shoulders. She hadn't told Karn a lie. Her uncle did say that all were to be rescued. She just didn't know how he'd feel about his sworn enemy's only son receiving so much hospitality.

'Maer, what is going here?' Her uncle, white-haired but still powerfully built, strode with a young man's energy towards them.

Maer swept into a curtsy. 'Uncle Sigmund. Gifts from the sea.'

'So that priest bleated at me. You've been floating boats. You took a terrible risk that it wouldn't jam the harbour. Did you think about the people you could have inconvenienced?'

'Uncle, I hope you are not going to be rude.'

Karn signalled to his men to stand to attention. The scarred warrior appeared far more formidable than Karn had suspected. Here was no simple fur and amber merchant. Everything about him screamed that he was more than handy with a sword. There were reasons why the petty kings of Islay wanted to hear his views.

His gaze flickered over Karn, making him feel like something unpleasant the man had discovered on the bottom of his shoe. Karn gritted his teeth. No one dismissed him like that.

'Who are our visitors?'

'Lord Karn and his band of sworn men,' Maer said. 'Men who owe us life debts.'

She was speaking far too fast, and her voice was higher pitched than normal. A great desire to stand in front of her and tell this warrior not to bully her nearly overcame him. With difficulty he swallowed it. Maer would not thank him for interfering.

The man's eyes became colder than a frost giant's. 'Karn of Agthir? The son of Thorfi but no longer a prince?'

'My father no longer recognises the relationship.' Karn bowed low. 'At his command, my men and I are now wolf's heads.'

The man's cold eyes appeared to bore down deep into Karn's soul. 'Thorfi made his only son a wolf's head? Why? What have you done?'

'Grew up.'

'Explain.'

'My father dislikes dissent, especially from his son. He prefers to seek a new son, one who will do his bidding, instead of one who wants what is best for Agthir,' Karn said, opting for a partial truth. 'We do not see eye to eye. Among other defects in my character, I refused to marry the queen's daughter, Ingebord.'

'Did you do something to make her think you would marry her?'

'Honestly, no. It was a scheme dreamt up by my father's advisor, Drengr.'

'Not a name I am familiar with.'

'I learned too late of his duplicity, but my father depends on him more and more, particularly since he suffered from a head wound last warring season.'

He heard Maer's swift intake of breath and ignored it, instead concentrating on Sigmund Sigmundson's scarred face. He was willing to bet that Sigmund Sigmundson was not the name he'd used in Agthir. The hostility rolled off him in waves, but Karn had never heard of his father quarrelling with such a person.

Sigmundson gave a catlike smile. 'Thorfi never could stand people wanting to go their own way.'

'You know him?' Karn asked, forcing his voice to be steady. Despite everything, had he found the man Queen Astrid asked him to discover without having to have the half moon shine in his face. He wanted to punch the air in triumph, but then he sobered. Neither Astrid nor Ingebord had mentioned anything about a niece.

'I knew him many years ago,' the man said with the smile leaching from his face. 'Long before he seized power and married Astrid of Agthir. Made it his business to marry a warrior woman. I swear that woman was more than half Valkyrie.'

Karn refused to get sidetracked by reminiscences about his mother. When she had been alive, his father had been a very different man, listening to her wise counsel and seeking to defend their lands rather than attacking any who dared insult him. Her final illness had sucked all the kindness from him. He instinctively touched the pouch where his mother's lucky pendant lay, nestled next to the queen's offering.

'Impossible to alter the sands of time.'

'Are you your father's son?'

Karn glared at him, trying to understand the hidden question. He knew he took after his mother's family, but he'd never heard if his mother had taken lovers before his father. 'What do you mean by that?'

The man blew on his fingernails. 'A simple question. Must you always insist on your own way and grind your opponents into the dirt? Or are you more pragmatic, like your mother was, and seek the bonds of friendship once differences are settled?'

White-hot anger flashed through him. The man had never seen him in combat but had already judged him. The temptation to grab his sword and challenge him threatened to overwhelm him.

'Being able to alter course in the face of new information is a mark of a true leader. It is a lesson I have learned several times and will no doubt have to learn again.' He put his hand on his sword and tried to keep hold of his temper, but if Sigmundson started anything, he would respond in kind.

'His father made him a wolf's head,' Maer said, stepping between him and his quarry, breaking the eye lock. 'That is all we need to know, Uncle. His past is his own. Just as ours belongs to us.'

'My niece is wise beyond her years.' The man inclined his head, and Karn relaxed his shoulders. 'He will hunt you, Karn formerly of Agthir, like an eel intent on its prey, hunting until one of you meets his death.'

'If he is hunting me, then am I not his enemy?' Karn asked, keeping his voice steady and silently willing the man to understand that they had come in peace. Whatever quarrel that man had with his father, Karn did not want to further it, he simply wanted to retrieve what Halfr had taken.

Sometimes at night, unable to sleep, he wondered if Astrid expected him to fail or, worse, return empty-handed and shame-faced, ready to do his father's bidding. However, in the clear light of morning he always decided she'd given him the task because she feared for the future and thought he was the only person capable of accomplishing the task.

'He has a point, Uncle.'

'Do you also know where I might find Halfr Hammdrson?' Karn asked quickly before his nerve failed. 'Has he survived my father's wrath? The skalds claim he is a great magician. I presume you knew him as well.'

Sigmundson and Maer exchanged speculative glances before the man's mouth became a thin white line and his face hardened, making a crescent-shaped scar stand out on his chin. 'Never heard of any rumours of him or rather, if I did, he ceased to exist many years ago.'

Karn creased his forehead and tried to push the confused thoughts away. Maer's uncle knew more than he was letting on. Had to be. Somehow, he had to find a way to win his trust. The queen's final admonition to be sure before he approached the man, the one which caused Ingebord to use her sing-song voice about half-moons, rang in his ears. What a half-moon shining in his face would tell him was anyone's guess, but Ingebord had a habit of playing such games. It made her feel superior to see him seethe and squirm. 'I see. I will bear that in mind, but still I have a mind to search for him.'

A muscle jumped on the man's jaw. 'Nothing for you here, son of Thorfi. Best to leave.'

He hated the way his stomach twisted. 'I will repair my ship first. I will honour the hard work Maer and her men did today.'

'Is it repairable?' The man shrugged, turning away. 'I

only ask because I've no wish to waste your time. You can perhaps buy another ship in the Black Pool.'

'Perhaps, but I waste no one's time but my own if I try.' He gave his best smile and willed Maer's uncle to agree.

He drew his upper lip down. 'We are not a charity.'

'If Thorfi's men come here, you will need warriors. Know that I will fight for you if we remain here, as well as helping with repairs.' He turned towards Maer who watched with wary eyes. 'We have already shown our worth. Ask your niece. We repaired the barn roof.'

Maer put her hand on her uncle's arm, but he shrugged it off. 'Karn and his men are hard workers, Uncle. They have done far more in a few days than I thought possible. It is why I agreed to try to tow the ship in. A just reward.'

Karn inclined his head. 'Something which I am profoundly grateful for.'

'We are in no danger from them,' Maer said holding out her hands to her uncle. 'Strangers can become friends as you always say. Even *dauthamathr* from Agthir.'

Sigmundson's eyes softened. 'Throwing my words back at me, Maer?'

Maer put a hand on her hip. 'When you forget your manners, yes. I'm sorry your trip did not go well, Uncle. We must look to our own. Right now, we should take advantage of Karn and his men. Secure the farm before winter.'

'We come in peace and seek no quarrel sir,' Karn said. 'I swear to Var…or whichever Christian saint protects oaths if you prefer, but personally I still hold Var to be sacred.'

'You are not a Christian. Pity. Islay is proud of its heritage.'

Karn made sure his shoulders were back and his head held high, just as he'd been taught. 'Are you? I know your niece goes to church, but she failed to mention your habits.'

The man's eyes assessed him for a long time. Karn willed him to make the right choice and allow them to stay for as long as it was necessary. Somehow, he had to win his trust and discover the exact circumstances of Halfr Hammdrson's demise. If he had to return to Astrid empty-handed, he wanted something to bargain with.

'There are many ways in which you could be a danger without even trying.' The man shook his head. 'Even the son of my enemy must be rescued. The way the Nourns spin a man's fate never ceases to surprise me.'

'Thank you, Uncle.' Maer made an ironic curtsy. 'Your lessons have not been lost on me, even if some appear to have forgotten them.'

The elderly man held up his hand. 'You must allow me to finish, Maer.'

The light went out of Maer's eyes. 'I do beg your pardon.'

'Right that you were rescued, Karn of Agthir, but you must depart from this place as quickly as possible. Your father will set his hounds on you. They will not give up tracking you simply because my niece rescued you.'

'What are you talking about, Uncle? Why are you speaking in riddles?'

'The runes I cast three nights ago troubled me, but now I can see clearly what they must mean.' He inclined his head. 'We must prepare for war, Maer. Old enemies become new ones. The snake eats its tail.'

'Old enemies can be defeated if new allies work together,' Karn said, willing the man to bend a little more.

'Any know you came this way?'

'I suspect the Northmen from the Black Pool believe that I perished in the whirlpool.' His breath caught as he remembered the whispered rumour in Dubh Linn which caused him to depart. The ancient man's words had seemed to be sincerely spoken, but were they? Or in his desperation had he been grasping at whisps of broken straw? 'A joke, and I rose to it. I put my men in danger, something I am not proud of.'

'Where were you headed in such a hurry?'

Karn firmed his jaw. 'I would hardly want to put you in danger by divulging information in case I'm wrong about my father's feelings toward me and others do come after me.'

'Uncle! Stop it! Karn is my guest!' Maer stamped her foot on the ground. 'I've given my word. You would not have me go back on my word?'

Sigmundson raised his hands. 'If you have given your word, my dear, then we must hold true to it. Next time consult me.'

Maer's eyes spat fire. 'How, precisely? When should I have consulted you? And by what means? I'd love to know.'

The man firmed his mouth. 'Just keep him out my way. He reminds me of his father and not in a good way.'

He marched off, his cloak twitching. Maer stood with her hands on her hips, shaking her head and muttering about stubbornness. Karn kept his face blank. Her uncle had inadvertently pushed her towards him, and he wanted to welcome it with open arms.

'Was it something I said?' Karn said, adopting an innocent voice. 'I have no wish to come between you and your uncle. Truly I don't. But my ship will take some time to repair. Should I—'

'Stay, please.' Maer relaxed her arms and rolled her eyes. 'He is out of sorts. The petty kings probably ignored his advice. If it hadn't been you, it would have been sour milk or a thousand other little slights. He was looking for a fight. Better you than one of the servants who might take it to heart.'

'I bow to your expert knowledge.'

She tilted her head to one side. 'And my uncle spoke the truth—Halfr the Bold ceased to exist many years ago. His name brought misfortune more than once to my uncle and me.'

A dark pit opened in Karn's stomach. Sigmundson might lie to him, but he didn't doubt the truth in Maer's voice.

Ceased to exist? Dead? Would the queen even know if Halfr was dead? Had he been sent on a wild hunt for a will-o'wisp? Was he going to have to return and beg? Be a sell-sword and turn his back on his promise to his men's families?

'Thank you. We will go as soon as we can. Once the ship is repaired and not before.'

She gave a shrug. 'I know you will, Karn. You are a man who keeps his word.'

Karn tapped a finger against his mouth. Somehow, he was going to have to find a way to get Sigmundson to reveal more. Perhaps Halfr had entrusted the object to someone before he met his end. Perhaps they didn't even know they had it. The trouble was he wasn't entirely sure what it was either. 'I always try to keep my word.'

# Chapter Five

Maer put her hands on her hips and glared at her uncle who sat whittling beside the fire in the hall as if he didn't have a care in the world. As if he had not been unforgivably abrupt with their guest.

'Are you going to explain your rudeness to our guests, particularly to Lord Karn?'

He made another scrape with his knife and shrugged. 'Why should I? What has he done to deserve politeness except prance about in a wet tunic and look at you with bedroom eyes? I thought I'd taught you to be wary of such men, particularly after the heartache you experienced in Dubh Linn with that warrior.'

'Will you at least explain your ire to me?'

Her uncle looked up from the stick he'd carved into the rough shape of Thor's goat. 'You know who his father is. You know the danger that puts us in. After all these years of being able to breathe free, to be confronted with such a man, asking for Halfr as if he had the right to know!'

'Not an explanation. Since when did you ever judge men by what their fathers had done? You taught me that was the height of folly.'

'I have a bad feeling about this situation,' her uncle said, putting down the piece of wood and stirring the embers of the fire until they glowed a brilliant red. 'He wants to spread you on bread like new-season honey and feast on you.'

Maer dampened down the little voice which whispered *Yes, please.* Instead, she smiled and continued in what she hoped was a flat, expressionless voice. 'He will depart as soon as is practical. He has always behaved properly with me, despite what the good father might have implied. Stop seeing shadows where there are none. I have enough self-respect not to be a notch on any man's sword.'

Her uncle dropped the stick and turned to face her. 'Over the years, one hears things. Rumours. Whispers.' His mouth became thin. 'None of them particularly flattering. Lazy. He darts from one thing to the next. One woman to the next. Never settling. Lucky in battle, though.'

'Just lucky, or did it take skill? He navigated the whirlpool in full spate.'

'A likely tale told to impress the gullible.'

'I believe him. I inspected the ship.' Maer pressed her hands together and willed her uncle to understand about Karn and his now-unjust reputation. Maybe he'd been like that once, but he'd changed. People were allowed to alter as they grew older. She knew she wasn't the same person who had left Agthir as a child. 'His men trust him with their lives.'

Her uncle tapped his fingers together and appeared unconvinced. 'What does that tell you? Thinking logically, Maer, rather than considering his shoulders or red-gold hair.'

Maer gritted her teeth. Her uncle had reverted to his teaching mode. He had adopted the wise teacher whenever he kept that there was a lesson he thought she'd missed. When she was young and they first escaped, she used to mull over the lessons for days, but not this time. He had it wrong. Karn was going to be a useful friend, and her uncle should stop trying to make it seem like he was in the same mould as his father.

'It tells me that there is some good in him and that rumours or whispers can be false. He may be reckless, but he also learns from his mistakes. He freely admits the stunt with the whirlpool was an error.' Maer picked up a stick and drew several runes in the ashes. 'He reminds me a bit of you or perhaps my father. The stories I heard about you two and the stunts you pulled. My father never settled until he met my mother. I remember my mother saying that you had lost your heart to Thorfi's late wife and never found it again.'

Her uncle frowned. 'Your memory is better than I'd considered.'

'One must be logical. Karn is also a *dauthamathr*,' she said using the proper word for a man who has been condemned to death, instead of just calling him a wolf's head. 'Becoming one alters people, as you well know.'

'If he has truly been condemned to death, why hasn't he run towards the east? A man can disappear for years in the rivers which run down to Constantinople. Why wash up here? Why ask for Halfr after all these years? Who is behind this is what I want to know.'

There was little point in telling her uncle when he was in this mood that he could just question Karn. He was far too stubborn. She stared at the fire. Patience was always hard for her, but she had to allow her uncle a chance to get to know Karn.

'You told him he ceased to exist, which I think he took for being dead.'

'Perhaps, perhaps not. He did appear to believe me, which is something.'

Maer forced a breath. The man wasn't asking any question that she hadn't already asked herself. Years ago, she'd have hoped that somehow her mother was sending word that she wanted her to return. She couldn't see that happening, not after all this time.

As her uncle had told her as they watched her father's hall burn from their hiding place and she had wanted to call out for her, her mother had made her choice. Maer knew that choice included naming Svanna as her daughter—something she was sure her mother had wanted to do long before that as Svanna was the better child, the more perfect child who never was in trouble. Even now, her throat closed at the thought—she had not been good enough for her mother.

No, Karn had not travelled all this way to retrieve her. Not after all this time. She quashed that sudden wild hope before it caused her to do dangerous things like confessing who she was to Karn.

'He didn't intend on coming here. His mast broke.' She attempted to keep all emotion out of her voice. 'We rescued him.'

'I suspect among certain sections of Agthir, the hunt for Halfr the Bold is a mythical quest. We know how many warriors have asked in the past.' He gave a thin smile. 'I've never been inclined to give them what they wanted. I'm quite fond of my head in its own way.'

'Not for several years,' Maer said slowly, trying to puzzle things out. 'Not since we travelled here, rather than staying in Constantinople and the east.'

He rolled his eyes. 'Are you searching for excuses for him, Maer? Hopefully I have trained you better than that. Use your eyes and tell me what he is.'

She drew a line through the runes. Her uncle had indeed trained her to be cynical about men. And she knew the sort of damning words he expected, but her heart kept screaming that Karn wasn't like the spoilt princeling who had had his way continually smoothed for him, something she was certain he must be. He had a genuinely kind heart and a fair bit of courage. 'I'm no longer the young girl you rescued. I've learnt my lessons well, particularly about men and their faithlessness.'

He caught her hand. 'I do worry about you. I promised your moth—your parents that I'd keep you safe.'

Maer allowed the slight lie. Her father would have wanted her kept safe, and her mother had just allowed him to take her. Easer for everyone.

She was grateful for her uncle keeping her safe, even if when it first happened, she kept waiting for a message that somehow her mother had made a mistake and she wanted her child back. That message never arrived, and she hated that a piece of her waited for it still.

'You've done. Let's not quarrel. We're two against the world.' She went over to the cooking pot and ladled several spoons of the pottage into a bowl. 'You eat your pottage. Then, explain to me why you are annoyed at the petty kings.'

'How do you know they were rude?'

She rolled her eyes. 'You're often rude when you are hungry.'

'You sound like your mother.'

Maer ignored the jibe. 'Eat the pottage.'

Her uncle took it and began to eat as if he was ravenous. 'Don't ask me to be pleasant to him.'

'I'll handle our guests, Uncle. You've enough to worry about.'

He reached out, and she squeezed his hand. 'But our

uninvited guests, as you call them, are precisely what I'm worried about. Strangers arriving and disrupting things.'

She squeezed his hand back and then let go, wrapping her arms about her waist. 'The archers and I have been practicing, even if our priest doesn't think women should be involved in battles.'

'I will recheck all our defences. Keep our guests entertained while I do it, as I don't want to reveal all our secrets to them.'

She laughed. Whatever had ailed her uncle appeared to have passed with his stomach filling up. And keeping Karn away from her uncle was not a hardship. 'You simply wanted an excuse to be angry.'

'I will be glad when that spoilt lordling leaves.'

Maer concentrated on her loom, but she knew her heart would weep that day.


The rain early in the afternoon had given way to clear skies. For once, the night sky showed twinkling stars and the nearly full moon, bathing everything in silver. The sort of night Maer enjoyed wandering in. Seeing the stars always brought comfort to her. She used to like to think of the people she loved seeing the same stars, but now she simply saw them as old friends and companions, unaltering in a constantly changing world.

Maer wrapped the shawl tighter around her shoulders and tried to think straight about her uncle and his refusal to entertain any notion that Karn being here was a good omen.

A stone hitting the water made her gasp slightly. Karn stood there tossing stones into the harbour, right at the marking point for the arrows. Her uncle's theory was that if they could hit them with the arrows first, then they would be less inclined to climb the steep slope to the hall, giving him and his men time to attack.

'Some problem with your ship's hull beyond the huge hole, Karn?' she asked after watching him skim a few stones. 'Has something else gone wrong? Because you will never be able to fill up the harbour by throwing stones in.'

He turned towards her, the bulk of his shoulders hiding the moon. She wished she could discern his expression.

'Maer, what are you doing out here? All is well. All is quiet.'

His voice rippled over her, warming her down to her toes.

'Perhaps you conjured me like you do with your magic tricks,' she said going to stand next to him.

'Sleight of hand. No magic required, but it makes people relax and smile.'

'Smiling is good.' She deliberately kept her gaze on the harbour, rather than staring up into his eyes, but her entire being tingled in awareness at his nearness. He moved slightly and her shoulder collided with his chest.

'Skipping stones across the water helps me to think,' he said, his low voice rumbling in her ear. 'Some men whittle. Others forge swords. But I find doing this helps when I find it difficult to sleep.'

'Not very productive to my thinking. Simply plonking stones in the harbour'

His shoulder bumped hers again as he skimmed the next stone, making it skip across the water three times. She tried to ignore the sudden pulse of awareness which thrummed through her. Karn was passing through and wouldn't look back when he went. She'd experienced that so many times before.

'A trick my mentor taught me. Forces me to concentrate on skimming and the intractable problem solves itself.' His chest shook against her shoulder with barely suppressed laughter at some memory. 'Or that is the theory.'

He leant down to pick up another stone, and as he did so, this time his hand brushed her side.

An accidental caress? She pushed the thought away and cleared her throat. 'Can you fix your ship, or should my uncle take you to the next market?'

'My helmsman swears he can.'

He moved so that her elbow was more firmly embedded into his chest. His mouth was a single breath away. All she had to do was to tilt her chin upwards. She forgot how to breathe. She swallowed hard and tried to regain control. 'I'll let him know.'

Her voice was far too breathless. She cleared her throat. 'What do you intend to do once you leave here?'

'Why doesn't your uncle wish to speak about Halfr Hammdrson?' His words were a seductive whisper, sliding over her skin, making her want to confess. 'Is he truly dead? Is that what he meant when he said Halfr ceased to exist? How and when did this happen? Does he know of anyone who was there when Halfr breathed his last?'

She forced a breath and regained a measure of control. He was trying to manipulate her. As if she'd betray her uncle for a kiss, even one which could send her senses spinning.

'Ask him,' she answered carefully and concentrated on ensuring her lungs filled properly with air. 'I was little more than a girl when we left Agthir.'

He put his fingers under her chin and tilted it upwards. 'Thank you, Maer, for the suggestion. Your honesty shines out from your face.'

Maer swallowed hard and tried not to drown in his eyes. She refused to lie to him, but neither would she betray her uncle, who would argue that the man he'd been before the invasion no longer existed, just like the girl she'd once been. He'd shed that name like a snake sheds its outgrown skin. And then he'd argue that she was no longer Ingebord, daughter of the former king and Queen Astrid. Maer knew, though, that deep down a portion of her remained that girl who used to cry every night for her lost dog, wondering if Tippi missed her. 'I'm pleased that is cleared up.'

'I am as well.' His fingers brushed her arm, sending warm pulses radiating through her. She knew she should step away, but instead she stepped closer. The moonlight highlighted the planes of his cheeks. Freyr help her, she wanted to feel his mouth against hers. She wanted to lean into him and forget the past which was lurking behind her like a great toad.

'I should go.'

'Why does your uncle loathe me?' he asked softly, catching her elbow. 'Surely you must know that. It goes beyond me being from Agthir. Something personal, but I've never quarrelled him.'

'He knows who your father is. He knows what he did.'

'I can't help having him as my father, can I?' Karn put a warm hand on her shoulder, and the heat made her legs melt. 'Sometimes parents are terrible examples rather than inspirations. I've no wish to be a leader like he has become, trapped in a loveless political marriage for the sake of the kingdom, continually seeking vengeance for petty insults, and imposing his will on innocents who had nothing to do with the quarrel. My dream is to become a leader whom men can look up to and trust, and who only seeks war when all avenues have been explored, because the cost in blood can be far too high.'

The faint twist of his mouth told her he suffered from his

father's rejection but was trying to hide it, just as she did with her mother's rejection. Proudly self-reliant. Her heart ached, and she knew she couldn't do the prudent thing and move away from him.

'He lost everything because of your father and the invasion,' she whispered. 'Including his family. I am all that remains.'

'Over a decade, and the world has altered.' He reached out and traced the line of her jaw. 'Irrevocably. I can do many things, Maer, but I can't undo the past. A hard lesson, but one I had to learn and one I keep learning.'

'I make enough of my own mistakes without being lumbered by my parents'.'

His mouth twisted upwards. 'You're wiser than me, Maer.'

'I know.'

'Good, because I require this and hope it will not be a mistake.'

She wet her lips. 'What is not a mistake?'

His mouth descended and claimed hers. Unlike the previous kiss, this one demanded she open her mouth which she willingly did. They drank from each other while their tongues touched and then retreated.

He brought his strong arms about her and pulled her close. The softness of her curves hit the hardness of his body. Solid and welcoming like he wouldn't ever reject her, like he understood without her saying that she too had been rejected by her parent and they shared a bond.

She tangled her hands in his hair and pulled his mouth closer, seeking relief from her thoughts. She wanted to float on this tide of dreams he'd unleashed.

'Maer!' her uncle called from the doorway.

His voice intruded, insistent on the kiss, and recalling

her to sanity. She felt the hard ground under her feet and the way her right slipper pinched. She had no time for dreams.

She stepped back, and Karn immediately released her. Her feet refused to move farther. She stood, with her chest heaving like she'd run a long distance. She knew she should say something, anything, and ensure the kiss was never repeated, but her entire body ached for more. And he would know her words for what they were.

Her uncle called again.

'He's worried about you. Go to him.'

She ran her tongue over her swollen lips. 'What we did was foolish. It should never have happened.'

'Sometimes the wisest things seem foolish.' He brushed her forehead with his mouth. 'See you in the morning, Maer. Sweet dreams.'

'That too.' She forced her voice to sound light and knew she'd dream of him. 'My uncle hates travelling. That's all his ire is.'

'You know him better than I do.'

'It will all work out, you will see.' She hurried towards where her uncle stood silhouetted in the doorway and tried to resist the temptation to glance back at Karn or run her tongue over her tender lips.

'Everything all right, Maer?' he asked. 'You were outside for a long time.'

'Why wouldn't it be?' she answered and hoped in the dim light that her uncle missed her swollen mouth.

# Chapter Six

'My uncle wants the top field's wall repairing. The sheep keep escaping.'

Karn turned from his inspection of the repairs to the boat and enjoyed watching Maer hurry towards them. Her impatient fingers brushed a lock of her hair from her face. He pointedly ignored the questioning glance from his helmsman.

'The ship requires—'

'I will deal with that later,' he said and sauntered over to Maer.

'The wall?' she said. 'Is it possible?'

'All things are possible for you, but I would fix the wall for your uncle as well.'

Her cheeks infused with colour. Ever since they'd shared the late-night kiss, his dreams had been full of her and the way her mouth tasted. He'd tried to steal another kiss or three, but the uncle appeared to have a sixth sense about it and kept appearing, calling her away for another task.

'My uncle thought you would be more amenable if I asked.'

'Why does he avoid me?'

'Not avoiding. He is a busy man.'

'He always sends you to convey his wishes.' He caught

the lock of hair and twined it about his fingers. 'Not that I mind. Is he pushing us together?'

Her cheeks flamed higher. 'Not that. He looks forward to the day you depart.'

'Do you?'

She ducked her head. 'You have done a great deal about the farm.'

'Not an answer.'

She lifted her chin and met his gaze full on. In that heartbeat, he wanted to spend a lifetime gazing at the curve of her bottom lip. 'Best you will get.'

'But you will show me this wall.'

She tilted her head, and her lashes swept over her eyes. 'Just you?'

'My men are busy with the repairs. I had best see what needs to be done before I make any rash bargains.'

He willed her to take the opportunity. He silently vowed to find a way to speak to the uncle, but Maer also held secrets he longed to unwrap.

She made a small curtsy, and the light sparkled in her eyes. 'If you insist…'

He tucked her arm within his and ignored the comments from his men. Somehow it felt right, and that unnerved him. He had no business thinking about this place or her as being right. 'I fear I must.'

'The wall which requires repairing is over here.' Maer strove for a natural and practical tone when they reached the field which had a sweeping view of the sea. When they first arrived, her uncle had wanted to build a new hall here but decided that it was better being closer to the harbour and fresh water.

Her vague idea of finding a way to be alone with Karn

in a gorgeous setting seemed blatant. She had to hope that Karn remained in ignorance.

He went over to the tumbled-down wall and nudged a fallen stone with his foot. 'How long has it been like this?''

'A few months,' Maer admitted, going to stand by it. 'My uncle remembered it today.'

'And he wants it repaired before we can go.'

Maer hated how the cold sweat broke out on the back of her neck. Of course he was going. He had his quest which consumed him. It would be better for everyone when he was gone, except she knew he'd leave a hole in her life. 'He wants a proper job, not a sloppy one.'

'It will delay us.'

'You can always refuse.'

He reached behind her ear and revealed a flower. 'Abuse hospitality? We'd deserve ill fortune for that. And this is the sort of peaceful existence my mother prized.'

She gingerly took the tiny purple flower and attempted to appeared unconcerned even though her body zinged with anticipation. 'She was a warrior in her own right, wasn't she?'

He tilted his head to one side. 'What do you know about my mother?'

Maer swallowed hard. She could hardly confess that her uncle had invoked her many times as the epitome of the sort of woman she should become. She'd tried and tried with her bow and arrow, but she knew she could never match that legendary skill. 'Her fame lingers. I remember the stories from my childhood.'

'Indeed.'

'And my uncle used to urge me on with the bow and arrow saying if one woman could do it, another could as well.' She clenched her fists and hoped he wouldn't ask why a fur and amber merchant wanted to train his adopted niece as a warrior.

His gaze travelled down her figure, lingering on her curves. 'Have you fought in many battles with this bow and arrow of yours?'

'Enough.' She held back the escapes from the assassins. 'The journey to Constantinople was fraught with danger. Being able to shoot gave me confidence and security, particularly...'

He tilted her chin so that she looked deep into the clear blue of his eyes and the remaining words about surviving when her uncle needed to be elsewhere died on her lips. 'Is that your desire—security?'

She tried to ignore the shifting colours of his eyes, how close they were and how she wanted to drown in them. 'And peace to be able to live quietly. My uncle and I have found it here. For a long time I had no home, just a place to lay my head. I like to think we have found a place to make a proper life.'

She stopped, aware that she'd probably said too much about her hopes and dreams for the future. But the ache which came as she was forced to leave Agthir had never left her; even now it lingered.

He let her chin go and turned from her. 'Security is not something I can offer. My home has been torn from me.'

She wrapped her arms about her aching middle. 'I know you are going to leave.'

He ran a hand through his hair. 'I want to be a steadfast warrior, bravely defending those I care about and giving them a chance to live in peace, but to do that I need to find out what precisely happened to Halfr.'

Cold seeped into her, and she suddenly knew what he was doing. He was using her attraction to him to obtain information. And she'd nearly fallen for it. Her uncle's caution had been well-founded. 'Why do you want to know about Halfr? I told you that he doesn't exist anymore except as a memory. Why is it important?'

Rather than answer, he stepped away from her and shaded his eyes, staring out to sea. 'You said that the assistant swine herder had seen a ship from the North the other day?'

'What does that have to do with Halfr? The herder often tells tall tales. No ship has come into the harbour. That's when my uncle says to worry.'

He shook his head and pointed. 'No, look. He was right.'

She forced her voice to be slow like she was speaking with the overly excited assistant herder. 'It is a Northern ship. They pass by here regularly.'

Karn shook his head. 'It is a ship from Agthir. I know the sails. Crew of about twenty-five.'

'They will pass on by,' Maer said with more conviction than she felt. 'They always do. This will be a different ship than the one he claimed he saw. They are not scouring the island, searching for you.'

He traced a line about her lips. 'My men need to be ready if they don't sail past, but we will continue our interesting conversation later, Maer.'

'What is going on, Maer?' Her uncle looked up from where he sat stirring the fire when she burst into the hall.

Maer put her hands on her knees and tried to catch her breath. 'Karn and I saw a ship. He claims it is from Agthir. It may be the one the swine herder saw the other day.'

'Panicking solves little. Only if they enter the harbour, remember?'

'Karn is readying—'

A horn started blowing, and shouts came from outside stopping her words. She stared at her uncle.

'Ship coming in too quickly!' came Karn's cry from outside. 'All shields up! Looks to be from Agthir! Hostile! That man of yours swears it is the same ship he saw the other day!'

Stopping only to grab her bow and quiver of arrows, Maer raced outside with her uncle following close behind.

Karn stood with the wind whipping his hair from his face, pointing out to the mouth of the harbour where a dragonship with its shields up was coming in fast.

'We make ready for them,' she said, swallowing the scream to her uncle who nodded.

'You know what to do, Maer.'

'My men and I stand ready to fight,' Karn declared.

Her uncle merely raised his brow. 'I'd expect no less.'

'Uncle!'

'Now is not the time, Maer,' Karn said. 'Too much is at stake.'

The older man harrumphed. 'On that we agree, at least.'

At her uncle's signal, the assistant swine herder raced off to light the beacon. Maer banged the gong which stood outside the hall, signalling people should be prepared. The women gathered their things and started with the priest and several of the farmers for the safe hiding place farther inland. Karn gave her a pointed look, but Maer simply raised a brow.

'It is different for me,' she said with a shrug. 'I can shoot, Karn.'

According to the priest, she should go with them. Her argument had always been a plentiful escort existed and she wanted to play her part in defending these lands. Her uncle had taught her well and she intended to use her skills.

She couldn't confess that she never wanted to be stuck in a hidey-hole, waiting again.

When her uncle lifted his brow, she shrugged and pointed to the roof. 'Like we practised. Make sure you get them to the mark, and I will do the rest.'

'Who am I to argue with you?' Her uncle's smile showed his pride in her choice.

A warm glow filled Maer at the rare praise. Getting his approval meant the world to her. It was the thing which stopped her tears and aching loneliness when her mother had abandoned her for Svanna.

Trying to ignore the sudden ache in her heart, she turned towards Karn who stood grim-faced with his sword strapped to his side and his helm jammed on his head and staring out at the ship which was sweeping ever closer.

'You were right, sir, and I was wrong,' he said. 'They are hunting me. I've put you all, including Maer, in danger.'

Her uncle waved a hand. 'Far too late to think about regrets.'

'Will you be standing shoulder to shoulder with us dressed like that?' Karn asked in a worried tone.

Maer glanced down at her gown and apron. 'Never fear. Where I'm going, I shall not require armour.'

'Where are you going?'

She gestured towards the roof. 'If you will excuse me...'

Her uncle nodded to her. 'Maer, do what we have practised. I trust you to get it right this time. Hurry, Maer. Much depends on you being in the right place.'

Not daring to look back, Maer climbed to the top of the roof where she would get an unobstructed view. She and her uncle had practised this many times. Several designated archers were already there. They moved over and allowed her to take her favourite spot, dead in the centre.

'Are you sure we can do this?' one asked.

'As long as we have arrows, we can shoot,' Maer said. 'Remember to wait for my uncle's signal and not be tempted before. Surprise is all.'

Her fellow archers gave vigorous nods. 'We know what to do, Maer.'

Beneath her, she could see the ship making its way to the shore, her uncle with his battle sword strapped to his side and Karn standing with his men, looking resolutely out to sea.

She notched her first arrow despite hoping that this ship had come in peace. She forced her hand and neck to relax. She'd find out soon enough. Silently she prayed that her uncle remembered to show Karn and his men where to stand. She had practised hitting the mark where the first volley had to go more times than she wanted to think about, but she had no idea what she would do if Karn and his men were in harm's way.

'I am in charge here, lordling,' Sigmundson stated with ponderous authority after Maer vanished. 'If they come in peace and wish to trade, we've no quarrel with them.'

Karn raised a brow and sought to control his temper. The grizzled warrior spoke to him like he was twelve. Who did he think he was? Halfr the Bold? A legend in his own mind, more like.

'Even if they are from Agthir?'

'Even then.' The older warrior made a disgruntled noise in the back of his throat. 'I've no quarrel with Agthir. I ignore their existence as long they ignore mine.'

'What do you want from me?' Karn asked, struggling to control his temper. That man had spent the last few days being unpleasant, and now he said that he had no quarrel with Agthir.

'To stand there and look pretty. You can do that, can't you, princeling?'

'My prowess as a warrior was earned, not bestowed.'

'Hopefully that remark will remain untested.'

'I know the sail. I know who commands that ship. There will be a battle.'

'Forgive me if I think differently.' Sigmundson turned, dismissing him like some wet-behind-the-ears boy who had never faced a battle instead of the survivor of a decade of warring seasons.

Karn concentrated on clenching and unclenching his fists rather than giving into the sudden surge of anger. Whatever Sigmundson thought, he knew the ship's sails and therefore the man who commanded it—Beorn Beornson, also called Beorn the Crook-nose, a warrior who shifted with the wind and always looked to make a profit. He had hated Karn ever since Karn broke his nose during a training session in his father's yard the year they both turned twelve, and the feeling was mutual.

Beorn had made the error of laughing at Karn's late mother, calling her an insult to womanhood and neither a man nor a woman because she once successfully led an army. Even then Karn knew he should have controlled his temper and not repeatedly struck Beorn's nose with his fist, but he refused to allow the insult to his mother's honour.

'What do you require from me, old man?' Karn asked softly. 'Because I am at a loss of how to win your friendship or even the barest portion of regard.'

The man's old eyes turned towards him and seemed to peer deep down into his soul. 'For you not to hurt Maer.

She means the world to me. I've dedicated my life to seeing her safe. If I should fall, keep her safe.'

Karn tightened his jaw. 'I've no intention on hurting her or putting her in any sort of danger.'

'I know your type—careless,' the man continued as if Karn hadn't spoken. 'In the past, you always had someone around to pick up the pieces. There isn't anyone now, and mistakes will get people killed. Think before you act from here on out.'

'Maer has nothing to fear from me or my intentions.' It was as far as Karn intended to go with this conversation. His growing feelings for the woman were far too new to take the risk of voicing them out loud to anyone, let alone to Maer's uncle who disapproved of him. If he hadn't spotted this ship, he'd have seduced her in that field. It had taken all his self-control to speak about Halfr's whereabouts instead of kissing her thoroughly like his body had insisted. 'I owe her a life debt.'

'Would you give your life for her?'

He balanced his weight on the balls of his feet. 'If necessary.'

'Let's hope it doesn't come to that.' The man's eyes twinkled as if something amused him. 'My niece is quite fond of your face.'

'Is she?' Karn firmed his jaw and hated how his heart leapt. 'She hasn't said.'

'I could be wrong. Women can be difficult to judge. Her eyes appear to follow you. Everywhere.' Maer's uncle took a step forward.

Karn pushed all thoughts of Maer away. 'I know these men. I know how they fight—what their strengths are and their weaknesses. Their leader is untrustworthy in the extreme and ruthless.'

'That is part of the problem. You know these men. I don't.'

Without waiting for an answer, the man marched down to the shore. He stood by the flat rock where Karn had kissed Maer so thoroughly several nights ago. 'We make our stand here. Behind me and to the right.'

'Here? Surely it would be better to go closer to where they are landing. Beorn the Crook-nose will be looking for any opportunity.'

'They will come to me. We will talk. Perhaps they will leave. Perhaps not. Then you will see why we wait.' The man had a certain implacable serenity to him as if he already knew what the outcome would be. 'You will remain where I direct you. Can you do that?'

'I wouldn't dream of abusing your hospitality.' Karn shrugged and motioned to his men who stood behind him.

He placed his hand on the hilt of his sword, ready for the fight which would inevitably come. To his left and right, the farm workers stood, some carrying pitchforks and other makeshift shields. A rag-tag bunch, but there was great purpose in their movements as if they had practised this many times. Maer had said that her uncle feared the Northmen from the Dubh Linn raiding, and perhaps they were better than he feared, but he doubted they would deter Beorn the Crook-nose.

'Why are you here?' Maer's uncle asked first in Gaelic to the Crook-nose, and then when the Crook-nose stared at him, asked again in Norse.

With his deadly grin, Beorn answered in Norse. 'What is it to you, old man? I can see what I came for. I mean to take his head. Move out of my way.'

'No.'

'What do you mean *no*?'

'My holdings, my rules.' Maer's uncle exuded supreme confidence. 'I keep the peace, and therefore, I ask again— why are you here, armed for war instead of for trade?'

Beorn nodded towards where Karn and his men stood. 'If you keep the peace, then give me the *dauthamathr* and his men you falsely shelter. My king requires their heads.'

'Why?'

'The reasons are many and varied.' Beorn waved his hand. 'All that is required for you to know is my king requires it done. And you don't want to anger my king. No, indeed, that would be a mistake, given your band of defenders.'

'Your king is Thorfi?' Sigmundson asked in a cold voice.

'You have heard of him and his might. Good.' Beorn's smile increased. 'That one over there is a slippery fellow. Anything he has told you is suspect. The jaarl Drengr demonstrated to Thorfi how ambitious his son was.'

'My father lost his temper.'

Sigmundson glared at him, and Karn shut his mouth.

'Thorfi hates admitting any mistake. He does not want the son of his late wife dead.'

'Yet he remains a wolf's head. Surrender him to me.'

'And if I refuse, as your king's writ does not run here and I've no idea who this Drengr fellow is?'

Beorn sent a long stream of spittle flying. 'Then, we shall take them, and many lives will be lost. Your life maybe.'

'These men are under my protection. Go tell your king that Sigmund Sigmundson says no, he has had a belly full of Agthir bullies.'

'You would risk your life for a man such as he? He blunders, constantly putting his men to danger.' The Crook-nose made a sorrowful noise and shook his lying head. 'I bet he will not say what he did to bring King Thorfi's wrath on his head. His father would not proclaim him worthy enough to rule on his own.'

'Nevertheless, Thorfi adores his son because he is all which remains of his late wife, a woman he loved beyond all reason.'

Karn stared at the older man. A hornet's nest of questions buzzed about his brain. How did he know Karn's parents' relationship that intimately? But he was right: his father had adored his mother, becoming insensible when she died.

Beorn blinked twice. 'What did you say?'

'The only lives which will be lost will be yours and your men's if you persist in this course,' Sigmundson said in a firm but carrying voice. 'I suggest you return to your ships and go away from this place while you still can. Maybe some other day, you and Lord Karn will encounter each other in another place, but here, he has sanctuary.'

'No!' Beorn roared. 'We will not. You chose wrong, old man! We will take this place and sell all as slaves.'

Beorn's men laughed and beat their swords against their shields.

'It is you who have chosen wrong.' Maer's uncle raised his hand and twisted it in midair before giving five long blasts on his whistle. 'A man who stops running starts living. Today I choose to breathe freely.'

Karn stared at him in astonishment. He'd never thought of it like that. Running meant he was always looking over his shoulder, waiting for the unexpected blow to fall. But standing there doing nothing like Sigmundson was doing solved nothing either. Why was he doing that?

In the next heartbeat, his question was answered. An arrow arched from the main hall's roof and connected with the throat of the man standing next to Beorn. Karn struggled to keep his face straight. Maer's first shot was brilliant.

Beorn stopped in surprise but roared again, raising his sword, seeking to attack Maer's uncle. In that brief heartbeat when Karn's attention had been on a barrage of arrows, Sigmundson had drawn his sword in anticipation.

Beorn clashed swords with him. The man might be old, but he moved better than most warriors Karn had seen, parrying and thrusting until Beorn was forced to retreat and regroup before leading another charge. Again, the barrage of arrows was loosed.

Beorn seemed to anticipate them this time. He lowered his head and charged. Whether it was age or merely a lucky angle, Karn did not want to say, but Beorn's blow connected with Sigmundson's leg, causing a large gash.

As Sigmundson fell to one knee, he gestured towards Karn to take charge. Signalling to his men to fall in behind him and protect Sigmundson with a shield wall, Karn rallied the remaining islanders. It seemed odd in a way to be clashing swords with men he'd called brothers and comrades at the start of the warring season, but it was the right thing to do. Neither he nor his men intended on going anywhere without a fight.

Once the wall was established, they started forward, driving Beorn's men back. Many of his company fell in that charge. Karn hoped they would run for their boat, but they regrouped and came again, swinging their swords and axes.

He gritted his teeth. Beorn had always been an overly ambitious fool. .

'Are you certain you want to enforce that demand for my head?' Karn asked as he beat off another advance and his sword clashed with Beorn's over the prone body of Maer's uncle, preventing Beorn from administering the fatal blow.

Beorn wiped a hand across his brow. 'Never been more certain of anything.'

'You appear to be losing, Beorn. You should go while you still can.'

'I don't lose. I win. Always. Drengr said that Ingebord would be mine if I returned with your head.'

'That has always been the problem with you. You believe sweetmeat promises too quickly, and you never know when it is best to give up.' Karn started to drive forward.

'Watch out! Get behind the flat rock!' he heard Maer's voice cry above the mêlée. And her voice gave him hope for a better future. He wasn't alone. Maer had his back.

Another volley of arrows rained down—from three directions. Attempting to dodge them, Beorn stepped into the swing of one of his axe-bearing warriors, and the weapon struck him in the neck.

Karn winced. Once they had been friends, after a fashion. He bent down and picked up Beorn's bloodied sword. He could remember the day Beorn bought the sword in Kaupang and how proud he'd been to finally own a well-crafted sword. Of course, he'd made a dig at Karn never having to lust after anything because his father would provide. Karn had ignored the remark, but it had rankled.

'Beorn is dead! He has gone to Valhall,' Karn shouted, holding the sword aloft and banishing the memories. 'Your ship belongs to Sigmund Sigmundson now.'

The fighting slowly ceased, and the remainder of Beorn's felag surrendered. Of the over twenty-five who had stormed ashore, five remained standing including the one who had killed Beorn.

'Karn?' Maer's uncle croaked from where he lay.

The priest was tending his wounds, but it was clear the old warrior had lost a great deal of blood. Karn hurried over. 'I... I...made a mistake. I thought of you as your father's son, but you are your mother's, and I owed her a great life debt, one which I failed to repay. I gave her—'

'Save your strength, sir.' Karn knelt beside him. It surprised him that the man had fought with his mother. 'I will get the news to Maer. But we won, sir, we won. The day is yours.'

'Good.' Sigmundson's eyes fluttered shut, and his face drained of colour.

'Tell me what to do,' he said to the priest. 'Can his life be saved?'

'Can you keep Maer occupied?' the priest asked in a low voice. 'I may be able to save his life, but I need to operate. What I don't need is Maer making demands on me. I will do my best, but then the rest will be in God's hands.'

'I will see what can be done. But Maer has a mind of her own.'

The priest laughed. 'You may be from the North, but I see you think with a Gael's practicality. Do what you can to soften the blow. I can't abide a woman's wails and gnashing of teeth.'

Karn gritted his teeth. The priest knew nothing of Maer. He hated the task, but he also knew that he would not entrust it to anyone else. 'I will do.'

# Chapter Seven

'My lady, have we won?' one of the archers called to Maer. 'I only have three arrows left.'

Maer shaded her eyes and peered out over the battle-field. It was clear there was no longer any need for the arrows. They had served their purpose. She had to hope that Karn and her uncle survived. 'No need for another volley.'

The man left out a huge sigh of relief. 'Then, we won against the pagan horde. God's will be done. I bless the day Sigmund Sigmundson and you arrived.'

Maer shaded her eyes and stood on her tiptoes. She couldn't see her uncle or Karn amongst those picking through the remains of the fight, and it bothered her. Both had been in the centre of the fighting.

'I should go and see what the news is.' Maer unslung her quiver which now contained only five arrows instead of the twenty-five she had lugged up here. Victory, but at what cost?'

'My lady, are we safe now? May I go check on my wife? She is expecting our first child soon.'

She wanted to ask if anyone was ever truly safe, but those were not the words the lad needed to hear.

'Go, tell her that we won the day, thanks in part to your steadfast shooting.'

The lad beamed from ear to ear before rushing off. Maer made sure the discarded bows and arrows were tidied before she left the roof as her uncle had always demanded happen. When it was done, she pressed her hands against her eyes and tried to prepare herself for the worst.

'Maer! Maer! Where are you, Maer?'

Her heart leapt. Karn was shouting for her. He'd survived. Maybe the carnage was not as bad as she feared. Maybe her uncle had survived as well.

'I'm coming down.' She rapidly climbed down. When she reached the final rungs, Karn's hands went about her waist and hauled her to him.

His mouth descended on hers. Deep. Dark and fierce. But very much alive.

'I have been searching for you,' he said against her mouth.

'Are you all right?' she asked, leaning back against his embrace, breathless from the strength and intensity of the kiss.

Her hands travelled all over him, trying to discern if he had deep wounds. He leant into her arms. His eyes crinkled at the corners, causing her heart to flip over.

'Don't tease me, Karn. How injured are you?'

'Me? A few bruises, a couple of cuts, nothing too deep.' He gave one of his heart-stopping smiles before sobering. 'Shall we go for a walk?'

A chill passed through Maer. Something bad had happened.

'A walk? Why? My uncle is always clear on what needs to happen after a raid—the clean-up.' She forced the words out, hoping her voice sounded normal.

'Because they are very busy here. I would like to get

washed.' He gave another smile, one which warmed her. 'You can check the state of my injuries for yourself then.'

She crossed her arms. 'You don't need me to wash your back.'

He lifted a brow. 'Only if you are offering. I want to be alone with you, Maer. The thought kept me going. A short walk, and then I will go for my lonely wash.'

She drew her brows together, trying to focus. Karn was speaking in a code, presumably because others were about. Karn obviously wanted to speak to her about something, away from prying ears. More than likely her uncle had refused to hear him out about pursuing the remaining Northmen. She risked a breath. That had to be it: he wanted to get a message to her uncle. She had to stop thinking about catastrophes. Her uncle was busy like he always was after a raid. He was one of the most skillful swordsmen she'd ever encountered.

'And my uncle? Where will I find him?'

His eyes slid away from her. 'Your uncle… Well now, the priest is with him. He asked me to find you, quiet like and not causing a disturbance.'

She put her hand on his arm and tried to keep her legs from collapsing. He put his arm about her waist, and she leant her head against his chest, drawing strength from him.

After a few breaths, she lifted her head and stepped away, even though it was the last thing she wanted to do.

'How badly injured?' she asked and then struggled to catch her breath. Karn looked like he was about to haul her into his arms again, but she shook her head. 'It is fine. Collapsing or giving way to hysterics achieves nothing. I don't need time to compose myself either. I appreciate what you were trying to do in getting me somewhere quiet, even though the method was unique.'

'He took several hard blows to his body and head, but he breathes.'

'Several blows?'

'Gave more back. Saved my life more than once.' His face turned sombre. 'Your uncle is a great warrior, Maer. I could learn much from him. I would like to learn from him, if he will permit it.'

Maer clung on to what he was saying rather than considering the alternative. Her uncle lived. He had to, and Karn thought he would get better, well enough to train him. 'You used *is*. Does that mean you think he will live?'

'The priest is hopeful, but you need to allow him to work his miracles and not pester him—his words, not mine. Your uncle grunted his agreement.'

The knots in her stomach tightened, and the world tilted. She put her hand to her mouth, and Karn's strong arms were instantly around her again. The steady thump of his heart resounded in her ear and made the world straighten.

'Will he recover?' she asked. 'I'm not sure I can bear it if he goes. We have been together for a long time. Us two against the world.'

He stroked her head. 'I could lie, Maer, but the truth is I've no idea. No one does. Sometimes we must trust, even if that is difficult. And there is no one I would trust more than that priest. Look at how he saved my men. I thought they were goners for sure.'

She looked up at him and cupped his face with her hands. 'You have already told me the truth. He is gravely injured. No one knows when the Nourns might break the thread of life.'

'If they do, then he will surely go to Valhall.'

'Is it wrong for me to hope that he will keep away from that feasting hall for a long while yet? We need him here.'

He gave a crooked smile. 'Not wrong in the slightest. As I said, I want to learn from him. Maybe in time, I can become that good. If I had his skills and technique…maybe I could save other lives.'

'Your men proclaim you a great warrior.'

'Men say many things after a victory, but your uncle possesses skill which I long to learn. Enable me to honour my mother's legacy.'

'Modesty does not become you, Lord Karn.' She tried for a laugh, but it came out as a shuddering sigh. 'You were the hero. I saw what you did.'

He pulled her close and held her as if she was made of precious glass. 'Cling on to hope, Maer. Don't give in to despair.'

Despair? She had no idea how she'd survive without her uncle. Her uncle would tell her to stop being silly, but she knew how much she leant on him.

She brushed her lips against his. 'I'm trying to.'

'That's what I like to hear.'

'I need to see him. I won't pester him,' she said against his mouth. 'Immediately. We have been quarrelling since… well…since he returned, and I don't want to—'

He put two fingers over her lips. 'Don't even think it. Time enough later. He's not going anywhere.'

Maer leant her head against his chest and listened to the reassuring thump of his heart. He understood her.

'The priest said you'd be in the way. You are apparently all thumbs when it comes to nursing.'

'He would say that!'

'I told him that I'd try. I didn't say that I would succeed.' He lifted her chin, so she was forced to look him in the eyes. 'You were the one who told me that the priest was the best surgeon you'd encountered, but he needs peace to do it.'

She stared in his deep blue eyes and knew what he was saying was the truth, but it did not make it any easier. 'This is my uncle.'

'And he is very strong.' Karn cupped her face. 'I owe him a life debt. He may hate me, but he refused to give me and my men up to Beorn and save the village.'

'He doesn't hate you,' she whispered. 'He has learned the hard way to be wary with his trust.'

'May I hold you for a while without talking?' he asked against her earlobe.

'I would like that very much.' She rested her head against his chest again and drew strength from the steady sound of his heartbeat.

They stood there for a long time, and Maer found it far more comforting than she thought it would be.

'He has looked after me for a long time,' she said into his tunic. 'Since I lost my parents. I loathe battles and war. I've seen too many, but you never forget the first one.'

She wished she could confess about everything, but that was impossible. She couldn't abandon her uncle and his ways now. But she knew if he asked she'd tell him the truth about when she'd first experienced battle.

Karn rested his forehead against hers. The gesture gave her comfort. 'I don't think anyone who has ever been in a battle likes war. They might see the necessity of it, but a battle is always a dirty business.'

The hard knot in her stomach eased. He hadn't asked. She was safe.

'Kiss me one more time,' she whispered against his mouth, because she did not want to think any more about past battles or of other dragonships which might arrive. She simply wanted to be, and the easiest way to do that was to lose herself in Karn's embrace. 'Kiss me like you mean it.'

'Like this?'

His mouth descended again. Their tongues tangled. She drank from him and somehow felt steadier. Her head seemed to clear. The temptation to remain here threatened to overwhelm her. She put her hands against his chest.

Instantly his arms dropped. He tilted his head to one side. 'Maer?'

'I must go and see him now. Thank you for allowing me the time to get my thoughts together.'

He touched her hand. 'What are friends for?'

She put her hand against his cheek and felt the silky roughness of his stubble. 'Get yourself cleaned up.'

He gave a heart-stopping smile. 'My lady's wish is my command.'

She walked quickly towards the infirmary, not daring to look back. The crowd that stood at the door parted at her arrival. Several patted her back, before dissolving into tears. Maer forced her back to stay as straight as a newly forged sword.

'Is it possible for me to speak with the good father before I must endure the gossip and innuendo?' she asked.

'He sleeps with angels guarding him, Maer,' the priest said to her when he came scurrying out. 'You must allow him to rest. Not bother him with details of running this place.'

'Will he—' Her tongue refused to form the words.

The priest's brow knit. 'In God's hands. But he made it through the operation, which is when I lose most of them.'

The world swam in front of Maer's eyes, but she managed to blink back the tears. 'A small measure of comfort.'

'We won the day, thanks to that warrior of yours, Karn,' someone shouted. 'Find a way to keep him!'

'He is not my warrior,' she said quickly, too quickly.

The priest smiled. 'I wonder if he knows that. The way he glowers at people when they look at you. But I was wrong about him. He is much more than a flirt. He has a good heart.'

Maer was aware her cheeks flamed. Everyone was suddenly a matchmaker. 'You will let me know when my uncle asks for me. Day or night.'

'If he does, I will send word. You need your rest, Maer.'

'My rest?'

The priest smiled. 'We all owe you a great debt. I never thought women should shoot, but you proved me wrong today. You were tireless in keeping the arrows raining down, I'm told.'

'My uncle's plan.'

The priest put a hand on her shoulder. 'We are all praying for Sigmund, my child. God blessed us the day he and you appeared amongst us, asking for shelter.'

Maer wrapped her arms about her waist. Waiting was the hard part. She knew she should sleep but she also knew her mind was too busy. 'Thank you.'

She stumbled aimlessly away, not feeling up to speaking to anyone and asking any god which might happen to be listening to offer some guidance, particularly where she and Karn were concerned.

Should she abandon a habit of a lifetime and couple with Karn, knowing that there wasn't a future for them? That he'd leave and she'd be alone again? But she wanted to be with him. After what she had just experienced, she needed to be with him and to feel alive in a way that only he made her feel.

Ask him and what if he refused, particularly if she confessed about never having been with a man? Some men might prize that, but Maer suspected Karn looked for women who knew how to play the game of pillows and tangled furs.

She soon found herself in a quiet glade, the one she used for thinking. She sank down on a fallen log and buried her face in her hands. Her entire body began to shake as the enormity washed over her.

After the shaking ceased, she gulped a breath of air and glanced about her. Still alone. No Karn suddenly appearing to hold her again. All alone, the way she liked it.

She nodded towards the ash trees which dominated the glade. The decision had been made. She'd left it up to chance and the Nourns like she used to do as a child. She'd asked for a sign. If nothing happened, if she didn't encounter Karn, then it was not meant to be. Simple. And she hadn't encountered him.

The Nourns had spoken. Her life would go on much as it had done. The thought made her slightly disappointed, but the decision had been made for her. She and Karn were not meant to be. A sense of deep regret over a future which would never happen filled her. She *had* wanted to melt into his arms.

'No longer a child, Maer. Just tell him.' Even saying the words aloud didn't make it more likely. She could easily imagine how that conversation would go.

She stood up and circled her shoulders. She needed to return and get on with her life instead of wishing for things which were not meant to be. Her uncle had told her that once when he'd discovered her weeping for her mother.

'Maer?' Karn said, making her miss her step and come down heavily on a twig. She stumbled, but his fingers caught her elbow before she fell. It was clear from his damp hair and clean clothes that he had had a wash. 'Who are you talking to?'

'No one.' She forced her eyes to widen. 'What are you doing here, Karn?'

'The assistant swine herder was concerned. He thought you might be here. Brooding. You did as much as anyone could.'

'He sent you to me?' The words came out too high-pitched. 'I mean, I don't think I told anyone where I was going. I just wanted time to think. Alone.'

His smile was crooked. And she was aware of how his chest went in and out with each breath he took. Her mouth became dry. Daring the Nourns had consequences, as her nurse used to say.

'Not exactly.' His voice flowed over her like honey fresh from the comb. 'I asked where you might be. His guess led me here. People do worry about you, Maer.'

The Nourns had used the swine herder. Typical. She opted for a wry smile. 'All makes sense now.'

'Were you able to speak to your uncle?'

Maer pressed her hands against her gown. 'It is in the lap of the gods. The priest seems to think there is a good chance he will pull through. He survived the operation.'

'Good. I was worried that you had had some bad news about Sigmundson and couldn't face telling anyone else about it.'

She forced her lips to turn up. 'The priest offered hope. Worrying about me is pointless.'

'Might as well tell the sun to halt in the sky or the rain not to fall.' He tilted his head to one side. 'A problem shared, Maer, can make things easier.'

She forced her hands from her gown. 'Thank you for your concern, even if it is misplaced. I've quite recovered from my earlier upset.'

She expected him to make his excuses and go. It was

how things had worked in the past with that other warrior. Every sinew of her being cried out that she didn't want that, but she attempted to focus on breathing.

He tilted his head to one side, and his gaze appeared to examine her from the top of her head to the tips of her toes. 'Maer...'

Suddenly she couldn't bear it. She knew what she had to try. She put two fingers against his mouth. 'Make love to me, Karn. Please. Here and now with no regrets. No promise for the future. Two bodies, making the best of a miserable situation.'

# Chapter Eight

Karn stared at Maer, her words circling around and around in his brain. Unable to think clearly but knowing he had to. His future depended on him getting this right with her whispered plea. He wanted her with every fibre of his being, but he feared getting it wrong and allowing her to slip from him.

How often in recent days had his dreams echoed with her saying some version of those words? He knew the flirtation with her to find out information had grown into something else, and that made him pause.

Only this morning, he woke with a variation of what Maer had just said ringing in his ears. He wanted to believe he had heard correctly, but he also knew he'd taken several blows to his head in his fight with Beorn.

'You want me to do what?' The words burst out before he could stop them.

Hurt and confusion flickered across her face, and he knew he had used the wrong words and in precisely the wrong intonation. She was going to slip away from him like water through his fingers.

She took a step backwards, preparing to flee.

'We shall just leave it, shall we? Forget I said anything. Momentary madness brought on by today's events.' She made a cutting motion with her hand and half turned away.

He ran a hand through his hair and tried again. 'I want to make sure I heard you correctly, Maer. Are you asking me to make love to you? Because my head rings from the blow earlier, and I don't want to do anything which might jeopardise our friendship. I value you too much.'

Inwardly he winced. His words were bland, and yet he knew he meant every word. He did value her friendship. In that short time, it had come to mean a great deal to him.

She raised her chin, showing him her blazing eyes in the sliver starlight. 'If I must ask twice, then there is little point in asking at all. I have my answer. Thank you.'

She started to walk out the glade. Her badly creased gown revealed the curves he wanted to unwrap.

A better man would allow her to walk away. A better man would instinctively know that her asking for him to couple with her was entirely due to the stress of the day. And that coming together like that would complicate both their lives, lives which required no added complexities. A better man would take her back to the compound and put her with the women until this fever in her blood drained away.

Deep inside, he knew he was not the better man, even if he wanted to be for her sake. He longed for her touch and wanted to bury himself deep inside her. He wanted to explore if his dreams about her were a mere shadow of what it could be truly like. He refused to think beyond this day and the next heartbeat.

He reached out and caught her shoulders, stopping her from moving. She stilled but didn't turn around. 'I merely wanted to make sure of the question.'

She glanced back at him with deeply shadowed eyes. 'Did you?'

He longed to ask her who had destroyed her trust, who

had broken her heart. He wanted to tell her that whoever they were, her spirit remained unbroken. She was a survivor. But his throat closed, and the words refused to come. How could they when he knew he'd have to leave her one day soon? Instead, he pulled her close back against him and moulded her curves to the hardness of his muscle.

'Do you doubt that I want you?' he growled in her ear.

She failed to melt into him, and he knew someone had badly hurt her. 'I… I wanted to give you the option.'

He traced the length of her jaw with an exploratory finger. Her flesh trembled like a new leaf in a spring breeze, but she remained still. He wanted to ask about the other men she'd lain with but knew he couldn't bear knowing about them or what they might have done to her. He wanted to erase all the bad memories and make her anew for him.

'You know this will alter things between us, don't you?' he asked nuzzling the slender column of her neck, and her body melted into his. He put a damper on his desire and resolved to take things slowly and at her pace. He slowly turned her around and looked directly into the pools which were her eyes. 'We won't be able to go back to how it was.'

'Things already have altered.' Her tongue flicked out over her lips, wetting them, and turning the colour of summer berries in the silver starlight. 'Asking for forever is an impossibility. I am asking for now.'

'For the now?'

'After all that I experienced today, I wanted the certainty.'

He pressed a warm hand against her cheek. His nostrils drank in her womanly scent, replacing the stench of war. He may have proved himself worthy today, but much remained to be done. His vow had to depend on his actions, not some object that a legend had stolen. And keeping that vow might hurt Maer but he needed to be with her because the future might never happen. 'We can seize the now. What more can anyone ask?'

'Indeed, what more could anyone ask?'

Maer reached up and firmly pulled his mouth against hers, preventing any more conversation.

Now that she had said the words about wanting to have sex with him out loud, a sort of calm had descended. Explaining about her lack of experience was irrelevant to the proceedings. Any explanation would muddy the waters. And she didn't want to explain about how she'd been prepared to give herself only to discover the then man of her dreams entwined with the high king's daughter and how she'd run away with laughter ringing in her ears.

The hard evidence of his arousal pressing against the apex of her thighs demonstrated he wanted her as much as she wanted him. She didn't want to think about the future or what might happen. Or how much at peace she felt in his arms earlier.

Her only other option was running far, far away from the mess that were her uncle's injuries and what it might mean for them and this place they had carved out. And that wasn't possible. She knew her duty, and that meant facing the future. But was it so wrong of her to want to lose herself in the peace of his arms and mouth in a way she'd never wanted to before? She had never understood the point of coupling, but now she was intrigued at the possibilities.

Karn's arms tightened about her. He lifted his mouth from hers. 'Do you mean it, Maer? Say it. Agree to it. No regrets.'

She loved that he gave her a choice. 'Yes, this is something I won't regret. We have the now.'

She opened her mouth and drew his tongue fully in. Hot,

wet and making her entire being sizzle. She arched forward, pressing her breasts into his hard chest.

He brought his hands about her and pulled her firmly against his middle. If anything, the evidence of his arousal was far more obvious than before. The curls of heat in her belly rose and consumed her being.

'See how I want you,' he said taking her earlobe between his teeth and nibbling.

Her hands twined about his hair and moved his lips firmly against hers.

His mouth began to rain little kisses on her jaw, tracing the line to her earlobes, where he suckled again. The heat burgeoning within her surged to white-hot.

Her hands clawed at his tunic, seeking his warm flesh, wanting to feel it under her palms. She groaned in frustration at the cloth. He caught her wrist and held it above her head.

'Far better to be horizontal' he growled in her ear.

She looked over her shoulder as disappointment washed over her. No way she could march through the hall with Karn in tow, seeking her bed. The very thought of the consequences made her shudder. How the Nourns must be laughing!

'No bed,' she said instead of confessing her ignorance. 'What a shame.'

'We can make do. Invention.' He smoothed the hair from her temple. 'No need for you to use that excuse. Tell me to stop if you wish, but no excuses between us. Only honesty.'

'I… I hadn't considered the necessity.'

'Consider this.' He gently laid her down on a bed of soft moss and bracken, spreading his cloak to keep her from the damp. Having settled her, he tangled a lock of her hair about his fingers. 'I'd prefer a soft bed piled high with furs, but this will have to suffice, my lady. Next time, though…'

A hard knot eased in her stomach. He was making it sound like there would be more than one joining. She knew she should confess about her lack of experience, but she didn't want to. Just in case… 'I suspect it will do very well.'

'Is there anything else?'

She ran her tongue over her parched lips. 'Nothing else.'

His fingers skimmed over her body, tracing her curves until they settled on her breasts, teasing the nipples through the fabric of her gown. Round and round in ever decreasing circles, at first seemingly to accidentally flick her nipples, lapping at their edges, until finally he deliberately targeted them, suckling and circling them. Under his lavish attention, her nipples grew painfully tight, and her back further arched the relief his mouth offered.

'Would you like this as well?' She slid her hands under his tunic and encountered his warm flesh. Her fingers quested upwards until she discovered his chest, and she began to explore its contours, rubbing her fingers against the flat of his nipples until they became hardened nubs under the pads of her fingers.

'I'll make it easier for you.' He leant backward and divested himself of the garment, revealing his golden chest, and then his trousers. Then he was rampantly naked. She drew in her breath at the beauty of him bathed in the starlight.

'May I?' he rasped, leaning back down to her and his breath once again caressing her sensitised earlobe.

She nodded, and he slowly removed her gown and undergown as if he was unwrapping some precious parcel. Her nipples hardened even further as the material slid across. Her body bucked upwards, seeking his heat.

He gave a very masculine smile and covered her body with his. 'Can't have you getting cold, my lady.'

She brought her hand around his back, feeling the various indentations and scars. 'You told the truth. You weren't injured.'

'Has all of this been a ruse to see?'

Her hand paused. 'Nothing like that.'

'Good, because I have been wanting to do this for ages.' His hands played on her skin like he was playing a harp, and where his hands quested his mouth followed. All the while her heart kept singing—he had wanted to do this to her. She wasn't some ill-favoured runt like Helga her nurse once called her. For tonight she was desirable.

Under his ministrations, the pulses of heat grew higher and higher until her body began to buck, seeking the cool relief that only he could bring. As if he sensed her need, his fingers slipped between the apex of her thighs and delved deep. The world exploded about her.

'Tight, so tight,' he murmured against her ear. 'Relax, I will make it better.'

'Now. I need you now.' She tugged at his shoulders, knowing that she required more. But equally not wanting to give voice to her fears about being adequate or confess that this was her first time of coupling.

'My insistent lady.'

'Karn,' she whispered, 'there is something I should say.'

He placed two fingers against her mouth. 'Are you trying to tell me to stop?'

Slowly she shook her head. Stopping would be the worst thing. Her body wanted him. 'Not that.'

'Good. Allow me to enjoy you, all of you. I've dreamt of this.'

'Does reality match the dream?'

'Surpasses it.' He ran his hands down her body, stopping to play in her tangle of curls, slipping his fingers in and around that burning centre of her. She lifted her body upwards and pressed her mound against his hand, seeking his questing fingers.

With one motion, he parted her thighs and drove upwards. After the briefest hesitations, her body expanded to welcome him. As if it were made to have him inside her. As if she had finally arrived home.

Everything in her world narrowed to him and their joining.

Slowly she began to echo his moves so that he thrust deeper. And then came a glorious explosion, and for a time she forgot about everything except for being with him.

Karn slowly came back down to earth. The coldness of the moss seeped through the wool of his cloak. He stared up at the starlit sky and tried to make sense of what had passed between them.

He'd thought that he was experienced in the arts of love, but nothing had prepared him for the mind-blowing joining with Maer. She'd surpassed his wildest imaginings. And he knew without her saying that he must be the first. He felt her barrier yield as he entered, but he'd driven onwards and she'd opened.

The knowledge made him feel very special. He alone of all the men she'd encountered had been deemed worthy.

The thought exhilarated and frightened him in equal measure. What if he had gone too quickly? Had he ruined her?

He looked down on her cherry-ripe mouth in the faint grey-traces of the dawn, and the way her tawny hair spread out against the carpet of green moss. His body hardened, but he clung to the few remnants of self-control.

'Have you done this often?' he whispered against her ear, knowing what her answer must be. He willed her to trust him with the truth about her experience. He'd meant what he said: no secrets between them.

Her eyes flew open. 'Have I done *what* before? Lie on a bed of bracken and watch the sunrise?'

He silently cursed his wayward tongue. However, rather than allowing her to pull away, perhaps forever, he gathered her close and pressed his lips against her temple and tried again.

'Because if you haven't,' he whispered against her temple, 'then I'm beyond honoured. I simply worry that I didn't take enough time to prepare you. I want it to be good for you. Increases my pleasure.'

Her brow knit. 'Prepare me?'

'My pleasure comes in a large part from my partner's pleasure.' He nipped her chin. 'No fun otherwise. But when it is a woman's first time, a man needs to take his time. Ensure she is ready to receive him. Ensure she has time to recover.'

'Have you had to do that often?'

He brushed the ringlets from her temple. 'I'm more experienced than you, Maer. Statement of fact. Not an accusation.'

He watched her face and hoped she'd understand. 'I see.'

'I very much want to couple with you again on a bed of bracken or a bed piled high with furs,' he continued onwards, aware that he was making matters worse and hoping that he'd find the correct words and make her understand what he was attempting to say. 'But I don't want to get you overly sore and stiff. I want you to want me as much as I want you.'

He waited, breath held in his chest, hoping that he had not allowed her to slip away like drops of molten iron in cold water.

Her face relaxed into a smile. He let out the breath he'd been holding. 'You wish to do this again? Truly?'

'Hopefully in a bed piled high with soft furs.' He bent his head and kissed each of her breasts in turn, watching her nipples tighten under his attention. 'A lifetime exploring you.'

'A lifetime?' She raised herself up on her elbow. Her brow creased. 'But what about your quest? You're leaving soon.'

No question in her voice. Nothing to try and hold him. He admired that from her. He owed her the truth, the decision he'd made when he stumbled on her in this glade.

He ran his hand through his hair. 'I fear it is already doomed.'

'Doomed? Why? Beorn is vanquished.'

'Beorn and his men were hunting me. True. I don't know if—' He stopped and knew he didn't want to burden her with his troubles and the lies he'd been telling himself that Astrid would protect those families. Astrid had sent him to find the one man who could protect Agthir. Except she'd been wrong: another man could, and that man was him.

His men looked to him to save their families, and it wasn't going to be solved by running away any longer.

He had to stop believing that a will-o'wisp was going to solve his problem. He needed to solve it himself. He owed it to his men to stop running and to start fighting. The words Sigmundson had told Beorn earlier spoke to what he knew had to be true. His greatest hope was to bring proper prosperity to those loyal to him and ultimately to Agthir. He was not going to do that if he ran away.

'*When a man stops running, he starts living.* Something your uncle said to Beorn, but it applies to me as well.'

Until today, he'd half wanted to believe that her uncle was indeed the man he sought, but now he didn't want it to be so. He wanted Maer and her uncle to continue how they were and not be entangled in his mess. Sigmundson had stopped running and started living and what a life he'd created for Maer. When he'd completed his task, he could return here truly worthy of participating in that life. But he knew saying it out loud was beyond him. He couldn't make promises that he could not keep, not any longer and not to her.

She gave a soft laugh. 'I suspect you were easy to track.'

'Me?'

She looped her arms about her knees and her hair made a curtain of silk which hid her expression. 'You would not have taken any care to hide your identity once you were out of Agthir. People will have remarked on how strange it was for the king's son to become a wolf's head, particularly one who swaggers.'

'Swaggers? Me?'

'You know the value of your sword arm.'

'That much is true.' He frowned. Everything Maer mentioned was true. If this man Halfr was indeed hiding from his father, he could have led the assassins straight to him. 'Even still your uncle believes the man to be dead, and I believe your uncle knows what he speaks of. I only hope that if he isn't, he has started living.'

'What are you talking about?'

'I want to give you this.' His hand went to the pouch and withdrew his mother's pendant—the amethyst globe covered in filigree—which his mentor had given him with final breaths. The amethyst would compliment her finely drawn features.

'What's that?'

He dropped it in her hand. 'Something for you. A morning gift if you will. It belonged to my mother.'

She held up the pendant and looked at it with wondering eyes. In the early-morning sunlight, the pendant sparkled and shone. 'A morning gift?'

Karn undid the clasp and put it around her neck so that the pendant nestled between her breasts. Somehow it looked incredibly right. He felt as if a tremendous weight had rolled off his back. She had something of his.

'Something between you and I. A man should always give a woman a token if he is the first.' He touched the corner of her mouth. 'You do me much honour.'

She laughed softly and her eyes sparkled, just as the amethyst had done. He wanted to haul her back into his arms and join with her again, but he knew people would start to look for them.

'I have never heard of that custom,' she said tucking her chin into her neck. 'A token if I should have child?'

'I hadn't even thought of that.' Karn closed his eyes and tried not to picture Maer holding their child. The chances of him getting to witness such a thing were slim to none, but he wanted to hold on to the image of Maer cradling their child and remembering him. 'Will you take it?'

'I will accept it in the spirit given.'

When he'd opened his eyes, she had pulled her shift over her head and was dressing quickly. The closeness which had sprung seemed to have vanished like mist in the summer sun.

'Thank you,' he said.

'For what?'

'For everything.' He closed his eyes and knew he had made the last roll of the dice. He'd reached a crossroads in his life, and now he started living. He needed to stand and fight to make his dream of repaying his men's loyalty a reality. He couldn't rely on the queen or anyone to fight those battles for him. He would take the amber pendant back and hand it to Astrid, telling her that he didn't need anyone else to fight his battles. 'Your belief in me means the world to me.'

Maer screwed up her nose and tried to remember how to breathe. Of all the pendants, she could scarcely believe that Karn had casually handed her this one as a morning gift. She wasn't sure if she should be insulted or honoured to receive the gift. He said that it had belonged to his mother, but it reminded her of another pendant, her mother's.

Her mother had acquired hers the name day before Maer's life changed. She had never said who gave it to her, but even at that young age, Maer had understood that it had not come from her father, but for some reason her mother adored it. In the final weeks, her father had often made cutting remarks about it, but her mother swore never to be parted from it except in some unspecified, dire emergency.

She breathed a little easier. This pendant was amethyst, not amber. Nothing to do with her mother.

'You are giving this to me? There is no hidden purpose behind except for it being a morning gift?' Maer asked cautiously, trying to think logically and not with her heart. Karn had not come here, looking for her.

'One might think you didn't like my mother's pendant,' he said, seemingly intent on dressing.

'Surely this pendant must be worth a king's ransom.

Hardly worth a night's tumble.' She willed him to confide in her.

He reached out and entangled a hand in her hair, pulling her face against his. 'Never, ever sell yourself or what we shared short.'

'But you may need it. Your quest…'

'My quest was all wrong. I was supposed to find Halfr Hammdrson and force him to listen to the queen's request for help.' Karn shrugged. 'Your uncle swears he is dead. The time to find him grows short. There was no guarantee that he would help despite what Queen Astrid thought. I need to make my own luck. To stop running and start living. Just as your uncle and you did here. It came to me as I held you, listening to your soft breathing. I make my own luck from here on out.'

She closed her hand about the gift. His own luck, instead of being her mother's errand boy. And he had it wrong: *ceased to exist* was different from being dead. She was surprised that Karn had missed this. What her uncle would have done with the knowledge that Karn carried a request from her mother for assistance was anyone's guess. And it was far too late. Her uncle could not travel now, not for a long time, maybe forever.

She took a steadying breath and tried to think how she could put this right. 'What were you going to show Halfr to prove you came from the queen?'

Her voice sounded high and strained to her ears. If she wasn't careful, she'd be spilling the entire sorry saga to Karn and where would that lead? Anger and recrimination.

Karn put his hands behind his head. 'A pendant very similar to this one. The queen said that I was to take it to him to make him understand that she had sent me in truth. But he has ceased. Therefore, I will take this pendant back to her and find another way. Another way always exists, Maer.'

Was this the sign her uncle had been waiting for all these years? The one he'd spoken of often during that initial period of escaping, but which he mentioned less and less as first the weeks, then the months and finally the years rolled by. When he was drunk, he'd claim that he knew how to defeat Thorfi if anyone would listen to him. He knew where the bodies were buried, but her father had turned against him.

She could remember, when he'd heard of her mother's marriage to the new king, how he'd become blindingly drunk and disappeared for more than a week, leaving her with an elderly woman. She'd curled up in a ball and refused to move, certain she'd been abandoned again. But he'd returned, and she'd hugged him tight, and he never mentioned defeating Thorfi again. 'Nothing more than that? Just a cryptic message.'

'Queen Astrid is a master tafl player and plays complicated games. I didn't bother to press her. Quite frankly I was too busy grasping for a way to keep people alive. She made it sound very simple.' He shrugged. 'Maybe she thought I'd give up and return, meek and mild, ready to do my father's bidding.'

'You mean she set you to fail?' Maer whispered, twisting the pendant between her fingers. 'Why?'

He sat for a long time, head resting on his knees. Finally, when she'd about given up hope of learning anything more about her mother, he spoke.

'I don't think she wanted me dead. She never has done. She helped me whenever she could, but sometimes she ensured I learned hard lessons because a future king needs to be able to make the correct choice, not the easy choice. My relationship with my father is far from the easiest.'

She gave a soft laugh. 'I gathered that. How many fathers declare their son to be a wolf's head?'

'From what Beorn said and what his remaining men have confirmed, Drengr, my father's close advisor, holds the true power now. He wanted the crown. And I let him have it, blundering fool that I am. I allowed my pride to get in the way, just as Astrid warned me I might do when she first married my father and boasted of my prowess in my first battle.'

Maer concentrated on the pendant. Her mother and Svanna were in danger, but she had no idea if they wanted her help or just her uncle's. 'Do you think Astrid and her daughter are in danger?'

'I think if he seizes power, then there will be a war. Many remain loyal to Astrid. He knows this. It is why he wants to marry Ingebord before my father dies.' Karn ran his hands through his hair and grimaced. 'You will not be interested in the ins and outs of Agthir politics. Take the gift in the spirit it was given. Let me put my past behind me.'

'You are returning to fight, even though you are a wolf's head and your life is at risk?'

He sighed and something in her heart twanged. Despite everything, he did care about Agthir. 'I shouldn't care, but I discovered in that battle that I did care very much. Maybe there is a way for me to make peace with my father before he dies. Failing that, maybe I can get those who wish to come with me to some place like this and carve out a new life.'

She forced her eyes to widen. Every nerve tingled. Her mother had sent him. But it was far too much to hope that her mother might send for her after all this time. She forced that sense of hope and expectation back down her throat.

'You might be able to do it without Halfr,' she said quietly, continuing to stare at the pendant and the reflecting colours on the wall. 'Things might have altered if your father is as ill as your men think. The queen might understand and rally her faction behind you.'

His mouth twisted downwards. 'Take it or not. My mentor told me to guard it well because it brought my mother great luck. Your choice, but I've never offered it to any before. And I make my own luck now.'

She silently cursed her uncle and his insistence that Karn not be told the full truth. She wanted to tell him the truth, but she required her uncle's permission. 'I will treasure it.'

'And if should there be a child...'

Maer curled her hand about the pendant. A child. Her own flesh and blood. She didn't want to think about Karn leaving or having to send a child to him with this pendant. She wouldn't. She'd keep that child with her and not abandon them. She knew how the villagers would react, drawing back their skirts, whispering behind their hands or simply pretending she didn't exist. But that child would be loved with all her heart, and that child would know it.

She opened her mouth to explain but closed it again, swallowing the words. How could she refuse such a gift? She crossed bridges when they came, not before.

She lifted her hair. ''ll wear it with pride.'

A spark showed in Karn's eyes. 'Then, you will wear it openly? You will declare yourself for me?'

Maer silently resolved to speak to her uncle at the earliest opportunity about the second pendant and ask whether its arrival meant anything to him. She suspected it might and wondered if that was the true reason why he had not wished to speak to Karn. But until she knew for certain, she would keep quiet. There had already been enough bad feeling between the two men. She had to hope that one day, they would become friends after a fashion.

'Hiding away is not my style. It is far better that such things are out in the open.' Her throat closed. 'Most will simply assume that it is a gift as my shooting saved your life earlier.'

He kissed her forehead. 'Thank you for being you.'

Her body tingled anew at his touch. 'We should return. It is nearly daybreak. Plenty to be done.'

'We should.' He put a finger under her chin. 'Wear this, and know I want you in a bed or under the sky. But you need time to heal. I won't have my desire for you ruining your pleasure.'

A small curl of heat rose in Maer. He did want her. It felt good to be wanted and desired, particularly by someone like Karn who could have his pick.

'I would like that.' She swallowed hard. 'I want to say that— this thing between us—I have no expectations of how long it will last. Marriage is not…it is not something I've ever considered.'

There was little point in explaining that she could never consider marriage unless she fully trusted the man. It would be a heavy burden for any man to bear.

His hand stroked her cheek, and she turned her face into his palm.

'I can't promise forever,' he said in a gruff voice. 'Not while I'm being hunted. Not while I need to discover another way to save those who are in danger back in Agthir. I can't have anyone share that burden. One day, if the Nourns allow.'

She put her hand over the pendant which held a bit of warmth from her skin. She could guess the answer to his conundrum and that it might involve her, but she couldn't be certain. Would Karn even believe her if she told him? Or would he think it another joke? And she'd promised not to pester her uncle. He wouldn't be able to travel anywhere for weeks in any case, if her mother required him for something.

'I'll speak to my uncle after he recovers. See if he knows anything more about Halfr's fate.' The words tasted like ash in her mouth, but she refused to break a habit of a lifetime. She might be willing to risk her own life, but she couldn't risk her uncle's. Not even with Karn. 'If he does, and you need to show this to him, I will give it back to you. I have no wish to be the person who prematurely ends your quest.'

'Thank you.' He touched her face. 'I don't deserve you.'

Her heart twisted. She wished she had the courage to confess about the truth about her parentage. She suspected her uncle would ask her what she hoped to gain. It would only put her life in danger. Or worse, Karn would think her a liar and treat it like a joke as he had done that first day. She'd no proof, nothing to show him that she was the queen's true daughter and Svanna the imposter.

He deserved someone who was much better than she was. All she knew was that she cared about Karn, and the last thing she wanted was to lose someone else to Agthir like she'd lost her father. 'All a matter of perspective, Karn.'

# Chapter Nine

'What do you have about your neck? Stop trying to conceal it.' Her uncle looked at her, bleary but alive and distinctly far more able to comprehend things two days later. He reached a trembling hand towards Karn's mother's pendant. 'Don't hide it from me. I demand to see it. That jumped-up lordling gave it to you. He will leave you, Maer. You must know that.'

'*That jumped-up lordling*, as you call him, saved your life. And the pendant belonged to his mother.'

'I know who it belonged to. I was there when she first received it.' Her uncle slammed his fist down on the fur covering him. 'Why did the son give it to you?'

Maer fingered the pendant's chain and silently cursed. She'd forgotten to hide it away before she entered the chamber. She'd been too busy thinking about how she'd woken up that morning to having him watch her and how secure that had made her feel. She had not planned it, but she knew the time had arrived to press her uncle to reveal the truth to Karn.

'He gave it to me because he wanted to. That should be enough of a reason.'

'It is catching the sunlight and blinding me.'

Maer moved closer dangling Karn's pendant by the tips

of her fingers. Just in front of his nose. The purple hues danced about the room. 'Did you give it to his mother?'

'Before Karn's mother met Thorfi, before he saved her life, we were close.' Her uncle took the pendant with greedy fingers. He held it against his cheek with great reverence. 'I told her once to send it to me if ever I could repay the life debt I owed her. And her son gave it to you.'

'He doesn't know anything about the life debt?'

Her uncle shook his head. 'He wouldn't. He was little more than a young boy when she died. More's the pity.'

'My mother had a pendant very like this one except with an amber stone. I think you gave that one to her too. She was wearing it the last time I saw her.' She waited to see if he'd lie.

'Was she? I don't recall.'

'She put her hand on the bauble and asked you to look after me, Uncle.'

'Sometimes you say foolish things, Maer. Your father—'

'The truth, Uncle.'

'Yes, she did.' He put out his hand. 'Your father badly neglected her in the last few years of his life. He was a weak man, Maer, and she required a champion.'

As a child she could clearly remember the loud arguments and throwing of objects which normally resulted in her father stomping off or sulking, as her mother called it, with a slight curl of her lip. Svanna had always giggled at the quips and asides from her mother, but the words had always made Maer feel vaguely uncomfortable, and she'd concentrated on examining the rushes, another reason why her mother had been displeased with her.

She should have seen the truth before. He'd not merely done this out of some misplaced loyalty to her father but out of love for her mother.

'She sent Karn with it. His instructions were that he was supposed to show it to Halfr whom you claimed ceased to exist some time ago.' She gave her uncle a hard look. 'He has now decided that his quest was a fool's errand and that he needs to return to Agthir to save it from a civil war. Was this her coded way of asking for me?'

Her uncle pursed his lips. 'Why do you know he has it?'

'He explained about it when he fastened this one about my neck. He is going to return it to her. I could hardly confess your true identity.' Maer forced her voice to be light. There was no need for her uncle to know the exact circumstances. And it was the truth, simply not the full unvarnished truth.

Her uncle's gaze locked with hers. 'Did he tell you what she wanted? Did she name her price?'

'Something Halfr took without permission. You took my father's arm ring without permission. He always joked that it gave him kingly authority. Could that be what she wants?' She pressed her lips together and willed him to say it was her he'd stolen and it was her that her mother required returned.

He silently tapped his fingers against the pendant.

'You know what they will do to Karn when he returns, don't you?' she asked into the silence, unable to bear it any longer. 'Was she asking you to rescue her?'

'His life, not mine.' He collapsed back against the pillows. 'How can I rescue her and that girl who took your place. What was her name—Svanna? Astrid made her choice when she married that pig.'

Maer tapped on the rushes and clung to the remnants of her temper. 'Stop feigning. Is there anything we can do to stop a war? Anything which might give Karn an advantage? You cared about his mother enough to give her this pendant. She'd ask you for her son's life.'

'I need to speak with Karn, Maer. There are things he must know before he goes back. Can you arrange that?'

'Yes, of course.'

'Alone. And you must keep this a secret between us two. The only thing I took without permission was that damned arm ring. I swear it, Ingebord.'

'But…' Maer tried to think quickly. Her uncle never used her old name unless it was a dire emergency and something he wanted her to promise on her absolute life.

He stared up to the rafters for a long time, not meeting her eyes. She wondered if he had drifted off to sleep and was about to go when he started to speak. 'I've no idea what Astrid wants after all this time, Maer, but I do know that I want to protect you and the life you have carved out until my last breath. You've become very precious to me.'

'Surely my true identity—'

'Until I know what Astrid wants or requires, keep it a secret,' her uncle said. 'The lordling has earned the right to make his request after his defence of me and these lands in the battle. Some of the secrets I hold are not mine to divulge.'

Maer rolled her eyes. 'You think if I hear the message, I'll do something foolish.'

'Not up to me to second-guess your mother or endanger her.' He gave her a stern look. 'I don't want you to become a counter in this deadly game. I never wanted that.'

Sometimes her uncle made it seem like they had just left Agthir, and she remained that headstrong and naive girl of ten, getting herself into trouble by talking about her father the king or mentioning her mother the queen. She'd learned the folly of opening her mouth shortly after they had left, and she'd innocently remarked about her father and his great hall in Agthir. That night, the first assassins had arrived and only her uncle's quick thinking and strong sword arm had saved them.

'Anything else?' she asked, crossing her arms and trying not to let the hurt at his lack of faith show. 'You've taught me well, Uncle. I hold our secret deep in my chest. If there is anyone to worry about, it is you.'

He again examined the rafters for a long time. 'I know what women can be like when they have stars in their eyes about some man.' His lips curved. 'I was young once, my dear. My eyesight remains clear. People are never as careful as they think they might be. What is best for the young lordling might be the worst thing for you. I trust you haven't given him your heart. He will only break it. Now, send Karn to me, and fetch the ring, in that order.'

'Your wish shall be done.' She curtsied, rather than replying to her uncle's jibe.

'Thank you, my dear.' The man closed his eyes and appeared to drift off again.

She carefully arranged the furs so that he wouldn't get cold and called for the priest, before taking a deep breath and trying to get her head around what she had to do next.

His eyes snapped back open, and his hands plucked restlessly at the fur. 'Promise me, Ingebord, you keep the secret until your mother or I tell you differently. The fate of the entire nation rests on her shoulders, and I will not add to that burden.'

'I've not forgotten my promise, Uncle. I won't fail you.'

'Good child.' He mumbled something else which Maer failed to catch and then appeared to drift off to sleep once more.

Her eyes filled with tears, and she knew she had to keep

that promise, even if her heart was screaming to properly confide in Karn, because she no longer wanted secrets between them. But she knew she couldn't take that risk and endanger other lives. The fact that she wanted that frightened her.

Maer had regained her poise and determination by the time she reached the harbour. The telling of her secret could endanger other lives for no good purpose, and she had to remember that.

Karn, his men and several of the villagers were busy transferring the trunks and other items from Beorn's ship to a more secure location. Karn stood, hands on hips, surveying the final stages of the operation. A ray of sunlight which had pierced the clouds shone on his hair, turning his hair golden. Maer stopped for several heartbeats to admire the view.

'This ship will do well, now that we have emptied her of the rubbish,' Karn said, beckoning her over. His eyes were as bright as any boy who was about to encounter battle for the first time. 'Can you ask your uncle? It would be a more seaworthy ship than my own. My helmsman wants several more weeks of sea trials with that patch.'

A great hollow opened inside her and sucked the air from her lungs. She wasn't ready for him to go. 'My uncle will allow you use of that ship if you ask. He has no use for it.'

'Kind of him.' He ran his hand through his hair. 'I've no idea what is happening in Agthir, but I know I must return as soon as possible to keep those families safe.'

She wanted to scream that her mother will have known the risk and calculated that she had until Jul. And that she was playing some sort of political game of tafl, but she doubted he would believe her. Far too many questions if she said that she only trusted the queen of Agthir as far as she could throw her.

Without saying anything, she went over to where he stood. Their shoulders accidentally bumped, and a pleasant frisson of anticipation coursed through her body. From the way something flared in his eyes, she knew he felt the white-hot heat too. She wanted to live and not ask for more, but the past loomed behind her, and the future appeared cloudy and lonely.

'Do you see why I must go?' he asked. 'Why I have to try?'

'You will do more than try, you will succeed,' she said, striving for normality in her tone. He hadn't asked her to return with him or said anything about returning to her. It would have been only words, but she could have held them in her heart. She swallowed hard and strove for a teasing whisper. 'Assignations? Trysts? Is that the sort of good use you can put this ship to in meantime?'

His eyes gleamed, and a warm curl started circling around her belly. 'I can think of a few other places if you are interested. Ones with beds and furs.' He dipped his voice for her ears alone. 'I believe you found it very satisfactory last night.'

She placed a finger against her chin and pretended to think about it. 'Perhaps I did. Perhaps I want a repeat demonstration just to be certain.'

'Happy to oblige, my lady.' He leant closer so that his voice caressed her ear. 'It will spur me on to finish my work here.'

'Your devotion to duty is admirable.'

He sobered. 'I want to make my dream of a safe haven for those families a reality.'

She touched a finger to his palm, and his strong fingers curved around it. 'You will. I've faith in you.'

'A reason I like you, but there are others.' Karn's wicked laugh sent a pulse coursing down her spine, and selfishly she wanted a few more heartbeats of this easy flirtation before she sent him to her uncle.

'Do you think it wise to abandon your quest?' she asked before she begged him to take her back to the chamber or, worse, to the bath house like he'd promised in the early part of the morning when they were lying entangled in each other's arms.

'Halfr no longer exists. You and your uncle told me this.' Karn shrugged and his eyes slid away from her. 'Beorn's ship has the added advantage that no one on Agthir will know about his defeat. I must make my own luck, rather than relying on pendants or portents. The queen will be made to understand.'

A place deep inside Maer opened. She was not ready to say goodbye yet, even though she knew that day was approaching. Particularly as she knew her uncle would leap at any chance to get rid of Karn.

'Let's say my uncle does agree.' She crossed her arms. 'You'll require more men than you currently command to row that ship. Some of your men are not fit enough.'

'I'm hoping to persuade your uncle to lend me a few of his men. I'll keep them out of trouble as much as I can.' He gave a smile which warmed her down to her toes, but she caught the slightest hint of uncertainty in the smile as if he knew he was minimising the risk to those men.

She wanted to scream that she knew what he was doing and he should stop it, but instead she smiled and murmured something which could be interpreted as supportive.

His smile increased, and he made an expansive gesture with his hands. 'I must return to Agthir, Maer, even if there are great risks that I might not come back. I see that now. I can't keep on trying to chase a ghost because maybe somehow, I and I alone, will discover this ghost before Jul. Equally I can't live the rest of my life looking over my shoulder for the next load of Agthir assassins. No way to live. No way to ask you to live.'

'For me to live?'

He gave a half shrug. 'I thought I had made it clear with my morning gift.'

She shook her head.

He put his hands on her shoulders. 'I would not have you dishonoured. I want you with me, but more than that I want you safe. You are safe here.'

'My uncle wishes to speak with you,' she said quietly before her nerve failed and she confessed to everything. The words appeared to hang in the air. 'There are things he must discuss with you before…before you start this voyage on whichever ship.'

He grabbed her hand. 'About what? What does he want from me?'

'He recognised your mother's pendant. His life debt to her weighs on his mind.'

His eyes bore down into her soul. 'You didn't have to show it to him. A gift for you from me. I've stopped relying on luck.'

'An absent-minded error. He wants to speak with you… about your quest to find Halfr. He may have some information.'

She waited for his shocked but pleased expression, or even his asking if her uncle was in fact Halfr, but his fingers tightened on her arm, and he led her away from the others.

'What is the matter, Karn? I thought you'd be pleased.'

'I've given up the quest,' he said slowly. 'You know that, but this could alter everything.'

'His story, not mine.'

His eyes narrowed. 'And you've told me your full story?'

'What little of it there is to tell,' she answered carefully. 'I left Agthir as a child. Nothing for me remains there. My uncle adopted me, even though I was a burden at first, but I learned and became useful to him.'

'I doubt he can tell me anything of real use. Halfr no longer exists.' He put his hands on her shoulders. 'I don't know if I should shake you or kiss you thoroughly for trying, but it will give me the chance to formally ask about using the ship. He won't refuse because of the debt he owes.'

'He regrets that you two haven't spoken alone before now.'

A variety of emotions flickered over his countenance. 'Your uncle knows where Halfr's belongings are? Or is Halfr not dead?'

She screwed up her eyes and hated the caution, but her uncle's instincts had proven their worth many times over, particularly in the early years. And it was more than her life at stake. 'Halfr will not be able to travel to Agthir, Karn, or indeed anywhere else. Not for a long time.'

'I see.'

'I hope you do.'

She watched him stride away. Even though it felt like she had made a mistake in not fully confessing, she knew deep down the time wasn't right.

'Better that he thinks me Maer and not the queen's true daughter,' she whispered and wished her heart believed that.

The chamber smelt of heavy incense, honey and blood. Karn stood and allowed his eyes to adjust. He hardly dared hope that Sigmundson might have remembered something which could assist him. The failure which had clung to him seemed to be dissipating like the morning mist after Maer's words sunk in. Sigmundson must know where Halfr kept his belongings.

He might be able to rescue the families without his men or indeed himself returning to Agthir. All he had to do was find Halfr and persuade him to return. Queen Astrid would do the rest. Karn tried to keep the hope that he might be able to stay with Maer from burgeoning.

'Come closer,' the old warrior said from his bed. 'I've no wish to raise my voice. What I need to say must remain between the two of us. I will not put my niece into any greater peril than she already is.'

'We both wish to keep Maer safe. It is why I have many things to say to you.'

The warrior's lips turned upwards. 'I suspected you might.'

Karn knelt. The queen's admonitions rang in his ears— *Halfr might prove to be tricky and unwilling, but persuade him.* 'You wished to see me.'

'The best way to speak of the past.'

'You accidentally saw the pendant I gave Maer. It belonged to my mother and not Queen Astrid.'

'Collecting life debts from me seems to run in your family.'

'Another pendant exists. Much like this one but belonging to Astrid.'

'I'd heard tell that she has one. I wouldn't like to say for certain after all this time.' Sigmundson gave a laugh like a rusty hinge.

Karn silently cursed. Of course he recognised it. He'd been a blind fool. Sigmundson was the ghost that old warrior from Dubh Linn saw. He was Halfr Hammdrson or had been once. Halfr had ceased to exist because he had become someone else, not because he was dead.

He peered more closely at the man and saw the half-moon scar on his face. He kicked himself. Ingebord in her flighty way had been giving him a clue, not mocking him. For her own reasons, she'd tried to help, not humiliate him. A first time for everything.

'Do you know its significance?' he said carefully, wondering how he could make Sigmundson or Halfr formally confess and give up that which he had taken.

'I ask you to think before you do anything which might set us on a pathway from which neither of us can return,' Sigmundson, or rather Halfr, said.

Karn frowned and moved back. The man sounded precisely like his father when he wanted to rebuke him. 'Like what? Saving your life?'

The laugh turned into a dry, hacking cough. 'Some will undoubtably think it was rash, but I'm thinking of Maer. I've grown quite fond of her.'

Karn frowned. Maer had nothing to do with Astrid. Halfr had adopted her for his own purposes after the fall of Agthir. Ingebord had never really explained about the mysterious companion, the one who'd kicked his shins when he wandered into the hall before everyone. Several weeks after the battle, his father had told him to stop asking about why the dog didn't follow his mistress about and instead sat pining at the door as it did. She might be Maer, but she had no influence on Astrid or indeed who might become king; at best she was Ingebord's childhood companion.

'My intentions towards your niece are beyond reproach. Nothing about the second pendant concerns her.'

The man grunted. 'Is that what you call it these days—

*intentions*? When I was young, we called it something different.'

Karn gulped hard. Of all the conversations he did not want to have with this man, this one ranked up there. What was between him and Maer was too new to be discussed, and he suspected the man actively did not approve. However, he had to hope that the uncle's views would not influence Maer while he was away. Something had seemed to be weighing on her earlier. 'I will not see her dishonoured. I will not see her humiliated. I will see her protected.'

'My innocent niece does not dissemble easily. Remember that.' Sigmundson put his hands behind his head and watched him with narrow eyes. 'How did you come by the second pendant? Did you take it in your headlong gallop to be out of Agthir? Helping yourself as its theft would remain undiscovered until too late? Tell me. I will keep your dirty secrets from my niece.'

'What?' The words burst from Karn. 'I've made mistakes, sir, but I'm no thief.'

The old man stroked his chin. 'The question had to be asked. I meant no harm with it.'

Karn clenched his fists and tried to control his temper. This man wanted to get under his skin. 'I explained about that. Halfr the Bold is the object of my quest. His tendency to vanish is legendary. Possessed of magical powers.'

A gleam appeared in the old warrior's eye. 'Pure speculation and fancy embroidery because your father dislikes losing at anything. I had luck, and the men he sent were pitiful.'

Karn clung to his temper with the slenderest of threads. Allowing the man to tell him in his own time had to be the key which unlocked everything. 'Am I supposed to play at riddles? Something to amuse you while you lie in bed?

We don't have time, man. That priest of yours will throw me out, and I am determined to leave for Agthir as soon possible. I want to be able to tell Queen Astrid the truth if it comes to it. Will you help me? Will you help Astrid?'

'I suspect you are rather good at riddles. Isn't that what the king's son excels at? That and conjuring tricks? I have seen you beguiling children.' He gave a hacking cough and lay back on the pillows.

'The last thing Ingebord told me was about the half-moon on Halfr's face,' he said, before the priest came back and shooed him from the room. 'I thought she was winding me up, but she was trying to give me a clue. The half-moon shines from you.'

'Ingebord said that, did she?'

'Yes, sir. Back in Agthir just before I departed.'

Halfr stared up at the ceiling for a long time before piercing Karn with his deep blue gaze. 'Ingebord said that before you departed. Not Maer. Just to be clear.'

'Why would Maer give me that sort of clue? She doesn't play games like Ingebord.' Karn said, opting for another version of the truth. The man did not need to know he'd taken Maer's virginity or that he hoped to convince Maer to spend the rest of her life with him. 'When I gave Maer her pendant, I thought I'd never find Halfr as he had buried himself so deep I doubted he remembers who he is, even if the queen's daughter does. I wanted Maer to have something which was precious to me because she is.'

'He remembers that, all right.' Halfr made an impatient noise in the back of his throat. 'He is undecided about helping you.' He stroked his chin, fingering the half-moon scar. 'Going back to Agthir will not happen for me if that is what Astrid requires. I'm done with that and Astrid.'

'She merely wants that object which you took restored to her. I am happy to return it for you.'

'I took nothing but that which she happily gave.'

Karn wondered if this was some sort of code. He wished he could remember the queen's precise words. 'I'm merely the messenger. I have done my duty, and that is an end to it. You are unwell and cannot travel. You deny having anything which Astrid could want. My quest has ended.'

'Where does Maer fit into all of this?' The old man smiled. 'Would you protect her first? Before the queen? Before Agthir?'

Karn swallowed hard. 'What exists between Maer and me has no bearing on what happens in Agthir.'

'You intend to leave her here? Even if I ask you to take her as there could be something Astrid might make use of? Would you ensure that there was no gossip about you two?'

'Do you think she'd leave you in this state?'

He stroked his chin. 'A question with a question. I like it. Shall we ask her? Shall we ask her what the best way for her to keep her honour is?'

Karn stared at the man. He didn't want to give Maer up, but the man seemed to be implying that he needed to marry her. Maer was not the sort to take kindly to an arranged marriage.

'The question of marriage has not been discussed. If it ever is, it must be Maer's decision.'

'Then, you'd have her as she is now.'

'I've few prospects to offer her,' Karn said, rubbing the back of his neck. Marriage to Maer? In time. After he'd put things right in Agthir. 'It must be Maer's choice, but I suspect many better men have asked for her hand. I do pledge to keep her safe to the best of my ability.'

He waited, feeling like he'd undergone some sort of test.

'An honest man despite being Thorfi's son. You shall be rewarded. You shall have what the queen requires.' Halfr laughed. 'If you are brave and trustworthy enough to do the right thing.'

'I am. I know I am.'

# Chapter Ten

Maer carried the arm ring gingerly into the smoke-filled chamber. The voices had been muffled through the door, but Karn must have said the required formula. Did that mean her mother wanted her home? The thought made her body tingle. Everything had altered, but she wasn't ready to return to being Ingebord; she wasn't certain if she could. Maer, the woman from the sea who defended her friends and longed for a home, was who she was now. Her uncle couldn't ask her to throw all that away.

Both men merely glanced at her, and Karn did not show any particular concern, the sort she was certain he would do if he knew the truth about her parentage. She silently cursed: playing tafl with people's lives could get people hurt.

'You wished to see me, Uncle?' She forced her voice to sound bright and breezy. 'I've brought the arm ring which you removed from the king of Agthir's arm.'

'Do you wish to marry this man?' her uncle asked without preamble.

All the air went out of Maer's lungs. Of all the questions, he had started with that one. She closed her fingers about the cushion and tried to keep from screaming that he was ruining everything. Karn needed to ask her; she mustn't be forced.

'Marriage?' Karn shouted. 'I explained it to you before, old man.'

The words cut Maer more deeply than she thought they might, puncturing the dream she hadn't even been aware that she'd been living in. Karn had no intention of forever or even of beyond the next few days. She needed to face that truth and not hang on to some cloud-dream about Karn taking her back to her mother and everything being made perfect, including him wanting to be with her for the rest of time. She drew on all her training to force the feelings of hurt and abandonment deep down inside her.

'You called me in here to speak of marriage to Lord Karn?' Maer asked when she trusted her voice. 'Why? Why would you think anything which passed between Lord Karn necessitated our being wed? Why would either of you think I'd be interested in such a scheme?'

Karn's swift intake of breath echoed in the silence, but she was beyond caring. Her uncle knew she'd have to trust her future partner with her secrets, and she'd just admitted that she couldn't or, rather, had not thus far.

Her uncle raised a hand but not before a small flicker of satisfaction crossed his face. 'Maer, swallow your anger. Best for everyone that you make your opinions about marriage clear and precise at this juncture. Now we may proceed.'

'I'm not angry, just confused.' Maer crossed her arms and kept her gaze away from Karn. 'We had this out months ago, Uncle, when the farmer's son asked. There'll be no forcing me into any sort of marriage.'

'We did, Maer, but women can alter. I'll not have villagers discussing you or drawing their skirts away.'

Maer went over, gathered his right hand in hers and spoke softly in his ear. 'I refuse to allow you to run my love life, Uncle. What happens between a man and me is and remains none of your business.'

'It is if you become pregnant and he is gone,' the elderly man muttered. 'Have you considered what then?'

'Karn and I are friends, Uncle. I refuse to allow you to destroy a friendship with poisonous talk of marriage.' She withdrew her hand and rolled her eyes. 'Do I leave this room and throw this arm ring into the sea, or are we going to choose a different topic of conversation?'

Her uncle slowly clapped his hands. 'Excellent, my darling girl. Worthy of your mother in her prime.'

Maer pressed her lips together and tried to avoid looking at Karn. There was no flicker of interest in his face.

'I'd rather we didn't discuss my mother,' she said, forcing the words from her parched throat. 'She has not been in my life since before we left Agthir.'

Her uncle gave an unrepentant shrug, but his eyes danced. 'Another time, my dear. Your mother shall play no more part in my deliberations about what to do with Lord Karn's request.'

Maer's knees went weak as she understood what her uncle was saying: her relationship with Astrid was to remain private and unacknowledged, even to Karn. A direct order, and she knew the folly of disobeying such orders.

She wanted to stumble to a stool and bury her face in her hands. Foolish sentimentalist that she was, some part of her hoped that Karn's message for Halfr had included something for her, but her uncle's words dashed that hope.

'As long as we are clear about that,' she said around the lump in her throat.

'We were speaking about Queen Astrid and her requirements,' Karn said. 'You are intent on upsetting your niece. I won't have it.'

'He won't have the upset.' Her uncle's mouth turned in a slight smile. 'Won't marry her, but won't see her upset either. Interesting.'

'Stop teasing, Uncle.' Maer made a show of smoothing the coverlet 'I know you hate being ill and are bored.'

Her uncle frowned. 'Goes beyond being bored.'

'You are not getting up until the good father says you may.' She put a hand on her uncle's shoulder. He brought his other hand over and gave it a squeeze. That little gesture eased the hard place in her throat. 'You are not going on some wild chase across the seas because the queen has beckoned with her finger. What does she require?'

'That which I stole from under her nose,' her uncle said, closing his eyes. 'What to do about that is my current predicament, but you tell me that I'm not to travel and I will listen to you.'

'If the queen requires this thing to be returned, then it should be done,' Maer said with her words tripping over each other in her haste.

'I'm happy to do it,' Karn said, making a bow. 'But I believe Queen Astrid expected Halfr to "return with the missing object from under whichever rock he inhabits."'

Maer arched her brows. Her uncle had guessed why her mother might have sent him which was why he'd avoided speaking to Karn. Men! She wanted to wash her hands of the whole lot of them. 'Did you promise to go whenever she asked and not bother to tell me?'

Her uncle struggled to sit more upright. 'I did, but I can send you in my place. I trust you to deliver it.'

'Send me?' Maer put a hand to her throat. Her uncle seemed determined that she should return and face her mother, but as who? He had not told Karn the full truth, that much was obvious.

'Quicker that way.'

'You're going to get better.'

'Time is a luxury Karn can ill afford.'

'I—' Karn said, but Sigmundson gave him a furious look, and he subsided into a glowering silence.

'Come here, my dear, with the arm ring.' Her uncle beckoned to her.

She handed him the ring. He solemnly took it and then placed it around her right upper arm. He fiddled with some mechanism, and the ring locked painfully about her skin. She gasped aloud.

'Wear it there until the queen removes it.' Her uncle's mouth turned upwards. 'She is the only living person besides me who knows the secret of its clasp.'

The heft of her father's ring weighed on her. She knew that it went beyond the simple wearing, but it was her uncle's way of ensuring her mother recognised her. It was going to be Astrid's decision, not his, about when to disclose her identity. 'I will.'

'And keep it hidden until the correct time. Many paid a terrible price so that arm ring could be worn by the proper person. You're only the guardian, Maer. I expect you to return.'

Maer swallowed hard, thinking about the men who had died so that they might escape. 'I know.'

'What is so important about this blasted arm ring?' Karn asked in a cross tone, ruining the moment. 'Surely I'm permitted to know that. All this secrecy is wrong. We are on the same side.' He paused and glared at her uncle. 'Or am I making the wrong assumption?'

'I find I grow weary,' her uncle said. 'I accept your suggestion that you should go in my stead, Karn, and protect Maer. The queen will listen to your plea, Maer. Remember she alone knows the secret of the ring's clasp, and all will be well.'

With each word, Maer's excitement grew. She was truly going to be able to do something for her uncle. She was going to make everything right. And once she'd seen her mother, she would be able to turn her back on her if necessary.

'Will Maer be safe wearing that ring in Agthir?' Karn asked.

Her uncle opened his eyes and stared directly at Karn. 'Up to you to ensure she is, and you must return her to me. I find she is very precious to me.'

'I'll do my best,' Karn said, standing straight.

And Maer knew she'd crossed a bridge without meaning to.

Karn struggled to control his temper as he strode from the infirmary with Maer scurrying along at his side.

A faint drizzle kissed the afternoon sky, but Karn ignored it. Up to him to ensure Maer's safety? How? The best way to keep Maer safe was to ensure that she never went within a hundred miles of Agthir. He knew what his father's advisors, particularly Drengr, were capable of.

'We need to talk.'

'Is there much to discuss? My uncle was very clear about our duties.'

'Yes, there is. And away from big ears and prying eyes.'

She sighed. 'If we must…then, we can go down by the bath house.'

What really irritated him was Maer had known all along that her uncle was the man he sought, and now she proposed taking that arm ring into Agthir and handing it to the queen as if there was no danger to her. Despite everything, she hadn't trusted him with her secrets.

'Are you going to explain what is going on?' he asked when they were clear of the infirmary and listening ears.

'Explain about what? What wasn't clear for you? My uncle trusts you to get the arm ring to Agthir and is willing for you to use the dragonship, along with an increased crew.' She tilted her head to one side and fluttered her lashes. That gesture had irritated him when Ingebord did it back in Agthir, but it annoyed him even more to have Maer doing the exact same gesture. In his experience, the gesture was supposed to disarm and deflect.

Said in a way that made it seem like he'd missed something. The few remaining shards of Karn's temper slipped further. He concentrated on the raindrops and regained some measure of self-control. 'Explain about that golden arm ring for starters. And the way Halfr performed that little ceremony binding you to it. I don't believe that any ring can't be removed.'

'The arm ring?' She blinked rapidly and cradled a hand over where the arm ring was now locked on her limb. 'My uncle was clear on that. He didn't steal it. He took it for safekeeping. Possession of it has now passed to me for a short while. The queen will know how to remove it. He saved my life numerous times, Karn. I can't go against him. Not with this.'

He suspected that she wasn't telling the full truth, but he blamed Halfr for that. Maer must have been a young girl when she left Agthir. All she would have been fed were bitter stories. There was no way she was mixed up in its intricate politics. Queen Astrid had once instructed him to focus on his duty whenever he felt uncertain. His mother had given her that advice many years before when they were fostered together as young girls, and it had always worked. Right now, his duty was to keep Maer from being used and needlessly throwing away her life.

'Why is it so important? Why does Astrid need the ring?' he asked quietly, willing her to tell him what she knew so that he could figure out a way to keep her safe. And the best way would be for her to give him the ring and the responsibility of returning it. There was no need for her ever to set foot on Agthir. 'What does the queen want to do with it?'

'It belonged to…' Maer bit her lip and concentrated on the ground for several long heartbeats.

Karn clenched his fists, willing her on. She wanted to tell him the full story. He could tell that in his bones. Trust did exist between them. That trust was an important part of the partnership they shared.

Finally, she looked up and met his gaze with blazing eyes. 'It belonged to the former king of Agthir, and traditionally the king of Agthir wears it. Its origins date back to when Odin first gave his ancestor this land. It is locked on his arm and remains there for the rest of his natural life. Symbolising his duty to his people. Halfr took it from the king's corpse.'

'But my father never searched for it.'

'Your father rules through conquest. He has no need of it, but any future king could find it useful. Maybe anyone who married the queen's daughter would have need of it to prove their legitimacy.'

Karn pressed his hands against his eyes. Astrid had required that because her daughter was suddenly going to inherit the kingdom and she wanted to give whoever the husband was legitimacy. The story seemed almost too fantastical to be true, but it was the sort of gesture Astrid liked: symbols of the past to ensure power in the present.

'What did your uncle hope to gain by keeping it for all this time?'

'I believe he was storing it until Queen Astrid had need of it. They had obviously worked out a scheme of contacting each other.'

'Contacting each other? He has been in hiding.'

'I've no idea if they have had other contact throughout the years. The queen will have had her spies. Wasn't she the one to tell you to look to the west instead of towards the east and Constantinople?'

Her voice grew less reedy and breathless, and he found himself believing her particularly as, now that he thought on it, Astrid *had* suggested the lands to the west. It was not Maer's fault if she'd been kept in the dark.

'You do believe me, don't you, Karn?' she asked, her mouth turning up in a sad smile.

He knew that sort of plea, and the anger coursed through his veins again. He was sorry that Maer used those words Did she take him for a fool? He'd heard it too many times from Ingebord when she did something he disapproved of. He pitied any man who ended up married to that woman.

'Was this Astrid's way of telling me to fight for the crown or to let her daughter have it?' he asked softly. 'Is that what you are saying? I'd thought her request was a plea for a rescue as my father is slowly dying.'

She widened her eyes. 'We must ask her when we speak to her, as how could I know her mind?'

'Are you sure she can take it off?'

'I believe my uncle. Queen Astrid will know the correct way to proceed.'

'What part do I play? I want to protect you. Allow me to have the burden. You can stay and look after your uncle.'

She shook her head. 'You simply need to get me there

and into an audience with the queen. You have a seaworthy ship now. Consider this task payment for the life debt you owe me.'

He frowned. It was not how this conversation was supposed to go. She was supposed to accept the simple fact that there was no need for her to come on this expedition. He could deliver the arm ring and any message. How hard could it be to take off? He refused to believe Halfr's proclamation that only Queen Astrid would know how to remove that ring. Good political theatre but serving no actual purpose in the business of ruling.

He inwardly cursed that he'd walked into the trap. He'd been so intent on ensuring that Halfr didn't force a marriage that he'd missed the killer blow. An elementary mistake, but he could find a way to recover.

'Do you think your uncle will be all right here while you travel?' he asked.

'Why didn't you mention the queen's price before?' she replied, crossing her arms. 'Why didn't you trust me? So much could have been avoided if you had trusted me with your secrets.'

'Have you trusted me with all your secrets, Maer?'

'Changing the subject won't help.'

'She requested I only speak to Halfr the Bold,' Karn said through gritted teeth. 'I gave her my word. You told me he had ceased.'

'Did she only ask for Halfr?'

He put a hand on her shoulder. 'I doubt she knows of your existence, Maer. She implied that Halfr travels alone.'

She flinched like he'd struck her. 'I see.'

'It wasn't quite like that.'

'Wasn't it?' Maer tilted her head to one side. Her lashes swept down. He longed to take her in his arms and kiss her until she gave in, but suddenly there was this barrier between them. 'Is that why you gave me the pendant? Because he would be bound to see it, and it was nearly identical?'

She reached behind her and undid the clasp, holding the pendant out.

'You know why I gave it to you.' Karn lifted her chin so that he could look deeply into her eyes. Suddenly it was important that she understood. 'It had everything to do with what we shared. With what we are sharing. But I must return, and I can't look to portents, lucky charms or even arm rings to save me.'

'I'm far from a child who has never seen battle or fought for her life.'

She tore her chin away. The rain was coming hard now, making her hair sparkle with droplets. He wanted to lose himself within her and make her understand how all he wanted was for her to be safe.

'We should go somewhere else,' he said, brushing the raindrops from her cheek. 'Somewhere where people are not watching. I promised your uncle that I'd keep you from being dishonoured.'

'My head is not made of feathers, Karn. Nor do I easily melt. I am not some fragile flower. You never fully explained the quest to me. You used me. You might want to lie to yourself, but don't lie to me. I would have helped you if I'd known the truth. I would have moved heaven and earth for you.'

He ran his hand through his hair. He wanted to believe her. 'I made a mistake, Maer. I'm sorry. Queen Astrid made me promise.'

She tore her chin away. 'Queen Astrid has been no friend of my uncle's or mine for a long time. I doubt her motives.'

'You knew her?'

'When I was a girl, back before your father invaded.' She smiled. 'Maybe she mentioned something about Halfr travelling with another person.'

'She never said anything about Halfr travelling with someone,' Karn admitted and watched something die in Maer's eyes. He inwardly winced, wishing he understood why it was important to her. 'If she is not expecting you, why is it necessary for you to take the ring to her? Why are you willing to risk your life for that old man's desires? He took something that he shouldn't have. Maybe he took it with good reason. Maybe he thought he could use it one day. Who knows? All I know is that no reason exists for you to risk your life.'

'Do you really think so little of me?'

'Think little of you? What do you mean, Maer? I want to keep you safe.' He willed her to understand what he was offering. He had to return and reach some sort of settlement with his father, but there was no need for her to be put in danger.

'Because my uncle demanded it. She will know it comes from him if I take it. She will understand who I am.'

'And who are you? Why will she know you?'

Maer screwed up her face and turned away. 'I'm sorry. It is all you need to know. My uncle made me promise long ago.'

All he needed to know, dismissing him like he was some wet-behind-the-ears boy who knew nothing about Agthir. It was she who knew nothing. Her loyalty to her uncle was commendable, but things could go badly wrong in Agthir.

He grabbed her arm. Her flesh quivered like she was a bird about to take flight. He'd discovered Halfr, but he was losing her. 'Maer—'

She stepped backwards, and he forced his arms by his

side. 'People are watching. People are always watching, Karn. And it has started to really rain.'

He watched her walk away as the heavens opened and knew he had to find a way to keep her safe. Somehow, he had to find a way to convince her to stay and allow him to take the arm ring to the queen. Somehow, he had to find a way to save her from herself.

Maer looped her hands about her knees and stared glumly at the flickering tallow lamp. She should sleep but the ring rubbed against her upper arm, reminding her of her duty to her uncle and above all to the woman who had abandoned her.

Her uncle had fastened it in a way that it would not move. She knew if she went to him and begged him that he would release her, but she also knew the disappointed look in his eyes would be unbearable.

She had to hope her mother would take the ring and release her, enabling her to return here where she'd been not necessarily happy but content. She had value here.

She wrapped her arms about her knees and sighed. She'd been abrupt with Karn earlier, taking out her nervousness on him. Everything which had been right between them now felt wrong.

'How am I going to repair it without betraying my uncle, my father and everything I was brought to believe in since I left Agthir?' she asked into the silence of the empty room.

She should have just confessed about the truth about her parentage and why it had to be her to give the arm ring to her mother. And why she no longer had the choice. But he had not believed her when she joked about it. And her uncle had reminded her that more lives than hers depended on her keeping the secret. She was to defer to Astrid's judgement as to if or when the truth would be revealed.

Karn had not appeared at supper. Some of his men explained that he was busy readying the ship and planned to leave as soon as possible. He'd even had her uncle send word to the neighbouring farms, asking if any young men wanted adventure.

Suddenly the time seemed very short. She refused to be one of those women chasing after a man. She wanted to ask him what she should expect when they arrived in Agthir, but how could she confess now? How could she go to him and ask him to hold her?

A loud knock on her door interrupted her unproductive thoughts. 'Maer?'

Her heart leapt at the sound of his voice, and a sense of relief washed over her. She wanted to run to the door and fling it open. And that feeling frightened her more than she wanted to think about it.

'Yes?' She hated how her voice squeaked.

'May I come in?' Without waiting for an answer, he stepped in. Large and vital with his red-gold hair faintly gleaming.

Maer pressed her hands against her gown and tried to ignore the warm curl of heat in her stomach. 'Is this another of your conjuring tricks—the ability to walk into rooms uninvited?'

'I wanted to apologise. I should have trusted you with why I needed to speak to Halfr.' He tucked his head into his neck. 'I'm truly sorry. It is important that no shadows exist between us.'

She stared at him in incomprehension. He was apologising to her? She should be the one apologising. 'I accept your apology but—'

He placed two fingers against her lips. 'Unreserved apologies need no qualifiers.'

His smile made her heart constrict. She knew she should tell him about her parentage and explain why the arm ring was a sacred trust, but the risks of him not believing her or indeed in her were too great. After she met with her mother, then she'd say something. He would understand her reasoning.

She couldn't risk being disbelieved and laughed at. It had been bad enough when some children at Kaupang had done that to her just after they had left Agthir, throwing stones and dirt and calling her a filthy liar for saying that she was truly the Queen of Agthir and merely biding her time until she could rule. Her uncle had swooped in and rescued her.

That night aboard a ship bound for Northumbria, he had quietly explained she must refrain from boasting ever again. It was a lesson she held close to her heart.

Besides, her uncle had already told Karn that he stole the arm ring, rather than it belonging to her by right. She needed to take her cue from him.

'Are there shadows between us?'

'I want to apologise, Maer. Everything was a shock. I took my anger out on you. I should have taken it out on your uncle or even Astrid for putting us in this situation. You're only a counter in this game of theirs, but you deserve much more. You deserve to be kept safe.'

She breathed a sigh of relief that all would be well. He understood now that he had considered it why she had to go with him. 'But you accept it now. You understand why, having given my word long ago, I must go and play my part.'

'I'm trying to understand.' He reached out and pulled her to him. Her body instantly moulded itself against his hard planes. She was aware of his arousal, and that awareness sent an answering curl of heat coursing through her. 'I want to keep you safe and wish with all my being that you didn't feel that you needed to go. I wish you'd trust me to do the right thing.'

'I trust you to keep me safe.' She looped her arms about his neck, tired of fighting and seeking words when explanations refused to come. 'You think this is the way to settle our differences.'

'One way,' he said against her ear. 'The most pleasurable way.'

She turned her face, and her mouth encountered his. The kiss deepened as if they were frantically trying to tell the other something.

Their hands roamed over the other's body, tearing at the other's clothing in the attempt to get closer and dropping it on the rush-covered floor. Suddenly, he stood naked in front of her, the flickering light turning his skin golden and making him seem more like a god than a human.

She drew a finger down his chest and watched his arousal jump. Giving in to temptation, she slowly sank down on her knees. When her face was level with his arousal, she flicked out her tongue and tasted him. Smooth and silky with the faintest tang of salt.

He placed his hands on her shoulders, holding her away from him. 'What are you doing? Seeking to unman me?'

She put a hand up to his mouth and traced the outline of his lips. He suckled her fingertip. 'Exploring.'

'Is that what you are doing?'

'I want to take my time and make memories.'

He cradled the back of her head with his hand. 'Memories, huh? What sort?'

'Like this one.' She took him in her hand and held him. He grew larger. Hard iron contained within soft silk. She began to move her hand, mimicking the way he was when they joined.

'Be careful.' His rasping voice sounded harsh to her ears.

'Careful?' She rocked back on her heels and glanced up at his face. His eyes were half-shut, and he appeared to be concentrating hard.

'I don't want this over before we have properly begun. My control is slipping away.'

A great sense of power swept over her. She had brought this proud warrior to this state.

'What do you suggest?'

A huge smile crossed his face. 'Mutual exploration.'

She pretended to think, enjoying the sense of teetering on the cliff edge. 'Mutual exploration?'

'Let me demonstrate.' He sank down on the furs next to her. 'Keep your hand on me while I do this.'

His hand wandered down her flank until he reached the apex of her thighs. There his fingers delved into her hidden folds. Her mound pushed into his palm while she concentrated on keeping her fingers curled about him, trying to mimic his movements which circled round and round her clit.

The heat within her kept building. She arched forward, longing for a full release, needing to feel him inside her instead of merely in her hand.

'Are you ready? You feel ready.' He brought his now-slick fingers up to her cheek. 'See?'

Wordlessly she nodded and put her hand to his cheek.

'Shall we?' he rasped against her ear before suckling on her ear lobe.

A mewling noise emerged from her throat.

He fully parted her thighs and entered. Hard and deep. She brought her legs about him, longing to keep him there.

Back and forth they rocked until the sweet tumult over-took them both. The sense of finally being safe and secure washed over her. Together they were invincible.

Much later, lying in the bed swaddled in furs, Karn smoothed the hair on her temple. 'This is how I want to think of you. Always.'

She raised herself up on her elbow. The hot haze which had engulfed her dissipated like mist before the morning sun. It had been an illusion of security. 'Think of me? Are you going somewhere without me?'

He collapsed back against the fur. 'Little need for you to risk yourself. I am begging you as your lover—be sensible, stay here. Ask your uncle to release you from the arm ring. I can take it.'

'My uncle ordered me to go. One of the reasons he gave permission for you to use the dragonship is to ferry me there. No me, no rowers from Gael. No ship which appears to belong to Beorn.'

'Are you saying I should wait for my ship to be repaired?' He sighed. 'I could wait. My men will go.'

An ice-cold chill went through Maer. Here she thought she was binding him to her and ensuring that he would cease all this prattle about her remaining with her uncle, but he obviously considered that her joining with him meant that he would get his wish. She hated that he wanted to betray their growing friendship in that way. She had thought that he was the one man who understood that she wanted to play her part and not simply hide away, waiting to be rescued.

'How naive do you think I am?' The words burst from her throat before she had time to consider. 'You will be in more danger than I will be. If anyone should not be going, it is the man who has a price on his head, but have I begged you not to go? Have I tried to seduce you into something like that? No! I have organised more rowers, agreeing to act as an interpreter, and I'm carrying the item which my—which Queen Astrid requested.'

She let out a long breath of air. She'd nearly confessed about her relationship with Astrid at the worst possible time. If he knew that, he'd do everything in his power to prevent her from what she considered to be her sacred duty And now that there was this possibility, she wanted very much to go. She wanted to see the landscape, the buildings and most of all the people. She wanted to hear her mother's voice again, but if she explained this, he'd refuse her, and this final chance would slip away from her.

'Naive? What are you talking about?' he asked softly. He tilted his head to one side and made no attempt to cover his nakedness. It bothered her that he was much more comfortable in his nakedness than she was in hers. She reached for her undergown, slipped it on and belted it about her waist. 'Why should I think that about you? You have an astute brain when you use it. I'm trying to think how best to keep you safe, Maer. I don't want gossip about you or people saying that I dishonoured you in any way.'

When she used it? Maer struggled to keep her temper under control. Was he implying she wasn't right now? That it was why she'd lain in his arms and allowed her body to say all the things she was frightened of saying.

An ice-cold chill went down her spine. Whatever had been between them had irrevocably altered.

'You came in here and seduced me so you could get the ring and sail away from my life. It is all you have ever wanted.'

'Seduced? Is that what you call it? I didn't hear any objections, and I considered you an equal participant. I made an offer which I thought you would not refuse. Up close I can see the weight of that ring and how it pulls your flesh.'

'Let me finish. You seduced me because you thought somehow, I would turn from my course, the course I agreed with my uncle. My uncle has kept me safe for many years, and this is my chance to repay him. His orders are that only the queen can remove this arm ring. And to die if anyone else should try.'

'With your uncle but not me. And there are very unpleasant ways in which that ring can be removed. I don't want you to suffer any of that. I wanted you to remain here, safe while I carry out this task. I would have returned with my men's families whom the queen has kept safe, having made peace with my father.' He clasped a hand over his chest. 'But you don't want that option, and I'm trying to understand why.'

'It won't work, Karn. I gave my word to my uncle years ago. He always guessed that a day like this one would arrive.' She leant forward and tried to peer deep down into his soul, attempting to reach that good part of him, the part of him which had first called to her. 'Why is my word worth less than yours? I do trust you to keep me safe so that I can fulfil my obligation. It makes me feel better that you will be there.'

He reached for his tunic and dressed quickly. 'You are determined to go, despite the danger.'

She rolled her eyes. 'Would you stay on the ship?'

His eyes widened. 'What? No.'

'The danger is far greater for you. Everyone knows you there,' she said and waited for him to acknowledge the simple truth. 'No one knows me in Agthir. How hard can it be to seek an audience with the queen?'

Karn ran his hands through his hair. 'You know why I am doing this. Why I dislike putting anyone into danger, but particularly you. I am not sure if I think straight with you near, but at least I can keep you out of danger if you are with me.'

'Why is that? Because you love me?' Maer poured all the scorn she could into her voice. 'Why must I obey you if we have been together? I am allowed my own choices. Never attempt to dictate to me.'

'I worry about you and what might happen.' He pressed his fingers to his temples. 'Denying my feelings is impossible.'

A fierce joy that she hadn't already confessed who she truly was filled her. She stood on her own feet and didn't lean. Always.

'Wrapping me in sheep's fleece will suffocate me. If you cared about me, you'd trust my judgement without asking for more.'

'Why is your wearing the ring important? Surely it would have been Halfr if he was not injured.'

'She needs to know who it comes from and that he put it on me.' Maer adopted long-suffering tones. 'I can answer any question the queen might have. I can vouch that none have worn it but me.'

His brow knit. 'She doesn't know you. Or am I missing something obvious? I feel like I am.'

Maer concentrated on the furs, thinking quickly. That was the problem. What if her mother refused to acknowledge her? She wanted to know one way or the other. 'She is certain to question me about my uncle. Those sorts of questions I can answer, but there you would flounder. She will want to make sure the ring comes from him and is the authentic one.'

He pulled at his cuffs. 'What sort of questions? If you know what to expect, you can give me the answers. There are ways to do this without risking your life.' He paused. 'Without risking the life of any child you might be carrying.'

'Far too soon to know anything like that,' she said around the lump in her throat. 'That future may never happen.'

Right now, she hated the thought that she longed to hold his child in her arms. She couldn't have any sort of future until she had done this, until they had both done this. It was on the tip of her tongue to confess that she needed to see her mother. Just this once. That somehow, she hoped against hope that her mother would recognise her and would tell her how proud she was of her.

'But it is a possibility, and I have a responsibility to look after you. Think on it. Speak with your uncle again.'

'My uncle is not a man to alter his course or his mind.'

She noticed Karn had dressed and was staring down at her. She pulled the fur tighter about her shoulders. 'What?'

'And you won't budge, not even for me.' A bleak sort of sadness tinged his voice. 'Not even though I consider it a grave error. In my bones I don't think you should be within a hundred miles of that place.'

'Neither should you be.'

'You know why I am going to stop a war. I wish—'

'Wish what? That you'd never given me the pendant? You set this in motion. Or maybe it was set in motion long before now. Who knows? We must see this through to the end, whatever that end is.'

His only answer was a drawn-out sigh. 'You are determined to go.'

Maer looped her hands about her knees. The arm ring seemed heavier than ever. She shied away from confrontation, except with Karn that was proving impossible. 'If you are willing to undertake the voyage, so am I.'

A ghost of a smile flickered across his face. 'Something like that. But I will take you, Maer, because your uncle has made it a condition. And to make certain you are not dishonoured in front of his men, what was between us ceases.'

The words cut her deep, but she refused to flinch. She made sure her back was straight and the arm ring gleamed in the flickering light. 'Thank you for accepting me on your felag, Lord Karn. You do this for me, and I shall say your life debt and all your men's life debts to me are paid in full.'

He bowed over her outstretched hand. All emotion had drained from his face. 'Against my better judgement, a member of the felag it is. And make sure you are dressed for travel. We leave on the morning tide.'

'I was hardly planning on dressing for a fancy feast,' she called after him.

'With you, Maer, anything is possible. Just be at the harbour for the turn of the tide.' With that he was gone without a backward glance, and she knew he took a large chunk of her heart with him.

# *Chapter Eleven*

The sun emerged from behind the bank of clouds, bathing everything in an eerie dawn light and making the entire world appear to hold its breath.

Maer walked slowly down to the water's edge to where the great dragonship lay. Her thick cloak swished about her strong boots as she tried not to turn over again in her mind the quarrel with Karn. He'd left her no choice. The men were a mix of Gaels and Northmen, including two from Beorn's old crew, but none from his own. The one who'd administered the final blow to Beorn insisted on coming despite his injuries. Maer decided to stay far away from him as there was something about him which made her skin crawl.

'Ready as requested,' she said with a cheerful wave to the men who would be her shipmates on the voyage, to show that she was unaffected even though her insides were in knots. She noticed the assistant swine herder sat at the bow with a huge grin on his face. 'I'm a good sailor. Always have been in the past. And I will translate anything and everything faithfully.'

Karn turned from where he was coiling rope. His eyes were sunk into his skull as if he had not slept, and his mouth was a thin white line.

Her uncle's bone whistle which he used to control his men hung about his neck. She gulped hard. Halfr must have handed it to him at some point, but what his instructions were she could only guess. All she knew was that her uncle expected trouble and had taken precautions.

'The voyage will hopefully be smooth. The autumn storms have yet to start.' He smiled and fingered the whistle. 'Your uncle gave me a few final instructions.'

'I'd expect no less of him,' she said, hating that she wanted that easy friendship to return, but the barriers seemed insurmountable. 'An interesting crew you have here.'

Karn shrugged, but his eyes slid away from her. 'They've all sworn fealty. I refuse to risk those who have a price on their head as your uncle has supplied more than enough men.'

'Yet you are willing to risk yourself.'

'I have to put my mistakes right.' He pressed her hand. 'Time remains. Ask your uncle. He will release you from this burden. He implied as much when he gifted me this whistle.'

She removed her fingers from his, hating that she wanted them to rest there longer. 'I already made my decision. I made it years ago when I chose to go with my uncle instead of remaining in Agthir.'

He reached behind her ear and made a tiny piece of white heather appear. 'For good luck, then.'

She hated that a sudden hope blossomed within her. She dampened it down. Her heart whispered that she should trust him with everything, but she ignored it. The time was not right. She would know when that time arrived and would confess the full truth then.

She took it from him and wove it into the pendant. 'We need all the luck we can get.'

\* \* \*

Maer clung to the rail, quietly cursing the rough sea which had upset her stomach for the second morning in a row. She hoped it would be like yesterday—seasickness at the start which improved as the day went on. She peered out in the grey gloom of sea meeting sky, willing her equilibrium to return. Always in the past, she'd been an excellent sailor. It was funny what several years on land could do to a person.

She shaded her eyes and tried to look over the swell towards the horizon. A definite line had developed. Her entire body thrummed with excitement. She was returning. She blinked rapidly and let the spray wash over her face.

'Is that what I think it is?'

'Aye, my lady,' one of Beorn's men answered with a slight sneer in his voice. 'That is Agthir dead ahead. I'd recognise it anywhere like. Whatever Karn is up to, I hope he has a good plan.'

'He will do.'

'Care to share it?'

Maer shook her head. 'That would be telling.'

The man laughed and went back to his rowing. The laughter sent a chill down her spine, and she wondered about the pledge he'd given Karn.

Her stomach roiled again, and she clung to the rail, praying she wouldn't disgrace herself. She watched her homeland slowly take shape, while just as it had done the day before the nausea vanished as if it had never been.

The outlines of a scattering of huts and a few larger halls became clearly visible in the rapidly clearing mist. Very different from the Agthir she remembered as a child, but she knew it was the same place. She could see that from the shape of the mountain beyond and the curve of the harbour.

Home once but not home to her any longer, except the tug of her lost childhood was there.

She touched the ring which now seemed part of her and missed her uncle. When she said her goodbyes, he had said very little except that he would be waiting for her return.

She wished she'd dared to ask Karn about her mother and Svanna but knew if she did, things would get too complicated because she still wasn't ready to trust.

A rogue wave lifted the dragonship up before setting it down with a thump. All her muscles trembled, and she would have fallen if she had not held on to the railing for dear life.

She looked again at the horizon. The knowledge thrummed through her: she had returned. If her luck held, she might even encounter her old dog. It would be enough to see Tippi. Not how she ever dreamt of returning, her stomach in knots and her former lover by her side, trying to not be noticed.

'You've done it! Excellent navigation,' she shouted to where Karn stood by the rudder. 'Are we going straight for the main harbour?'

'Agthir as promised, my lady.' He gestured with a smile which made her heart turn inside out. His face then sobered. 'But I'm not so foolish as to risk this boat on the main harbour. They may see Beorn's sails, but the instant we land, I lose the element of surprise.'

Taking his speaking to her beyond monosyllabic grunts as he'd done all voyage as a sign, she made her way to him. He moved over to make room for her. His eyes roamed her figure. She was immediately aware of how travel-stained she must look.

'Do you have an alternative? Won't all the harbours be watched?' she asked, pushing the unwelcome thought away.

'Several of my uncle's men have asked me what comes next.'

'Your uncle's men.' His eyes crinkled at the corners. 'We can use a small harbour around the next headland. We will approach it cautiously.'

'I will let them know.'

He put a hand on her elbow, detaining her. She looked at it pointedly, and he let go.

'Queen Astrid suggested the harbour as a landing site as they are part of her dower lands. She swore that it would be safe. Precautions have been taken.'

'You mean I'm underestimating you.'

'It wouldn't be the first time.'

'I trust your skill, Karn.'

'But you don't trust me to deliver the arm ring.'

'It is firmly attached to my arm. Only Queen Astrid knows how to remove it without injuring me.'

He turned his face away. 'At the time I discussed the return journey with Queen Astrid, I did wonder if she was humouring me.'

'She has the measure of your character. She had to know you would keep your word. Anyone who knows you knows that you'd try.'

He looked down at her, and his blue gaze appeared to pierce her soul. She wished that this barrier of awkwardness would pass between them. Once she'd done what she promised her uncle, and they had left Agthir behind them, then she'd explain about everything. She could make him understand then. 'Something like that.'

'Do you think what the queen plans will be enough to expose the plot and keep everyone alive?' she asked, allowing some of her nervousness to creep into her voice. 'Provided she accepts the ring as genuine.'

'I do have an alternative plan. The families of my men will be rescued. I refuse to allow them to suffer on my account.'

'Do I get to hear that plan?'

He touched the side of his nose. 'Secrets work in all sorts of ways, Maer.'

She winced and tried to find the words to explain. 'Karn, my family, the one I left behind in Agthir—'

Before she could complete the thought, the lookout shouted about two fishing boats off the port bow, and Karn motioned her away while he took evasive action.

Later, she promised herself. She'd tell him the whole story later but before they encountered the queen. He deserved that much. She just needed to find the correct words to break it to him gently and hoped that he wouldn't hate her for it.

Karn concentrated on piloting the ship into the half-hidden harbour, rather than thinking about the shadows in Maer's eyes or how he wanted to find a way to break down the barriers which had grown around her. He had no idea why she was being so stubborn. Halfr had taught her to be very cautious and trust no one, but he knew she was keeping something important from him, and that hurt.

The only thing which gave him hope was that she continued to wear his pendant.

His neck muscles relaxed as he saw the queen had been as good as her word. No lookouts or ships. Just white sand leading back to a wood filled with larch.

In times past, barely anyone used it, preferring the much larger harbour.

He glanced towards where Maer stood with her nostrils quivering and her hands clinging to the rail as if she could not wait to get off. Whatever sickness she had experienced seemed to have vanished, just like it had the other day.

He still retained hopes of preventing Maer from travelling to his father's hall where she could fall prey to any number of foul villains, starting with Drengr. He needed to smooth the way first.

The trick to releasing the arm ring should not be too difficult to discern, if she'd let him. He could tell it pained her by the way she rubbed her arm when she thought no one was looking.

All his instincts screamed that she would be putting herself in grave danger, even though he knew intellectually that she had no ties to Agthir and was an unknown here.

Whatever this plot was and however Astrid was going to counter it, Maer played no further part. His nonnegotiable demand to Astrid.

Maer would probably argue that he was doing the same—deliberately putting himself in harm's way by returning—but it was different for him. He could look after himself, and at least he knew there was a price on his head. Maer appeared to be oblivious to the lurking danger.

'Are you going to go disguised?' Maer asked, placing her hands on her hips. 'Many people will be looking for you, wanting to collect the reward. You should allow me to go and request an audience with the queen. I can take some of my uncle's men.'

'They don't know Agthir as well as I do. And I do have a scheme. You and I can go to the hut where Astrid set her watchman. We will send a message that way.'

A tiny frown developed between her brows. 'Even still you are taking unnecessary risks.'

'Who would think the banished heir would be fool enough to return?' He smiled the sort of smile which he hoped would make her cheeks flame. 'Part of my charm. And the men can stay here, ready to row if we have to move quickly.'

'Someone might come. Beorn came after you. Someone might have guessed that you had gone hunting Halfr and what you might have found.'

He pursed his lips. Maer had hit on the flaw in his plan. Drengr had sent Beorn to the west. Someone was manipulating the whole thing.

'What are you suggesting—that I go dressed as a woman?' he said with a laugh. 'That skald's tale about Thor going to the wedding dressed as Freyja in order to retrieve his hammer always made me laugh as a boy.'

Her eyes sparkled like summer sunshine on the harbour. He missed that sparkle more than he'd considered possible. And it gave him hope that they could mend things. 'Somehow I don't think you will fool anyone dressed as a woman.'

Karn scrunched up his face and hoped he'd avoid hitting whatever the next barrier surrounding her was. 'Somehow I suspect you're right.'

Her merry laugh rang out like a bell, warming him, and made him long for a future with her, one where they could sit in front of a warming fire with their child in a cradle.

'I suspect hunched shoulders and not visibly wearing your sword would be a good start,' she said.

He put a hand on her arm. His fingers brushed the arm ring. She flinched and drew away. 'I'm hoping that neither of us will have to go and that Astrid might come to us.'

'Is there a special signal to bring the queen down here to this deserted area? A beacon we need to light in this watchman's hut?'

'Ingebord's old nurse lives near the cove, long retired but utterly loyal to Astrid. She will go to the hall once

I explain the situation.' He hesitated. He had thought to go alone, but that would mean worrying that Maer would somehow set off on her own. The entire crew seemed to consider her their mascot. Several had sidled up to him on the quiet and told him that he was to treat her right, particularly as she had developed the sea sickness. 'Come with me. Clear your head.'

Maer put her hand to her throat, and her eyes slid away from his. 'Ingebord's old nurse? You didn't say that we would be meeting her. Is that wise? You refused Ingebord's hand.'

'Believe me, the queen's daughter has no desire for me.'

'That may be so, but I doubt this nurse wanted to see her humiliated.'

He frowned trying to understand her nervousness. He didn't especially like Helga. She often stuck her nose where it didn't belong and had decided views, particularly on male and female relationships. However, if anything she would be rude to him, not Maer. He'd never witnessed her being rude to a stranger. *Strangers could be gods, and one must always be polite to the gods* was her frequent saying.

'Why is that a problem? Helga is utterly loyal to Astrid. Part of the reason my father wanted her retired out here. Before I left it seemed she was living more in the past, like talking about how the Nissar, the little sprites who help about a farmstead, were up to their mischievous tricks, stealing her wits one small piece at a time because she refused to put out porridge for them.'

'I never believed in such creatures.'

'Pity. Helga swore to me that they were real when my men and I departed from here.'

Maer plucked at the cloth over the arm ring as if it pained

her. 'I've waited a long time for a simple explanation for why some lose their wits. I must say it is as good as any.'

'Helga can be a bit gruff, but she used to save a piece of honeycomb for me. A golden-haired boy who would one day be a great king and a warrior, a man fit for a golden bride.'

'She likes gold? That could explain a lot.'

'Astrid sending us to Helga was the reason my men and I were able to escape at all. Drengr and his men were watching the harbour like hawks. She led us to where the boat was stored and ensured we had plenty of food and water,' he said, feeling that he had once again missed something important.

'Are she and Astrid close?' she asked, a light shining in her eyes.

He inwardly shook his head. He'd never understand women and their ways. Why should that matter?

'Maybe if Astrid refuses to visit, Helga will be able to release you from the ring.'

Maer stopped abruptly and glared at him. The Ice Maiden had returned. 'Halfr said that only the queen knows the precise way to release the mechanism. I must confront Astrid with it, not this old nurse.'

'I was under the impression Helga knew most of the queen's secrets.'

'Not this one. Halfr was quite insistent on that. Only the queen knows.' Her voice rose sharply.

Several of the men turned around and gave him dirty looks. He smiled back at them and gestured that all was well.

He put his hand on her shoulder. Her nostrils had flared, and her flesh trembled. He silently cursed the old man who held so much sway over her.

'You have brought it this far, why not allow someone else to take the burden? Get it the final few yards.' He hoped his voice sounded gentle and reasonable. 'Now, could you please smile and tell the men you are not upset.'

A sad smile crossed her face. 'The arm ring is far from a burden. It is my current and only purpose.'

'Your purpose?'

'My uncle would not have given it to me if he thought I'd be tempted to fall short. He expects me to find a way to succeed. Finally, I am of some small use to him and can repay my many debts.' Her smile deepened. 'Why should I want to disappoint him? No, I shall be coming with you to Helga's and then onwards to see the queen. It might prove educational.'

'Very well,' he said pretending to give into the inevitable. 'We will meet Helga and decide where we go from there.'

She closed her eyes, and all tension went from her shoulders. Karn longed to take her into his arms and whisper that he intended to slay all the demons who pursued, but she had to explain who they were first. One step at a time.

'Maer, is everything all right?' one of the men called. 'Lord Karn recovered his temper yet?'

Several more joined in, making it clear their sympathies lay with Maer rather than with him. He blew a blast on Halfr's whistle, and they fell silent, even the assistant swine herder.

She opened her eyes and gave him a brilliantly false smile. 'Everything will be well. Meeting Helga will help clarify things. Thank you for allowing me to join you.'

'It is something I'd do as well—refuse to be left behind.'

'If that is an apology for your fierce behaviour on the way over, you will have to do better,' she said quietly.

'A challenge?'

She lifted her chin. 'A statement of fact.'

The sun broke through the mist, sending everything into a golden haze. And Karn knew that somehow, against the odds, he had not destroyed everything between them.

'Cheer up.' He lifted her hand to his lips and placed a kiss on her palm. 'Everything is under control. Allow me to go in first and explain. My scheme will work out brilliantly.'

'When you start speaking about your plan working out brilliantly is when I start getting worried.'

'You of all people should have some faith in me.'

'I do, and that worries me' was what he thought she murmured, but the men started shouting, and he had to concentrate on ensuring the boat was properly beached.

# *Chapter Twelve*

Everything was most definitely not under control. Everything was about to come crashing down about her ears. The knowledge thrummed through Maer like the steady beat of a drum.

Her entire being was in knots. With every step she took, she wished she'd had the sense just to tell Karn to stop and then confess the truth and be done with it. She knew how he'd react and that he'd refused to allow her anything more to do with the mission, and that was the problem. She needed to complete it. She needed to confront her mother. All she wanted was the smallest sign that she cared.

Somewhere a dove cooed followed swiftly by a raven's caw. She chose to think those were good omens if she could get through meeting Helga again without losing her temper. It was probable the woman wouldn't recognise her. She tried to hang on to that thought. She wished she could ask Karn to hold her without having to explain why.

As if he heard her wordless plea, Karn stopped and drew her into his arms once they were hidden from view. She rested her head against his chest.

'Should I apologise?' he asked against her hair.

'It depends on what you are apologising for,' she said leaning back against his arms.

'I've thought about doing that ever since we departed.' He gave a half smile. 'I promised Halfr that I wouldn't dishonour you, but I require your touch.'

She smiled back at him. Maybe everything was not over. 'My uncle made you promise?'

'He wants to keep you safe, Maer. We both do.'

His mouth descended on hers. She gave herself up to the kiss, melting into him, knowing that she needed this and knowing it could be the last time she did it. He tasted of sea salt, fresh water and something which was Karn.

He lifted his mouth and looked down at her. 'Even now, you could go back onboard.'

She tilted her head to one side. She'd nearly confessed everything, and he had simply thought to confuse her senses. 'Your kiss might have been welcome, but my purpose remains unaltered. I gave my word.'

He sighed and allowed his arms to fall away. 'Then, we had best go forward, my stubborn lady.'

'Do you really think this woman, Helga, will help us?'

'She has a soft spot for me.' He put his hand behind her back. 'Now, come on.'

'Here we are. Safe and without any trouble.' Karn beckoned to her from the front of the secluded hut. 'All will be well. Trust me.'

'I thought to wait outside until you had a word. I don't want to startle her.' She winced at her words, and a little voice inside her head called her a craven coward.

He tilted his head to one side and gave her a look which caused her insides to melt. She suspected he did that sort of look on purpose, just to make her feel off-balance. It would be easier if she hated him, but she liked him. She liked being with him, and her heart was easier with him near.

She simply wished the seasickness would vanish. It was taking far longer than usual for her land legs to return.

'Come in with me. Please.'

'Is that wise?'

'Any good commander will tell you to alter your plans once you have the lay of the land before you.' A smile touched his lips. 'I now have the lay, and my plans are duly altered.'

'You want me to go in there. With you. Unannounced.'

The small wooden cottage with a curl of smoke rising lazily suddenly appeared to harbour all sorts of potential for evil things. Memories of Helga's many scoldings flooded back. She would find a way to mess up. She always did.

'Best way.' He gestured back to the ship. 'The alternative lies before you. My men will keep you safe. We will figure out a way to free you from your burden, but it won't be pleasant. Or you do as your uncle Halfr asked.'

Maer absently rubbed the raw skin above the arm ring. 'Perhaps we should talk about it some more.'

'What is there to talk about?'

She heard Helga's voice on the breeze, asking who had come calling on an old woman. A shiver ran down her back.

'I've made my choice,' she said crossing her arms. The simple act helped to restore her confidence. 'In fact, I made my choice years ago. I always knew this sort of mission was a possibility. My uncle never hid the reality of our situation from me. We can go in.'

'I find that hard to believe.' Karn's eyes crinkled at the corners. She hated that her heart leapt at the crinkle. 'I suspect he gave you a honey-coated version of the truth.'

'He wanted to ensure that I was ready to take on the challenge. And I am. I will go and meet this person and see if she will assist us. If not, we try another way.'

It wasn't precisely a lie. Karn could remain in ignorance about their previous association. She doubted if Helga would want to clasp her to her scrawny bosom in any case. It would suit the old woman to have Svanna remain as the undisputed Ingebord.

'That's what I thought my woman would say.' He squeezed her hand and placed a kiss at the corner of her mouth.

'You are being presumptuous. I currently belong to no man.'

He laughed and gestured towards the door.

Maer swallowed hard. There was no hope for it. She had to go in. A part of her hoped that Helga would not recognise her, but a larger part hoped she would.

She drew her brows together and wished she'd confessed to Karn because this was fast becoming far more difficult than she thought it would be. And her mind refused to offer up any sensible excuse. Maer the woman from Islay should not be worrying about meeting Helga, a nurse who had never travelled. She had to remember who she was now and not who she had once been. Her feet refused to move. 'Go ahead. I've a stone in my boot.'

She made a show of undoing her right boot.

'Are you coming, Maer? We need to be here for as short a time possible.' Karn stood in the doorway, with his brow knit in confusion after she had refastened her boots three times. 'Helga is here on her own. She has told me to come in and to bring my guest.'

Maer forced her feet to run the remaining few yards. Whatever happened now, she'd thrown her stones and she had to go where they landed. Far too late for regrets.

She skidded to a halt at the doorway, knocking her knee against the pillar. She winced at the sudden jolt of pain. It took several heartbeats for her eyes to adjust to the smoky gloom. The wizened figure huddled next to the smouldering fire resolutely ignored her, muttering something under her breath.

Despite the near decade, a flash of recognition raced through her, and she was immediately aware of the ways in which her current dress and hairstyle fell short of her old nurse's exacting standards. She drew a breath and tried to concentrate rather than panicking.

'Doesn't someone look after you, Helga?' Karn asked in a soothing tone like he was attempting to gentle a horse. 'That fire needs building up. You mustn't catch a chill. I will fetch some more wood.'

The old crone smiled up at him, reaching out a claw. 'You were always good to me, Lord Karn, not like some I could mention.'

Karn knelt beside her and gathered Helga's hands in his. Maer's stomach roiled at the gesture. The thing she remembered most about Helga was her willingness to tattle and to use a switch if Maer failed to comply with her unreasonable orders.

'The queen promised me that someone would ensure your comfort. Has this been done?' he asked. 'I know several of my men's wives were willing to volunteer. Queen Astrid promised she'd choose the most suitable person.'

Helga made a cat's paw with her hand before making a rude noise. 'Ingebord will be along shortly. She has grown up to be such a kind person. A true lady. She will make some lucky man a wonderful wife. They say she may even be queen once her mother dies. The whole of Agthir will rejoice to have two such wonderful women guiding them.'

'What a future to look forward to.' Karn stretched out his hand towards Maer. 'I have someone I want you to meet, Helga. Maer has something important for the queen, something she greatly desires. You can assist us in getting it to her. You can send a message for Astrid to visit us here, can't you?'

Her old nurse turned her head towards Maer. Her eyes were now opaque with cataracts, but her features had become more like a raven's than ever. Her nostrils quivered as if she caught an unpleasant stench. 'Why does the woman hang back?'

'I wanted to let Lord Karn greet you first.' She took a step closer and retched as the stench from ash and the wide variety of dried herbs hanging from eaves assaulted her nostrils. A massive pain in the back of her head. The sickness returned with a vengeance. She rushed outside, retched again, and then gulped in great mouthfuls of clean air. She closed her eyes and leant her head against the rough wood of the doorframe. The sudden dizziness dissipated.

'Is she breeding? Is that why she retched?' Helga demanded, her voice rising to a screech. 'I'm rarely wrong when it comes to a woman breeding. Ask anyone.'

Maer put her hand over her stomach and tried to stifle her sudden hope. Far too soon. Just Helga trying to exert her authority. Just as she had always done in the past with the serving women, accusing them of breeding or behaving badly. She wrinkled her nose and pushed all thoughts of a child away. Time enough for that sort of dreaming after she'd delivered the arm ring. 'I'm quite comfortable where I am. The hut is stuffy. I suspect I ate something which disagreed with me onboard ship.'

Helga made a considering noise, one which dredge up memories. Back then it had invariably led to some punishment.

'Helga can see shadows and nothing much else. It has

been this way for a few years,' Karn said beckoning for her to come back inside. 'She is only guessing. Her idea of a little joke.'

Maer fought to keep her voice steady. 'Odd to play a prank against a stranger.'

'Shadows and not much more.' The woman held out a gnarled hand. 'Is this your bride, Karn? Because she certainly is not Halfr, like you promised the queen. Ingebord will be most disappointed, but I suppose Thorfi will have to accept the bride.'

'I can live with Ingebord's disappointment,' Karn said, rolling his eyes. 'But my bride? Alas no, nothing like that.'

Helga's hand fell onto her lap. 'Pity. One way to solve your problem would be to find a suitable bride, instead of the usual women you get involved with.'

'Does his father miss Karn?' Maer asked loudly to distract Helga from going off on a rant about Karn's women. She didn't need to know about them. They were in Karn's past. What she was concerned about was the present, and she knew she was the only woman who currently mattered.

'His father listens to the poison Jaarl Drengr drips in his ear.' Helga banged her stick on the ground. 'It upsets my lady Queen Astrid most dreadfully. The man has become foolish. It seems the Nissar are more intent on taking his wits than mine.'

Her cackle filled the hut.

'But he loves his son, if only for who his mother was,' Maer said, repeating her uncle's insight.

'Do you have a name, woman who is not Halfr? Where do you come from?'

'Her name is Maer,' Karn said in a loud tone. 'She is Halfr's niece from what I understand. And she comes from across the seas. Halfr sends his greetings.'

Helga's toothless mouth turned upwards in the vague approximation of a smile. 'Halfr's niece. Interesting. I thought she died. Convenient for all concerned if she'd stayed dead.'

'Obviously not for me. I like being alive, but he adopted me after Agthir fell,' Maer said, hating the way her stomach lurched again. Had Helga guessed, or were her wits that addled? The Helga she remembered had always enjoyed game-playing. Now that she was an adult, she could see it for what it had been, but as a child, Helga's little digs and asides had upset her dreadfully.

'You lost your family?'

'My entire family. Thankfully Halfr decided I was worth protecting.' A bleakness crept into her voice as she remembered his grumbles and sighs in the early days.

'First time for everything,' Helga muttered.

'Halfr gave me the king's arm ring to present to the queen,' Maer said, forcing her voice to steady. Helga wanted her unbalanced. She wanted to say to her that she was an amateur in manipulation compared to some of the women she'd encountered in Constantinople, but that would involve an explanation to Karn. She had no choice but to play the game of shadows, mirrors and insinuation. 'Fulfilling this duty for my uncle is why I have travelled all this way. He regrets that recent injury prevents him for fulfilling his duty. I trust you are willing to assist...for an old friend.'

Helga made a cat's paw with her hand.

Maer waited, poised on her tiptoes, for Helga to say something about the girl who must have escaped with Halfr.

'Halfr was never my friend. Far too many schemes. Always in love with some woman, including Astrid. He never got over losing Karn's mother to Thorfi, even though he only had himself to blame.'

'Why would I know such things? I'm only his adopted niece.'

'Were you aware that Astrid must have returned Halfr's affection because she accepted the pendant and then kept it, knowing that my father would recognise it for what it was if he ever discovered?' Karn said in a quiet voice. 'It is she who set these events in motion. Are you going to betray her now?'

'Easier said than done, my dear Lord Karn. Easier said than done. The queen…well…the queen is unlikely to want to see Halfr's niece.' Helga poured a lifetime of scorn into the word *niece* as if she knew precisely who Maer was and was giving vent to her opinion of her. 'I doubt she ever wants to set eyes on such a person.'

The words were like a double punch to Maer's gut. Helga had guessed and was pouring her spleen out, daring her to object. The worst thing was that she was probably correct. Her mother had no desire to see her. It was why she had not been waiting at the harbour like Halfr had promised she would be.

'Is there something wrong with Astrid?' Karn asked before Maer could adequately collect her thoughts to respond. 'I would have thought she'd want to hear about Halfr from his niece. She did go to the trouble of dispatching me to fetch him. I would have thought she'd have run down the pathway as fast as her legs could carry her.'

Helga waved a gnarled hand. 'Witch's curse just after you departed. She has remained in bed ever since, seeing neither the king nor any of his advisors. And she would have wanted the warrior, not the girl. Never her.'

Maer forced her head to remain still as the words cut her soul, confirming her worse fears.

'In bed?' Karn asked. 'Why would she do that? It sounds unlike her.'

'In bed. Drengr keeps trying to get her to agree to a quick marriage between him and Ingebord. But she refuses to see him.' Helga leant forward, and her opaque eyes blazed with malice. 'Some whisper the curse was just punishment for convincing the king to deny his son and favour her daughter. Others say it was because she helped that son to depart in safety and foiled a plot against his life. I wouldn't like to speculate, but I suppose you will know all about that, Lord Karn.'

'We must see her. I've crossed an ocean for her,' Maer said, before Karn erupted.

Helga shrugged her shoulders before leaning over to stir the fire. 'I think very few will be able to see her. Certainly not you, Karn. Drengr has his spies everywhere, and your pretty head will be fastened to a spike before you reach her private chamber.'

Maer pressed her hands against her eyes and tried not to panic. Somehow, on the way over, she'd convinced herself that Karn would be at her side when she confronted her mother.

'But I must see her. I've brought Halfr's answer. She must hold true to her promise to Karn.'

'That promise remains unfulfilled because Halfr avoided travelling with you.' The old woman gave a cackle which sent shivers down Maer's spine. 'He is slippery, that one. He caused my lady to weep bitter tears after he slipped during the final battle for Agthir.'

Maer concentrated on the glowing embers. Slipped away? Maer remembered it differently. He'd made it into a game and had tarried in the harbour, clearly expecting her mother, Svanna and even Tippi the dog to arrive. They managed to clamber onto the final fishing boat leaving the port, with Halfr's curses ringing out over the harbour while she wept.

'Will you at least tell us where the women and children are hidden? The families of my men Queen Astrid promised to keep safe until I returned with Halfr's treasure or Jul started.'

'You should have made your peace with Ingebord before you left, Karn.' The old lady drew several runes in the ash. 'You should do so now. Throw yourself on her mercy. If she forgives you, maybe your father will. This whole mess could have been easily avoided if you hadn't humiliated her at that feast.'

'There will be no match between us,' Karn said. 'No marriage between the queen's daughter and me. Ever.'

The woman's mouth turned up into a toothless grin. Her loud cackle echoed about the hut 'No match between you and the queen's daughter. That's a good one.'

Chills went down Maer's spine. Helga knew and was enjoying taunting her.

'Stirring that particular nest of hornets does you little credit, Helga,' Karn said, making an irritated noise. 'Ingebord agreed with me. My father would have come around if Drengr had kept his long nose out, but he'd been pushing for the final break for months.'

Karn's words set off another loud cackle from Helga.

'I'll find another way.' Karn shook his head. He started to edge towards the door.

Maer shifted her weight from foot to foot. She could clearly remember her old nurse enjoying such mind games when she was little and complaining to her father, who refused to see it. 'Will you help us, or are you going to keep speaking in riddles?'

'Riddles have a deep meaning for the discerning, Halfr's niece.'

Karn slammed his fists together. 'Are my people well? Can you tell me that much?'

'Astrid has kept her word and seen to their safety. Jaarl Drengr has not harmed a hair on their heads.'

Maer's breath caught. Her mother must have sent them to the hidden valley. It was a half day's march from here. She clamped her mouth shut, belatedly remembering that her explanation could cause difficulties.

Karn buried his face in his hands, and his shoulders shook. 'Thank the gods for that.'

Maer shifted uncomfortably. She needed to quickly find a way of informing Karn without revealing the full truth in front of Helga. Perhaps she could explain that Halfr had confided the location to her? She screwed up her face. Tenuous, but it might work.

'Will we be able to send word to them?' Maer asked, striving for a bright tone. Practicalities rather than recriminations solved situations like this in her experience with various warring factions on Islay. 'Have them assemble here, and then we can go. No need to trouble your father, Karn.'

'And your burden?' Karn asked.

'I will figure out a way to fulfil my promise, but the most important thing is to get those women and children to a place of safety. If the queen is failing and guarded, her protection may cease,' she said in a low voice, willing him to understand. 'The queen is by all counts a pragmatic woman who will understand. Get me to her, Helga. Someone must deliver you food. They can take me up to the queen's chamber. I'm no danger as I'm merely Halfr's messenger.'

She glanced over to Helga who seemed to be engrossed in stirring the fire.

Karn frowned. 'Are you proposing to remain behind, should your task not be accomplished?'

Maer ignored the tension in her neck. If her mother recognised her, it would be a short reunion before she returned to Halfr. Meeting Helga again had brought back all the horrible parts of her childhood, the parts she tried to forget except in her bad dreams.

'I'm used to looking after myself.' She willed him to accept her arguments. 'Those women and children have more value than a lone woman who matters little in the grand scheme of things.'

'You matter more than you might like to think.' His grip tightened, pressing the ring into her tender flesh. She pointedly looked at his fingers. He slowly released them one by one and stepped away from her, his cheeks flushing slightly.

She absently rubbed her arm. 'Be sensible, Karn.'

'Even though I am beyond grateful, Maer, you are going beyond what I agreed with Halfr. You are taking risks that no woman should.'

'Plans alter.' Maer investigated the rushes rather than meeting Karn's eye. 'Surely you of all people must see what is important here—your people's lives, the ones you bargained for, rescued.'

Helga began to laugh. 'You appear to believe in skalds' tales, my lady. How do you know where they are hidden?'

'Do I?' Maer held out her arm. 'I suppose you know the correct combination of moves to release the mechanism, but then from what I understand, you often exaggerate for your own advantage.'

'You are being difficult for the sake of being difficult.

No doubt your uncle told you stories about me.' She shook her head. 'Halfr and I were often rivals.'

'You know he didn't mention you once.' Maer bobbed her head.

Helga snapped her fingers, and Maer was instantly transported back to when she was a little girl and had done something minor that Helga had decided was naughty. 'You are being impertinent. I once knew someone like you. They failed to meet a pleasant end...my lady with the mouse-coloured hair.'

Maer rolled her eyes. *My lady with the mouse-coloured hair* was what Helga used to call her when she was in trouble, usually followed by dire predictions about what happened to naughty children who disobeyed their nurses.

A bead of sweat trickled down Maer's back. Helga was never her friend.

Before things progressed further, she needed to confess to Karn. But not here and not now. Helga might deny everything simply to be awkward. She prayed to all the gods and saints that Helga remained silent.

'How is it impertinent to adhere to one's word?'

'My poor legs will not carry me to the hall. Who will speak for you?' Helga gestured to Karn. 'How are you going to enter the hall without putting your man in jeopardy?'

Maer tightened her jaw. 'He is not my man, as you say. Our interests coincided for a time.'

Helga made a clucking noise in the back of her throat. 'Bah. You remind me of someone and not in a good way. And I repeat—you have the look of one who is breeding.'

Maer tilted her head to one side. 'I can hear footsteps on the pathway outside. Someone is coming, Karn. We need to go now as this old woman is refusing to assist us. She only wants to speak of breeding and other rot to make us tarry. She is expecting someone.'

'It will be Ingebord. If Karn had a brain in his head instead of it being stuffed with feathers, he would have seen her worth.' Helga turned her nearly sightless eyes towards Maer. 'When you first came in, I thought you were her. It quite took me back years. But now I see you are simply an untutored woman who fails to understand the reality of the political situation. Ingebord understands the sort of counsel a king needs.'

Maer did a brief curtsy. 'Sorry to disappoint you.'

'Leave me to speak to my old charge. Alone. One of the few pleasures I have left.'

Sweat coursed down Maer's back. Svanna was coming here, and Svanna had no reason to acknowledge Maer.

She wanted to walk away and never come back. But if she did that, she'd fail Halfr. Maer swallowed her pride.

'We had best hide until we know,' she said to Karn. 'And I'm sorry if I offended you. Unintentional.'

The old woman made a clicking noise in the back of her throat. 'Some people just can never help their nature.'

Karn appeared more perplexed than ever. 'Why do we need to hide?'

'To allow Helga the opportunity to gently question S— Ingebord and see if she will take the message to the queen or ideally me.' Maer willed Helga to understand. 'Whatever Helga thinks of me and my untutored Gaelic ways, I feel certain she would never go against a direct order from her mistress. The queen wants this arm ring, badly. She ordered you to retrieve it from a ghost.'

Helga swung her near-sightless eyes towards Maer again. Maer had the uncomfortable feeling that the woman could peer down to her soul. She gave a brief nod. 'There may be more to you than I first considered. Remain here, and I will ask your question.'

'Thank you.'

'It would be for the best, Lord Karn, if you hid.' The woman gestured behind her. 'There is an alcove. If you are quiet, all should be well. Allow me to gently investigate the matter. Ingebord may have someone with her.'

Karn pressed his lips together. 'Fine, but I have my doubts about enlisting Ingebord. She is feather-brained and apt to lose her head at the worst possible time.'

'You refused her hand without truly knowing her or appreciating her many qualities.' Helga gave a sniff. 'On such things kingdoms are lost.'

'The feeling was mutual.' He gave a half smile, which made Maer's insides flip and made her think that whatever was between them remained simmering under the surface.

'Think what Ingebord will say when she meets you, my lady,' Helga muttered. 'And prepare your speech. See if you can reach her tender heart as this one won't try.'

Maer regarded the door and thought back to the last time she had parted from Ingebord. They were friends after a fashion. Once. 'I can't wait.'

# *Chapter Thirteen*

As the footsteps and the woman's voice grew louder, chatting away to some unknown, Maer scurried to the alcove. Karn joined her a breath later. He pulled a heavy tapestry across, making her eyes sting and nose tickle from the dust. She stifled a sneeze, but the tight space meant that her chest bumped against his. Her body thrummed with renewed awareness of him.

'Inge is often wrapped up in her own little world,' he said against her ear. 'She sees what she wants to see and disregards the rest.'

'Let's hope Helga decides to be cooperative.'

'You are doing well, Maer. Helga can be a tricky customer. Personally, I don't understand what Astrid and Ingebord see in her,' he said against her ear. 'Try not to antagonise her.'

'She and I...well...it is complicated.'

'Stop holding a grudge against someone who has no recollection of you.'

Maer caught her bottom lip. She suspected Helga remembered all too well. 'Me? A grudge? Helga objects to my breathing.'

Karn craned his neck. 'Let's hope Ingebord has not enlisted her latest admirer to carry Helga's food basket.'

'Helga! It's me!' Svanna's voice rang out, making Maer swallow her retort.

Svanna's voice had not really altered over the years. Maer shifted uncomfortably. They were once friends, but now she had little idea of how Ingebord would react and indeed if she would accept that Maer was who she said she was. She hated that she couldn't decide which was worst—having her secret revealed or being blanked.

'Oh, help,' she muttered. 'We should have discussed things, Karn.'

'Breathe.' Karn's voice caressed her ear. 'Ingebord has a good heart. Far too kind in an irritating way, but genuinely kind.'

Maer stared out through the small crack, hoping for a glimpse of her former friend. *A good heart?* That is what Helga used to say, and it had always made her feel inadequate. Deep down she knew no matter how much she tried, she would never quite live up to Svanna's perfection. After all, her mother had chosen Svanna over her own daughter.

She put two fingers over his mouth. 'Hush. Ingebord and her friend are here.'

A sharp bark resounded in the hut, drowning out all other sounds. It was a bark she'd know anywhere. Maer tried to suppress a rising sense of excitement.

Tippi! Tippi was here.

She stifled a shout and tried to tell herself that it could be another dog or that Tippi would fail recognise her for it had been more than decade. But every fibre of her being strained to see the briefest glimpse of her beloved dog.

'I can hear you brought that dog. Amazing the old thing walked all the way down here,' Helga said with a sniff. 'Her paws will be dirty and new rushes have recently gone down.'

'She wanted to come. Wouldn't let me leave without her. And growled at Drengr's men who wanted to carry my basket,' Svanna said with that winning tone she always had. 'She loves you, Helga. And you love her too. Really.'

'Do I? News to me. I dislike dogs in my house, *Ingebord*.'

'You wouldn't be so heartless and cruel to banish her outside.' Svanna gave a light laugh. 'Not after she walked all the way down here to see you. Her back legs are so stiff these days. I worry that one day she will sit down and never get up.'

Helga made a noncommittal noise in the back of her throat. 'Keep tight hold of her. I don't want her upsetting any of my pots. You know what she can be like.'

'Bad luck,' Karn murmured in Maer's ear. 'Nice dog, but a pest. We will be discovered because no way Ingebord will keep tight of the dog.'

'Did anyone else come with you, *Ingebord*?' Helga asked in a loud voice.

'Just me telling Tippi my secrets. Freyja knows I've very few people to speak honestly with these days.'

Maer peeped out. She had an imperfect view over Karn's shoulder, but she caught a glimpse of Svanna's blond loveliness. The pretty child had grown into a stunning woman with golden tresses and comely countenance. She was the sort of person who seemed to live a gilded life, even if she thought she had very few people to speak with.

'Whose fault is that?' Helga asked. 'Why do you think you will get anything for defying the king?'

'Hardly defying.' Svanna gave a tinkling laugh. 'I simply want to wait until Beorn returns from his voyage before deciding whose hand I accept. My stepfather thinks it is a wise decision, as does my mother.' Svanna paused.

'Won't be long now. Someone said they spotted his sail this morning, but it vanished.'

'A mystery to be sure.'

Both Maer and Karn shrank back in the alcove.

'I can only hope my stepfather will give me time to properly make up my mind. Mor said that I would have until the middle of Jul, and then he'd name my husband. Drengr keeps pressing him.'

Helga gave a little sniff. 'Are you saying you wish you'd gone with Prince Karn?'

'Him? Why have you brought him up? He is just going to get himself killed. Silly fool. Always thinks he knows more than anyone about everything. When he makes a mistake, he thinks he can get out of it with a smile and conjuring up a blossom or a trinket. Drives me to immense destraction.'

Karn's brows went up at that characterisation, and Maer fought hard not to break into a smile.

Another sharp bark came from Tippi, and Svanna gave a little cry. There was a scramble of paws against the rushes.

'Ingebord, you promised to control that dog, but you let her run wild.'

'I'm trying, Helga. I've no idea why you are so cross today. Or why Tippi is being so naughty.'

Maer peered over Karn's shoulder through the gap in the tapestry just beyond Svanna's shimmering goldenness and spied her old dog. Older. Fatter. Moving with stiff legs and greyer about her nose, but still unmistakably Tippi, with her tail wagging furiously as she gave little whimpering noises like she used to do when they were playing hide-and-seek. Maer bit her knuckle to keep from crying out.

'Muddy feet all over my clean rushes. Always the same with that scamp.' The old woman sighed. 'Come here for your treat, then, dog. I've saved you a bit of hard cheese.'

She rustled in her pouch and withdrew a lump of cheese. However, Tippi ignored Helga's offering and went straight for the alcove, tail still wagging. In front of the tapestries, she gave a series of sharp barks, did three playful bows and then started to chase her tail.

Karn put a finger on Maer's mouth, signalling to keep quiet.

Maer nodded.

'What is going on with you today, Tippi?' The exasperation in Svanna's voice was clearly audible. 'First you are desperate to come down here, and now you are completely ignoring Helga. You adore hard cheese.'

'That dog always had a mind of her own.' Helga gave a sniff. 'A bit like her mistress.'

Svanna crouched down and beckoned to the dog. 'No one else is here, you silly dog. You've upset poor Helga.'

'Actually, that is not quite true, Ingebord.' Karn stepped from the alcove. 'I reckon the dog could smell me. Will this do for a pathetic conjuring trick?'

Svanna gasped and put her hand over her mouth. 'Karn? Why did you return? Did you find Halfr? Did you find the half-moon shining in his face?'

'Come here, Tippi. That's a good dog.' Karn hunkered down in front of the tapestry and held out his hand, but Tippi ignored him and rushed straight into the alcove.

With a joyful yelp, she launched herself at Maer. Maer caught her in midjump, gathering her in her arms and burying her nose into Tippi's fur. There was something about the dog's scent which had remained unaltered after all the time they had been apart. Maer swallowed hard and attempted to hold back the tears.

'I told you that I'd come back, you silly thing,' she murmured over and over. 'I hope you've been a good dog and not a little scamp.'

Tippi licked Maer's face and continued to make little seal noises of delight.

'Who is this?' Svanna asked, pulling the tapestry fully back. 'Come out at once. Tippi is wary of strangers. She may bite.'

'My travelling companion, Maer, Halfr's adopted niece,' Karn said, lifting a brow. 'Halfr regrets he is unable to travel. Maer has something which belongs to your mother, something she wants desperately. Not precisely the specific instructions, but near enough, I think.'

Svanna's eyes narrowed. 'Does she indeed? *Maer* did you say? Where did you meet this person? How do you know this is what Halfr said?'

Maer took a deep breath and knew she had to confess, despite what it might make Karn think of her. She prayed that Svanna would be sensible, and Helga would resist sticking her knife in.

She walked from the alcove, keeping tight hold of Tippi. Karn looked at her with questions in his eyes as if he was suddenly starting to put the pieces together. She concentrated on Svanna instead of him, even though her heart twisted. This wasn't how she wanted to confess, but she had no choice. She had to hope he'd understand why she'd kept it a secret.

'Hello, Svanna. It has been longer than I predicted, but it was unavoidable. Honest.'

Svanna's mouth dropped open. 'Ingebord? Is it truly you?'

'They call me Maer now.' Maer stroked Tippi's ears. The dog instantly leant into her and licked her palm. 'You can keep Ingebord. I never particularly cared for it. Never really thought it was my sort of name. Maer is much more to my liking. I came up with it after I tried a few names out.'

'That sounds like something you'd say, Ingebord,' Helga stated. 'Always wanting to be different. Always wanting to cause trouble.' She inclined her head 'Wanted to see how long it would take you before you coughed. I see you kept him in ignorance.'

'What is going on here?' Karn asked, crossing his arms. 'Are you saying that you know Helga and Ingebord, Maer?'

'In a manner of speaking—yes.' She shifted her weight. 'Sorry for the deception, but Halfr decreed it necessary.'

'Deception? What deception?'

'A long story, Karn.'

Karn crossed his arms. 'I've the time.'

Tippi twisted, and Maer set her down. Tippi toddled over to Helga, took the treat and toddled back to Maer before lying down at her feet with a huge sigh.

Tippi's settling freed Svanna from her paralysis. She rushed over and enveloped Maer in a huge hug, glaring at Karn. 'Be kind.'

'I'm always kind, Ingebord. I dislike being lied to.' Karn's words were chipped from a block of ice.

'Maer suits you,' Svanna said in a loud voice. 'I never thought I'd see you again. We tried to make it to the harbour, but you were gone and…and… I don't know what Mor will say about this. She has worried about what happened to you. No word. No rumours. I have prayed to the Nourns that this day would arrive, and we'd be reunited.' She lowered her voice to a barely audible whisper. 'I've hated living this lie.'

Maer put a finger over Svanna's mouth. 'We will talk later. Right now, we require your help.'

'Look at you all grown and three times as smug,' Helga

said with a faint sneer. 'You were always the same—thought you were cleverer than me. Thought you could run rings about me. But I knew. I knew.'

'It is good to think I continue to live down to your expectations, Helga,' Maer said, ignoring the way Karn glowered at her. 'You should have said earlier. It would have made life easier.'

Helga made a cat's paw. 'Bah, and ruin the surprise? I wanted to see how far you'd go.'

'The person I was, I am no longer. I'm not planning on staying.'

'You look like your mother when she was a young woman, even if you have your father's chin. Only a blind fool wouldn't see that,' Helga muttered.

Karn's glower increased.

'You do look like Mor,' Svanna declared. 'I knew you straight off.'

'Mor sent Karn for Halfr and, I presume, the arm ring he took from my father's corpse. But he was injured so I came instead.'

'Your man looks like he has swallowed a particularly sour plum.' Helga cackled. 'My day has become interesting. Not attracted to the queen's daughter? I beg to differ.'

Karn let out a violent oath. 'She never deigned to tell me.'

'I did say when I unloaded your ship on the second day.' Maer shook her head.

'I thought you were making a deeply unfunny joke!' He pointed to the door. 'We need to speak, *Maer.*'

'You are looking lovely, Svanna,' Maer said, ignoring the command.

Svanna went a rosy pink. 'You as well. Mor... I mean the queen...your mother.'

'It's fine,' Maer whispered. 'I'm glad my mother is now your mother as well. Sisters by blood oath. Remember?'

Svanna's face cleared. 'Are you? Truly? I used to think I was borrowing her until you returned, but then it seemed like you never would, and she has been mine for such a long time. Having a mother was the only part I liked.'

Maer nodded because she didn't know what else to do and she knew in her heart that it was the truth. She was pleased that Svanna now considered she had a mother. She remembered the nights that Svanna wept bitter tears for her dead mother. 'We're friends. Sealed in blood. Nothing which has happened has altered that. Nothing could.'

Svanna smiled. 'You always had the best ideas, Inge—Maer. Do you want the name back?'

'Truly I loathe it. Belonged to my father's mother, who used to pinch me.'

'Far from a late-night catch-up over a goblet of mead, ladies,' Karn grounded out. 'I meant it, Maer. You and me. Alone.'

Svanna squeezed Maer's hand. 'Mor did what she had to. You and Halfr were missing in the confusion at the harbour. Suddenly Thorfi was there, and he threatened to make her a concubine, but then he saw me…'

'You kept me in ignorance. All of you,' Karn muttered, giving her a hooded look.

'The past was supposed to remain past,' Maer said, throwing his words back at him.

'The past has a way of biting you on the arse because it's behind you,' Helga called out, and Svanna gave a shocked giggle.

Karn's mouth opened and shut several times. 'Maer!'

'Poor Karn. Always shouts when he isn't getting his way,' Svanna said, holding out her hand to him and making a little moue with her mouth. 'This secret kept my mother alive and possibly Maer as well. I refuse to apologise for that, even if I found it burdensome. If you'd kept your temper with your father, Karn, Mor would never have needed to set things in motion. For once consider other people.'

'Can I speak to you outside, Maer?' Karn asked in a deadly quiet tone. 'In private and alone.'

Maer's heart twisted. 'I suspect Tippi might want to go with us. She might howl, otherwise.'

'Is there something between you and Karn?' Svanna whispered. 'I never understood the appeal. Far too growly.'

Karn made a disgusted face. 'If the dog must come, then so be it, but we have things to discuss. In private. You owe me.'

Maer crossed her arms and glared back at him. 'Do I?'

'I need to see to Helga's meal, Ing—Maer,' Svanna said in an overly bright voice. 'After that, we can plan how I will sneak you into Mor's chamber. Just seeing you will cheer Mor up to no end.'

'I don't think that will be happening,' Karn muttered. 'Acknowledging Maer would bring the carefully constructed edifice down and plunge the country into civil war. Astrid won't do it, not even for her long-lost daughter.'

Maer pretended that she had not heard him and that his words had not cut her deeply. All the reasons she'd kept her identity secret remained, particularly if he was going to start acting like this.

She belonged to no man, least of all Karn. What they had shared was never meant to last long, but she simply wished it would have lasted longer than it did and that the thought of losing him didn't frighten her so much. She could only lose what she already had, but this felt final.

Karn stopped beside a small clump of trees and tried to keep hold of his temper. His entire insides were lacerated.

What he thought he'd shared with Maer had turned out to be a mirage. She'd used him. She had no consideration for him, none at all. He'd poured out his heart to her, telling her intimate secrets about his life, his dreams and his hopes, but she'd withheld the most important secret of all—her identity. She hadn't trusted him.

'Are you going to explain?'

'Do you deserve more of an explanation?'

'Yes, I think I do.'

Maer closed her eyes. Looking at the fine bones in her face and the way she carried herself, Karn wondered how he'd missed the resemblance between her and Astrid. Save for the shape of her mouth and the slight curve in her nose, she looked like a younger version of the queen. He should have guessed something was up years ago when Ingebord looked nothing like her mother. He had simply assumed that she must take after her father's side.

'The time never seemed to be right, after you dismissed my declaration as an unfunny joke.'

'You were looking for the right time. Right.' He stared at her in disbelief. After everything they had shared, she did not feel she could trust him with the one simple fact about her life—that she was the queen's true daughter.

She pressed her hands against her eyes. 'What reason would you have to believe such a far-fetched tale without proof?'

His stomach ached worse than when a battle was about to start. He had no idea what to think. 'Not believe you! You never gave me the chance!'

'Halfr swore me to secrecy. When we first escaped, I nearly destroyed everything because I mentioned who my father had been. It was only Halfr's sword which allowed me to escape. After that, he ensured I could look after my-self, but the price of his protection was silence.'

'You knew I wanted to speak to him.'

'I'd no idea what you wanted as you failed to confide in me. Many assassins have come for us. And adventur-ers, who simply wanted to say that they had met a legend.'

Karn's jaw went slack. 'You thought I might want to kill you, but you were willing to join with me anyway?'

She gulped hard, and the pain flickered across her face. 'When you put it like that, it sounds foolish. What was be-tween us just happened. My uncle's secret was not mine to give.'

'You deliberately made a fool of me. You must have known that your identity would become known.'

'Not intentionally.' She buried her face in her hands. 'It was never my intention to humiliate you. I was trying to protect Halfr, who protected me for all these years. What happened between us…was supposed to stay private and wasn't necessarily long-lasting.'

Even though he'd half expected the words, they still hurt. Many times when he was younger, he had had liaisons which had barely lasted a night, but he'd grown dissatis-fied with that, and he wanted something more meaning-ful. He thought he'd found it with Maer. Only she was not the person he thought she was at all. She couldn't even tell him who she was.

'But you succeeded, and you were trying to protect your-self in case no one recognised you. In case your mother repudiated you in front of everyone. You failed to consider me at all.'

She tucked her head into her neck, hiding the sudden flash of extreme hurt which flickered across her face.

'Would you have believed me if I had done? I nearly tried again when you gave me the pendant.'

He forced the pity back down his throat. She'd trusted him with her body but not with her mind.

'It's easy to say an intention when you never did it. You had no idea how I'd react. Coward.'

'There was never a good time after that.' Her teeth caught her bottom lip. 'Maybe I was a coward, but I wanted to know that you would believe me, and I couldn't be certain. Everyone I have ever loved has abandoned me. I couldn't bear it from you.'

'I would have listened. I would have believed.'

'Truly?'

'You didn't give me the chance.'

She wrapped her arms about her middle and turned away, her shoulders shaking. He wanted to draw her into his arms and comfort her, but he was beyond furious. Her coming here put her life in danger.

His father might have forgiven the false Ingebord, but he doubted his enemies would forgive Maer. What she represented was too great of a danger, particularly if Helga was right and she now carried their child.

'I have no idea how I'm going to keep you safe,' he said to her back.

She spun around. 'My safety is my problem.'

'You are too reckless.' He began to count the points on his fingers. 'You are wearing the arm ring which belonged to your father. You are about to expose your mother for being a liar. It looks like you are trying to overthrow my father. My enemies will have every cause to exploit this.'

'All I am trying to do is see my mother and have her take it off me. She could refuse to acknowledge me. But I'm not responsible for what she does with it.'

'Likely story!'

'Karn, you are shouting. Helga and I can hear every word,' the false Ingebord called out from the hut. 'Do you want everyone in Agthir to hear your lovers' tiff? If you truly wish to protect her, you will need to say what you want to say quietly.'

Maer put her hands on her hips. 'You have no right to use that tone of voice with me, because I don't scare easily. I should just leave you here and have nothing more to do with you.'

Karn tucked his head down into his neck and tried to control his anger. Slowly he felt the control returning. 'I wish you had trusted me more, that is all. It alters things irrevocably.'

His words were no more than a furious whisper.

A single tear trickled down her cheek. She brushed it away with furious fingers. 'I did what I thought was right for everyone. I would do it again in a heartbeat to protect those I love.'

Those she loved obviously didn't include him. That hurt. She didn't think him worthy of her love, just as his father had admitted. He loved her, and she didn't love him. She could be carrying their child, something he devotedly hoped for, but she wasn't the person he thought she was; rather she was someone else entirely, a stranger who hid her most intimate thoughts.

'The same again. Even though I would never try to hurt you.'

'But you wouldn't have believed me,' she said in a sad voice.

'You don't know. What are we going to do now? How am I going to protect you like I promised your uncle I would?'

She glanced up at him, her eyes wide and dark. 'I look after my own safety. No one else is bothered.'

He gulped hard and gripped Maer by the shoulders. He brought his mouth down on hers hard, pouring all his fear and frustration into that kiss, willing her to understand that he was bothered, and beyond that he wanted her to be safe more than anything in this world.

For a heartbeat she melted into him. His shoulders relaxed. Maybe she understood what he was trying to tell her. The kiss became hot, wet and dark. He moved his hands to her waist and ensured their middles collided.

She tore her mouth from his. 'What was this in aid of? Keeping me safe?'

He held her chin between his fingers and knew he'd been wrong. She was going to move forward with her plans even if it meant her end. He couldn't stop her, but he couldn't watch either.

'That? That was goodbye, Maer. This is where we part. You are on your own. You can pursue this reunion with your mother, but you can count me out. I will never return to that snake-pit of a hall. My father made his feelings quite clear. Astrid's machinations alter nothing.'

She fingered her mouth. 'Goodbye? But we nearly have everything. Svanna will take me to my mother, and she will give you what you desire—the location of your men's families. We then get them and return to Islay.'

It was a pretty tale, and he half wanted to believe in it for her sake. Her mother was going to do what was best for Astrid, not necessarily Agthir. And she was going to use Maer and ruin her. Karn knew remaining and watching would destroy him, but he could not stop her either.

'What part about the queen being heavily guarded did

you miss? She did not ask for you, Maer. She asked Halfr for that which he stole—the arm ring.'

She flinched like he had struck her. 'She wanted to keep me a secret to keep me safe.'

'Keep telling yourself that. Astrid wanted to be queen.'

Maer drew herself up. 'No one knows who I am. Svanna will keep my secret. And my mother…will do what she will. I'm not planning on staying, Karn. This is not my home. It was once, but that world vanished a long time ago.'

Despite everything, Karn thought she'd never looked so beautiful with a resolute determination in her eye so certain in her self-reliance.

He shook his head. 'It is a risk you must take alone, then. Utter folly, which I can have no part of. I must see to rescuing my men's families. Where my duty lies. Everything has altered between us. Maer… Ingebord…whatever you want to call yourself, I wish you well.'

'My father gave me the name Ingebord.'

He willed her to understand. 'I prefer Maer.'

She was silent for a long time, and hope grew in his breast. Maybe she would see reason, and they could find a way around the problem together.

'You don't know where your men's families are,' she said finally. 'You require my mother's help.'

Karn knew he'd lost her. She probably was never his to begin with. The Maer he was in love with had been an illusion of his heart. 'From what Helga said I am pretty sure I know where they are being held. I want to get them out safely rather than trusting in Astrid's benevolence. Then I shall dust the dirt of this land from my feet. Only reason I'm here.'

A flash of hurt crossed her face. 'I see.'

'I hope you do.' He reached for her hand, but she drew

away. 'I gave Halfr my word that I'd bring you back to him. Once I have them, I will wait for the next tide for you. It should give you plenty of time to give your mother the arm ring and return. Three days.'

'But you will need me to communicate with the men.'

Karn patted his pouch. 'Halfr gave me a whistle to use in emergencies. I figure they'll respond to that and my shouts. No need to worry about me, Maer.'

'I plan on being there,' she said, setting her jaw. His heart ached to see her fierce determination. 'I promised Halfr that I would return. I will do my best to keep that promise. He always returned. Eventually.'

He choked back the words about how much he cared about her, knowing that they would not make the slightest difference, and forced his feet to turn and walk away without looking back. It was one of the hardest things he had ever done, leaving her to her fate, but he'd honoured her wish.

When he reached the bluff over where the ship was beached, he frowned. The men were supposed to be keeping watch.

He spotted one of the lookouts with his head against his knees. Asleep. Typical. And of course it would be one of Beorn's old men.

Karn inwardly sighed. The Gaels were all well and good with the promises, but he could be anyone.

'Hey,' he said going up to the man. The man's head lolled to one side.

A distinct chill ran down the back of Karn's spine. Dead. Strangled and left like that. Someone had betrayed them. Someone knew what to look for and where. Someone had waited for him and was exacting a terrible revenge.

Maer was in terrible danger.

A great warrior he'd turned out to be. He'd promised

to keep her safe, and at the first hint of trouble he'd abandoned her. Just like her mother had done, just like Halfr.

He needed to get back to her and to prove that he was different than all those others. He needed to do that now. He needed to be there.

Time he stepped up and proved himself worthy, rather than always wanting others to think that of him but never really earning it. Time he proved she could trust him to keep her safe. That he was capable of being her shelter in any storm.

He glanced towards the eerily silent ship. Where were those men? Halfr would have given instructions. He put the whistle to his mouth.

'Ah, Lord Karn, I had wondered when you were going to show your handsome face. It won't be handsome for much longer, I can promise you that.'

# Chapter Fourteen

'Allow me to do the talking, please, if we encounter any-one before our mother's chamber. You should remain silent. Is that possible for you Inge—Maer? I can remember how you used to talk and talk,' Svanna said, leading the way up the steep and winding path towards the hall while Tippi trotted along at Svanna's side, giving Maer longing glances.

'I suspect they will be more likely to listen to you as you are her daughter,' Maer said, trying for a light touch, but her insides twisted. Astrid was more Svanna's mother than hers now. She'd changed into an old gown of Helga's rather than remaining in her travel-stained gown so that she would blend in better, but she personally considered that she looked like a scarecrow with the hem of the gown several inches too short and revealing her ankles and sturdy boots. Svanna had fastened two box brooches on the front of the gown, saying they were the height of fashion.

'You don't know how touchy Thorfi has become since Karn went. Any little thing and he loses his temper. I am sure some of it is why Mor has become so ill. Every day we seem to lose a little more of her. She seems sad. And me? I just want this lie to end without hurting anyone.'

Maer tried not to think about her mother refusing to acknowledge her. Svanna might think it a foregone conclusion, but she knew her mother might deem it prudent to keep the relationship a secret. 'All I want is to have the arm ring off. Once off, I will return to the ship.'

Svanna squeezed her hand. 'She will want to see you. Stop wearing that fierce face. You used to wear that face when you thought you were going to get in trouble.'

Maer concentrated on keeping her face bland. When they were little, Svanna had the trick of saying what she thought someone wanted to hear. She doubted if she had outgrown it. 'Am I? I thought I was concentrating on the job I was given, nothing more. And my mother will do what she does. I accepted that long ago. I can't force anyone to love me. Not even Halfr.' She was about to add Karn but stopped herself in time. She'd wanted Karn to love all of her without question, but that was impossible after their recent argument. Some things were best left unsaid.

'And our mother? I know she thinks about you.'

'Svanna. Ingebord. Telling pretty tales is pleasant enough for Helga, but I don't require my life to be wrapped with an intricately braided ribbon.'

Svanna stopped and turned towards her. 'She misses you. She has worried about you for years. She wished that she had had an alternative.'

Maer raised a brow. 'My mother confided in you?'

'Who else could she speak to? You had to be kept a secret, don't you see? For both our sakes.' Svanna chewed her bottom lip. 'Neither of us thought it would go this far, or for so many years. She'll insist on you staying…and seeing you honoured. I know it.'

Maer forced a smile. That was a sweet thought, but she had her doubts. Her being here exposed her mother's lie and upended whatever carefully constructed life she had made for herself. And there was Halfr to think about. She wanted to return and ensure he recovered properly. She owed him that much and more.

She refused to think about Karn and the life they could have had. Maybe later but the ache was far too raw. And what was worse, he was right—she hadn't trusted him enough to share that deep down piece of her.

'I'm doing what I was ordered to do, nothing more. Then I return to Islay and my home.' She forced a smile. 'Part of the reason why Halfr's men form the bulk of the dragonship party.'

Svanna chewed her bottom lip. 'And Karn intends to leave as well?'

Maer concentrated on Tippi's ears. 'How can he stay? His father wants him dead. Karn has no wish to cause a war.'

'He may not have a choice,' Svanna murmured.

Maer's feet skittered into each other. 'What?'

'Ingebord, there you are. I've been searching everywhere for my little swan.' A portly warrior with a florid face advanced on Svanna, preventing any further conversation.

Svanna jumped like a startled rabbit before going into a sweeping curtsy. 'Jaarl Drengr, I had no idea you had returned. I thought you had left for Kaupang on this morning's tide.'

The man tapped the side of his nose. 'Stopped a few miles out and returned. Had an instinct that your stepfather might require me.'

'He does depend heavily on your advice, Jaarl Drengr, but all is well here.' Svanna's giggle was far too high-pitched and her voice more sing-song than ever. Maer recalled that when they were little, whenever Svanna was nervous she spoke in that sort of tone. 'You said so yourself only last night when you took your leave.'

Jaarl Drengr, the man whose machinations had caused Karn's banishment. Maer's throat went dry. Svanna had ample cause for her nerves.

'He does indeed, particularly now that your mother has taken to her bed, refusing to see people. Most unlike Astrid.'

'Any itsy-bitsy news my mother should know about?'

The man's tiny mouth pursed. 'Beorn's ship has been spotted. We may not have to wait for Thorfi's son to come to his senses after all. Beorn is several times the warrior that Karn could ever be.'

Svanna fluttered her lashes. 'What do you mean by that?'

'My nephew was determined to avenge your honour, my dear. Even though I counselled caution, he replied *no* and set off in hot pursuit.'

'I thought he'd merely gone to trade trinkets in Kaupang. Isn't that what you assured my mother?'

The man's smile became feral. 'He, like me, does not believe Karn will come to his senses before Jul as your mother calls it. He was determined to force an answer from that arrogant bedroom warrior.'

Maer's insides twisted. This jaarl had no idea of what had truly happened. She silently cursed her fight with Karn and his blind refusal to see that she had been doing her duty. And that she'd forced him away. She wanted to scurry back to the ship and warn him that Drengr was busy setting a trap.

She had to figure out a way to keep the trap from snapping shut and to save him, but her mind was fresh out of ideas. She forced a breath and tried to remember the lessons she'd learned.

To save him, she was going to have to confront her mother and force her to reveal the lie. It was the only way.

'Are you certain he found Karn? There could be another reason for his return,' Svanna said, fluttering her lashes again. 'He does have the habit of returning before a battle to secure more men. You remember last summer when he left Karn and my stepfather stranded?'

'Why else would he return except with Karn's head?' The man gave a lecherous grin which appeared to undress Svanna. 'Thorfi will admit my way is the only way.'

'I believe the king misses his son,' Svanna said. 'He said as much the other day.'

Drengr's smile increased, revealing sharpened points for teeth. 'I'd hardly like to increase the king's sorrow. We must hope that Beorn was persuasive then, and Karn realised the folly of defying his father and his expressed wishes. The son must learn to take proper direction.'

'He is a man grown.' The words burst from Maer.

Drengr's dead gaze swivelled to encounter her entire form. 'And you are?'

'No one of importance, Jaarl Drengr.' Maer swept into a curtsy.

'Just see you remember that.'

Svanna also made a curtsy. 'I will let my mother know of your return and Beorn's.'

His cold gaze flickered over Maer again, making her feel like she'd been touched by some sort of reptile. 'And who is this, precisely?'

'Nobody of import. A relation of Helga's.' Svanna's laugh reached ever higher levels of pitch.

Drengr stroked his chin. 'A relation of Helga's? Meddlesome old bag.'

'Helga thought my mother might enjoy a fresh face and lively conversation in her confinement. My mother had a certain fondness for Maer when she was a child.'

The man stroked his chin. 'I'd heard rumours there was another girl who was brought up with you for a time. I simply did not know her name.'

'Now you do.' Svanna linked her arm with Maer's. 'My mother will enjoy seeing Maer again. She has been low lately, worried about Agthir's future. She could use some good news.'

'I suspect she'll enjoy the news of Beorn's return more.' He bowed low, and his tongue flicked over his full lips. 'Ladies, I look forward to seeing you both at the hall tonight. I predict we will be feasting well.'

Maer stood next to Svanna, shoulder to shoulder, until he disappeared.

Svanna's shoulders immediately crumpled. 'I despise him. I really do. His eyes make me feel unclean.'

Maer firmed her mouth. If he tried anything with her, he would meet a swift knife to the stomach. Halfr had ensured that she was well equipped to deal with men like Drengr. 'He is…?'

'He is Thorfi's chief advisor.'

Maer regarded the blackened beams. 'What else does the queen say about the situation? Quickly, Svanna, I need to know.'

'That Drengr has his eyes on the throne and wishes to marry me or have me married to one of his sons.' Svanna's fingers dug into Maer's arm. 'I couldn't bear that. He is horrid and has buried three wives, plus he has a mistress. And his sons are worse.'

'Busy man. I wonder that he has the time or energy.'

The corners of Svanna's mouth twitched. 'What do you think they will do when they discover Beorn is not onboard?'

'I prefer to think about one problem at a time.' Maer

stared at the large wooden door. She had to find a way to warn Karn, but she was fresh out of ideas.

Karn slowly regained consciousness. The back of his head ached, but he was alive, breathing and with all his limbs intact, but his life was in ruins.

All he knew was that he'd failed Maer when all he'd wanted to do was keep her safe. He should have guessed there was more to Maer after Halfr confessed, if not before. The insistence on carrying the ring only made sense if it was the ring-bearer who was important. His error, not hers.

He should have told her the story about the little girl who had kicked him in the shins to snatch back Tippi from him, and how he'd looked for her until Astrid told him that he was imagining things. Perhaps it would have allowed her to trust him with the full story.

All along she'd been expecting him to fail her, like everyone else had in her life, from her parents to her nurse and even Halfr who had sent her back without knowing what Astrid truly wanted. He wanted to be the one person who hadn't failed her, but at the first sign of trouble he had done precisely that.

*Ignorance is no excuse, and neither are hurt feelings*— something which his mother used to say when he was little.

Maer's words were correct: above all he should have trusted her more and believed in her. He should have shown her that he was bothered about her safety, and that even if he didn't understand why she had to do this, he supported her.

He should have found a reason to stay with her despite everything. Instead, he'd made matters worse.

Now he needed to find a way to undo the damage he'd done and to give Maer a choice on who she truly wanted to be, but whoever that was, he knew he loved her.

He opened one eye. The hut was a mean one. Three figures stood huddled about the fire.

His nose itched but unfortunately his hands were secured at his back.

'I say we cut off his head and deliver it to Drengr,' one man said. 'Collect the reward that way.'

'No, no. Thorfi has started to miss his son,' a woman said from a corner of the hut. 'Doing that Drengr's dirty work for him? No, thank you. Our necks in the noose if Thorfi takes against the notion, not his.'

Karn tried to concentrate. It was his head on a platter if they decided to go with the first speaker. He tried to work the ropes loose but only managed to make them tighten.

'You may be right,' a second man said. 'Drengr only cares for himself and his family. The king has granted a stay until Jul. It is why we were able to go back to our lands and farm. He believes the queen is right that Karn will recognise the error of his ways, return much chastened and agree to Ingebord's gentle hand in marriage.'

Karn breathed a sigh of relief. He had wondered how Astrid had convinced his father to spare the lives. She always had a penchant for spinning a pretty tale. And ironically, he wouldn't mind marrying Ingebord, the queen's actual daughter, but Maer wasn't the woman his father meant. If there was some way of making him see Maer's qualities were much like his late mother's, then it might be possible.

Karn stuffed the idea back where he kept impossible dreams. It was never going to happen. Astrid would ensure the truth never came out.

'Take me to my father,' he said against the filthy rag they had shoved into his mouth.

'Are you saying something?' The first man hunkered

down beside him. 'Pity I can't make it out, princeling.' He laughed as if it was a joke.

'Ask him where Beorn is,' the second man said. 'Why did he allow Karn to return alive?'

Karn shouted, 'Dead!'

The man took the rag out. 'Goes back in if I don't like the answers, but I can't understand you like.'

'Beorn is dead,' Karn explained patiently. 'Halfr the Bold and I defeated him in battle. I've rarely seen a finer warrior than Halfr.'

'Halfr is a story to frighten old women.'

Karn wished he had not lost the whistle and could conjure the men up. 'Didn't you find the other men guarding the ship?'

The men shook their heads. Karn frowned. He suspected they were safe, following Halfr's orders, not his. Once he'd have been angry about it, but now he welcomed the foresight.

'Where is he? About to knock the door down?' The first man gave an uneasy laugh.

'I will put you out of your misery. Halfr failed to travel with me. I came with a small crew to try and rescue my men's families. However, you tell me that there is no one to rescue because of the queen's benevolence.'

'I would hardly be here, elsewise,' the old woman said curtsying. 'But what of my son? Where is he?'

'He lives in Halfr's compound. He was injured when we went through the whirlpool, but he has recovered thanks to the priest's skill at healing.' Karn forced his shoulders to relax. 'When I leave this place, you may come with me if you like and tend to him.'

The men laughed. 'Arrogant as ever. Drengr may have other ideas about you leaving, princeling.'

'My father rules here, not Jaarl Drengr.' He paused and decided to follow Maer's advice about making friends. These men weren't Drengr's. He'd be dead if they were. They had something to do with Astrid's machinations. He needed to figure out how to use that without putting Maer in any more danger. 'Or even Queen Astrid. Although she will be very interested to see me because she sent for the king's arm ring, the one which Halfr stole.'

The laughter died, and the men shifted uneasily, confirming his suspicion. They were Astrid's men, but restless for action.

'Where is the king's arm ring?' the first man asked.

'With the queen. I was returning to my ship when you attacked me.'

Muttering filled the hut.

'Take me to my father. You will be well rewarded, whatever happens.'

Silently he prayed that Maer had met the queen and concluded her business and was safely back with Helga. But the best place for him to ensure her safety was in that hall, confronting Drengr directly, or otherwise Drengr would continue to cause trouble.

He also had to find a way to make his father see that he would remain his son, but he was his own person and would lead his life as he chose, a life which he wanted to have Maer in. But right now, he'd settle for exposing Drengr's plot.

'Listen to what Lord Karn says,' the woman said. 'When has Drengr ever been a friend to us? We are Agthir born and bred. I believe him about the arm ring. I witnessed Halfr cut the ring from the late king's arm. If anyone has it, it will be Halfr.'

'Quiet, woman,' the first man said. 'We're thinking.'

'Your son believed in him, which is why he sailed with him.'

'Drengr tried to take our lower field three years ago and was only stopped when Lord Karn intervened at court. Astrid did not lift a pretty finger then,' the second man said. 'I'd practically forgotten about that.'

'Your son helped me and the rest of the felag survive the whirlpool,' Karn said quietly. 'My men are all heroes. They wait with Halfr. I can take you to them, but first I must go to the hall.'

The first man rubbed his chin. 'Thorfi has always been more honest than Drengr. We will take you to him—alive.'

Karn let out a breath. He could give Maer a chance. 'Thank you. And my other men?'

'I swear on Var there were no other men except Beorn's old men. The one we encountered and the one who is dead.'

'Pity, that one tried to tell us what to do. We know about the gold he took from Drengr.'

Karn frowned. Where were the Gaels? He'd dropped the whistle when he'd been captured, but they should be there. What had Halfr told them?

'Hard to cross an ocean with such a small crew,' he said and wished he had the whistle, but he would make do with what he had. 'Shall we get the journey started? No point wasting time.'

The woman plucked at his sleeve. 'I found this.'

She opened her hand to reveal the missing whistle.

'Thank you. I may have need of it.' Karn fastened it about his neck.

'Find a way,' the woman murmured to him. 'For the sake of my son, find a way. Be very careful. I heard a rumour that Drengr didn't go to Kaupang and expects to be crowned king this evening. Agthir will suffer if that happens.'

'Were you saying something, old woman?' the first man called. 'We need to get going if we are to be at the hall before night fall. Your father better be prepared to pay handsomely for you.'

'She merely wishes to be remembered to her son,' Karn said. Her words of warning echoed his current thoughts about Maer's danger. He needed to get to his father's hall and stop whatever Drengr had planned, but he didn't have enough men.

The woman gave a curtsy. 'Yes, that. Precisely that, my lord.'

He smiled at the two men. An opportunity would present itself. He just had to be patient and allow everything to play out. As far as schemes went, it was full of holes, but it was the best one he had. He had to believe in second chances and Maer. He had to find a way to demonstrate his love and support for her. 'Shall we go to my father's hall, then?'

Maer entered the smoke- and incense-filled chamber. The smoke hung so heavy that her eyes stung, and her stomach roiled. She stood for a few breaths, allowing her eyes to adjust. A woman lay in a bed, piled high with furs. Her hair was streaked with grey, and her skin resembled crumpled parchment, but she was recognisably her mother.

Maer put a hand over her mouth to keep from crying out.

'It will be fine,' Svanna whispered before raising her voice. 'Mor, Mor, someone has travelled a long way to see you.'

'Tell Karn to go away. I'm tired. He can apologise tomorrow.' She lifted an arm and allowed it to flop back down. 'I'm not sure I can go on much longer, my dear. My last hope is gone. Thorfi is dying. And his son is not ready to be king. He couldn't even find Halfr for me.'

'Queen Astrid?' She swallowed hard and continued. 'I've come from Halfr. He sends his regards. He returns that which he borrowed. He never stole, nor sought to keep it one heartbeat beyond the time it was required.'

Her final words hung in the air. Her heart pounded in her ears. Up to her mother now.

Her mother instantly sat up. 'Ingebord? Is that you? Have the gods answered my entreaties?'

'Yes, Mother, it is me,' Maer said, her throat closing. Her mother had prayed for her return. 'I've returned the requested arm ring.'

Her mother held out her arms. 'I have prayed for this day for so many years. Come here, my dear. My arms have been empty for so very long.'

Maer took several faltering steps forward before she was enveloped in a fierce embrace. Her mother held her tight, exclaiming repeatedly that her little girl was home.

That small of piece of her which she had kept hidden for so many years relaxed into that embrace. She had been wrong. Her mother did care for her.

'Oh, my daughter, my daughter. It is you. A woman grown. Let me look you. How many years I've missed.'

'I've missed you as well,' Maer whispered against her mother's wet cheek.

Her mother put her away from her and examined her face. 'Did Halfr explain why I had no choice? It was to keep you alive, Ingebord. I didn't want to, but we both feared for your safety.'

'I go by Maer. Ingebord belongs in the past, or rather it belongs to Svanna now.'

'But you remain my daughter.' Her mother's face crumpled, and fresh tears leaked from her eyes.

Maer reached up and brushed them away. 'Hush, now. I am back. Halfr trained me well like you'd have wanted him to. My archery skills surpassed his years ago.'

Her mother caught her hands. 'Is he here with you? Do you understand that Thorfi is dying? I don't expect him to last much beyond Jul. I don't know if Karn explained that. He can be clueless at times about such things.'

There was no disguising the eagerness in her voice.

'Halfr was injured in a battle, the one where Beorn died.' Maer rapidly explained the situation, dancing around her relationship with Karn.

Her mother frowned. 'Who brought you here, then? Surely you are not a woman warrior in command of ships.'

Maer laughed. 'Karn did, using the dragonship he and Halfr won in the battle with Beorn. One might say I played a small part with my archery, but the sword and I have never been close companions.'

Her mother cursed softly. 'Why are men foolish? Don't answer that question. All I know is that the world would be a better place if they acted more sensibly.'

'What do you mean?'

'Karn was supposed to stay away. It was why I told him… I thought Halfr would understand if he didn't kill him first.' Her mother firmed her mouth. 'Where is that errant stepson of mine?'

'We had a fight. He left to rescue his men's families. He thinks he knows where they must be. I promised to return. Do we need to develop a plan to get you, Svanna and even Helga away? Is that why you required Halfr?''

Her mother's eyes widened. 'There are none to rescue. I made a bargain with Thorfi after he calmed down. He

does love his son, even if he likes to get his own way.' Her
mother pressed her fingers against her temple. 'Why is
Karn always so headstrong? He should have trusted me to
keep my end of the bargain. He should have come to me
before trying any rescue attempt.'

Maer crossed her arms. *Headstrong?* Her mother could
give lessons on stubbornness. 'Because he has principles,
something which seem to be in short supply in Agthir. He
cares about the people who serve under him. And he has the
courage to see his scheme through. You do him a disservice
if you don't think he is a good leader, because he is one.'

'You care for him.'

Maer rubbed where the arm ring sat. The last thing she
wished to discuss with her mother was the implosion of her
relationship with Karn. Her feelings were too new and too
deep. He was right. She should have trusted him more. He
would have found a way to keep her safe. Now she had to
find a way to keep him safe and repair the damage she'd
caused.

'Will having the arm ring make it easier for Drengr to
marry Svanna? I really don't think she wishes to marry
him.'

'You avoid the question.' Her mother and Svanna exchanged cat-that-got-the-cream identical looks. 'I believe
I have the answer.'

'Karn and I are friends. I value his friendship.'

'They had a big fight,' Svanna said in that tone she always used to tattle. 'He's overprotective.'

'Someone has to be,' her mother said. 'I doubt somehow Halfr is.'

Svanna put her fingers to her temples. 'Why do I think
that this is going to be a mess?'

'No mess. We simply must get Thorfi to accept his son

has done the impossible and brought back the king of Agthir's arm ring. He has proven that he has the right to be king,' Maer said thinking aloud. 'We can send word to the ship. Karn will return there once he discovers the families are safe. Easy. Isn't that why you sent him to find Halfr?'

Her mother raised an eyebrow. 'Must I divulge all my secrets?'

She stared at her mother. She couldn't have wanted to play matchmaker, could she? Maer rejected the idea. Her mother had lived the lie for too long to wish to bring her carefully constructed world down about her ears in that fashion.

'I think you want to do whatever is politically best for Agthir. You always have,' she said slowly, trying to persuade her. 'And you know Karn will make a far better king than Drengr.'

'Why do you think that?'

'I'm the daughter of the great Astrid, after all. Some of my knowledge I learnt in the womb.'

The corners of her mother's mouth twitched. 'I was your teacher for the first decade of your life. Remember that!'

Maer smiled back at her. She knew some sort of bridge had been crossed. Her mother did care for her deeply. 'High praise coming from you.'

Her mother put an arm about her. 'I'm having trouble believing it is really you.'

Maer sobered. 'Svanna said that you were ill.'

Her mother shook her head. Her face was wreathed in smiles. 'How can I be, now that my daughter is restored to me?'

'Only for a little time. I did promise Halfr that I would return. There will always be a home for you with him.'

She put her hand on her stomach, hating how the hollow opened in her stomach when she thought about a future without Karn in it.

Her mother made a noncommittal noise.

Maer squared her shoulders and lifted her chin, meeting her mother's amber gaze. 'I would like the arm ring off now. I believe you are the only person who knows how to do this before we put the plan in action. I've no wish to rule here.'

'But you do wish to save Karn. Interesting.'

By the time Karn and his escort of men left the hut, a thick mist from a sea fret had risen obscuring the landscape. One of the men started talking about ghosts and other creatures in the mists. The leader told him to be quiet and to stop being such a baby. But he, too, kept looking over his shoulder at the shifting shapes.

'Stop. We are not going towards my father's hall,' Karn said after they had gone aways in the dense fog. 'We need to go back to my ship. We need more men.'

'More men would be good, but how are you going to magic them up?' the leader said, stopping and mopping his face with a handkerchief.

Karn patted the whistle. 'I have my little ways.'

'Where this mist has come from I've no idea. Maybe that old demon Halfr Hammdrson sent it.'

Nervous laughter from the other three. Karn kept his face steady. He'd half forgotten that the skalds liked to portray Halfr as some sort of demented magician, and that was why so many of the men his father had sent over the years had failed to return. The fact that Halfr Hammdrson was an excellent warrior and tactician seemed to have passed over these men's heads.

Karn grit his teeth. 'I can only apologise for mistakes I've made, but I believe I have proved my worth on the battlefield, keeping Agthir safe. Trust me on this. We need to go back to my ship.'

'We shall have to see. Maybe we should try our luck with Drengr.'

Karn tilted his head. The mist-shrouded rocks appeared to be moving. The missing Gaels? He had to hope that one or more of them were following him. If not, what he was about to do would be very short-lived.

'Sorry, but you should have trusted me.' He abruptly stopped and blew on Halfr's whistle four times.

The whistle resounded eerily through the mist, echoing until it eventually died.

'What are you doing?'

'Calling up Halfr's ghosts,' Karn said with a half shrug. 'The ghosts of those truly loyal to Agthir linger in these parts. We shall have to see if they're loyal to me.'

'If they are loyal to you, I'll follow you.'

The other men glanced over their shoulders. A wisp of mist blew obscuring everything, but there was no movement. Karn frowned.

'No one is coming, Lord Karn. I doubt you even met him.' The leader gave an uneasy laugh. 'Now that we have Karn's little party piece out of the way, shall we continue? Whistling up the dead, my big toe!'

'Look!' One of the men pointed to where the mist had started to clear. 'Someone is coming, and they are definitely wearing armour. No way I want to meet Halfr's former felag, fresh from the battlefield at Valhall.'

He began to run and stumbled, lying flat on the ground, whimpering. That left two besides the leader. Karn crouched down, getting ready to charge. The odds weren't great, but he suspected that he might be able to take them. The Gaels moved closer.

'You fools!' their leader shouted, but by now the other two were scampering away, screaming about Halfr's ghosts.

Karn sprang, timing his leap to perfection. The man went sprawling. Karn put his foot on the man's wrist and snatched up his sword. 'I think I should have this. Shall we go where I say, now?'

The man gulped hard. 'I don't believe in ghosts, more's the pity. Agthir lost many good men that day.'

Karn watched him. 'Are you saying that you are still loyal to the former king and his daughter?'

The man tugged at his tunic. 'Queen Astrid commanded us to obey Thorfi until the arm ring of Agthir was found. That arm ring remains missing. All I'm saying.'

Shapes appeared and solidified in the midst. The assistant swine herder led the way. All of them were bristling with axes and swords. They had captured his former captors and were herding them back. 'Lord Karn? Where is our Maer?'

Sweat tumbled down the leader's face. 'How...how did you conjure these men?'

Karn raised a brow. 'Halfr gave me a magic whistle which allowed me to raise spirits. Isn't that what the skalds will claim?'

'Karn? Where is Maer?' the assistant swine herder asked again, sounding out each syllable with difficulty. 'Is she in trouble?'

'We need to rescue her.' Karn hated to think about the arm ring and what might happen to Maer, particularly as Drengr remained in Agthir. 'She needs to have a chance to choose her own life.'

He hoped that he could persuade her to stay with him in wherever that place might be, but first she had to have the choice.

## *Chapter Fifteen*

Maer's arm ached. She had stood for what seemed like an age, waiting for her mother to release the arm ring. Thus far, everything her mother tried had failed.

'This is far more difficult than I remember,' her mother said. 'Did Halfr store it somewhere damp?'

'He kept it safe.' She winced as the mechanism pinched her underarm for a third time.

'But he didn't trust Karn to bring it on his own.'

'Karn saved his life.'

Her mother tilted her head to one side. 'What do you think of Karn, Ingebord? The truth. Was I right to send him to Halfr?'

'I prefer Maer.'

'Don't play word games. Could there be a match between you two?'

Maer stared at her mother, open-mouthed. She hardly knew what to say. Her mother had had hopes for her and Karn. 'What? Why?'

'The king declared his son had to marry my daughter. He simply did not specify names.' A faint smile played on her mother's lips. 'A neat solution occurred to me.'

Maer was glad Karn's pendant was tucked beneath her

undergown. 'I must be allowed to choose my own husband, rather than marrying for the sake of a kingdom.'

'Halfr neglected your education. Women marry to weave the peace.'

'Helga said that Maer was pregnant with Karn's child,' Svanna chimed in unhelpfully from where she perched on a stool.

Her mother lifted a brow. 'Is this true?'

'Too soon to tell,' Maer admitted, her cheeks growing hot. 'What existed between Karn and me has ended. I neglected to tell him the truth about my parentage until after Svanna informed him of it.'

'He had not asked to marry you before he knew?'

'No. We were as long as it lasted. The end came.'

Her mother fiddled again with the arm ring, pressing the stones in quick succession. This time, the clasp gave way. Maer eased off the ring. Her arm was sore and raw.

'Forgive me, Maer. I didn't mean to hurt you.'

Maer knew her mother was talking about the ring, but she chose to hear the deeper meaning in her mother's words. 'My choice. My life.'

Her mother nodded and indicated that Svanna should leave the room, telling her to find a fresh gown for Maer.

Maer crossed her arms and waited in the silence. 'What do you need to tell me?'

'Thorfi married me because he required me to help rule a divided country. The country remains divided. More than ever. He is a practical man,' her mother said in a flat voice. 'He buried his heart with his wife. I…well… I refused to be his concubine.'

'Yet, he has treated Karn terribly. He made him and his men wolf's heads.'

'He lost his temper with Karn. He wanted to shock him

into behaving. I had not understood Drengr's influence.' Her mother shook her head. 'I was indisposed, and it was too late. I've done what I could to make amends. I sent Karn to find Halfr.'

'Are you sure you haven't made matters worse?'

Her mother ducked her head. 'It doesn't matter what I think. It matters what you think. You said that Karn was principled and courageous, good qualities for becoming a king. A far better one than Jaarl Drengr. We will find a way to get the ring to Karn in time.'

Maer pressed her hands to her eyes. She wasn't ready for this.

'Mother! Inge—Maer!' Svanna burst back into the chamber, carrying a heavily embroidered dark blue gown. 'We need to move quickly.'

'Why? What is it?'

'Karn. He has arrived with what they are calling a ghost army, and there is a huge commotion with Drengr threatening. Rumours fly that Karn is saying there has been a huge lie. You need to come. Now. Before the entire country erupts into war.'

Maer started forward. 'Then, I shall go.'

Her mother caught her arm. 'No, not like that, Ingebord. That gown is practically rags. We must present you like the queen I know you could be.'

'Do we have the time?' Maer asked.

'We make the time,' her mother said.

'It is what we did when we knew you'd left,' Svanna said. 'Thorfi will expect more from the daughter of the great Astrid. We will have to confess, Mor, to stop a war. I see no other way.'

'There is always another way,' Maer said and rapidly

changed into the dark blue wool gown which flared slightly about her hips.

'Now you look like my daughter,' the queen exclaimed, pinning two box brooches on Maer. 'The colour brings out your eyes. Look in my mirror and see.'

From her mother's dark mirror, a face stared which she barely recognised. Was she Ingebord, Maer or a combination of the two? All she knew was that she had to save Karn.

'Lovely.'

'Then, we're ready,' Svanna said, linking her arm with Astrid's.

Maer spotted the trepidation in her mother's and Svanna's eyes. It was kind of Svanna to lend her a proper gown and for her mother to lend her jewellery. But she also knew she was about to ruin their world.

Her hand curled about Karn's pendant, trying to think of a plan but failing. Suddenly she had it. It was risky but doable. Maer arranged the pendant so it would be the first thing the king spied. 'The arm ring. I require the ring.'

Svanna's mouth dropped open. 'Are you going to wear it?'

Maer smiled. 'No, carry it. I've found a way to save us all.'

The hall teemed with men but not as many as the last time Karn had encountered his father. When the guards saw him and the band who followed, they fell back and allowed him to pass unmolested.

Karn kept his gaze fixed firmly ahead. He tried not to think about everything which could go wrong and instead concentrated on the prospect of keeping Maer safe and returning her to her home.

'I am surprised you returned so quickly, my son,' his father said from where he sat. He appeared to have aged thirty years in the weeks that Karn had been away. His eyes were sunken, and his nose more like an eagle's than ever.

'I discovered that I had unfinished business, Father.'

'With new followers and hopefully a better attitude. Are you going to do as I asked? This country needs a steady hand, Karn.'

'He whistled them there Gaels up from the mist, King Thorfi!' one of the Northmen shouted. 'He has Halfr's army with him.'

The colour drained from his father's cheeks. 'Since when did you start believing in skalds' tales?'

Drengr frowned from where he stood, looking more like an overfed seal than ever. A seal with reptilian eyes. A cold smile played on his lips. 'Lord Karn, an unexpected pleasure.'

The back of Karn's neck prickled. The man could not have intended for him to come here like this. 'Jaarl Drengr.'

Drengr stepped to one side. Next to him was the man who had killed Beorn, with a self-satisfied look on his face and a new gold chain about his neck.

'A magic whistle to explain why you do not require a bodyguard and no one attempted to claim the reward. Interesting, but we have other business, King Thorfi. More pressing and urgent business.'

Karn kept his face bland. The man wanted him to lose his temper. 'What could be more urgent or pressing than my reunion with my father?'

'The cold-blooded murder of Beorn the Crook-nose. I've a witness—'

'Are you certain that witness is trustworthy? He seems to break his oaths as easily as he makes them.'

His father raised a brow. 'You now possess actual magic instead of cheap conjuring tricks?'

'I leave magical powers to the gods and skalds.' Karn inclined his head. 'I had no wish to risk my men. These men from Islay are well-trained. No one attacked me because they understand that I love Agthir and my father.'

'Who trained the men?' Drengr asked.

Karn permitted a smile to cross his lips. 'Halfr Hammdrson. Beorn overestimated his own ability and paid the ultimate price for underestimating the strength of the opposition. He was always like that.'

'Beorn is dead? Who killed him? Jaarl Drengr says you killed him in an ungovernable rage.'

'The man who stands next to you lies because he administered the fatal blow in a heated battle.' Karn gestured to the Gaels. 'They are willing to testify.'

His father stroked his chin. 'Have you thought about your answer to my question?'

'My answer to which question?'

'Who will you take as a bride? You must marry, Karn, to ensure your temper remains steady. I will have my succession settled. I have chosen the bride.'

Karn laughed. 'Is that why you think I returned to do your bidding?'

'Could there be another reason?' Drengr cleared his throat. 'I must protest, King Thorfi. Your son is unsuited. His temper will have caused the battle.'

Karn furrowed his forehead. 'He came for my head.'

'My nephew was simply carrying out your orders, King Thorfi. He wanted to ensure that Karn knew that he would be welcomed back. Once again, it would appear your son acted rashly. He caused this battle with Beorn and Halfr. Just as he caused so many unnecessary battles in the past.' Drengr bowed. 'I look forward to saying more in court.'

'I was prepared to forgive you, Karn, but your temperament is proving grossly unsuited to being a king. You arrived here with an army to force your will,' his father said. 'You must pay Beorn's family a significant debt.'

'He lies. Drengr—'

Before Karn could answer, Maer strode in, with Ingebord and Astrid following in her wake. Maer had changed into a dark blue gown which emphasised her curves. She carried the arm ring on a pillow and, most surprisingly, the pendant he'd given her was clearly visible on her chest.

Karn cursed under his breath. Maer should be miles away from this place. He wanted to scream at the men staring open-mouthed at her that she was not a sweetmeat ripe for plucking.

'What have we here? A procession of women?' Drengr asked. 'I thought King Thorfi left orders that he was not to be disturbed. We are discussing an important matter.'

'Such orders never apply to me,' Queen Astrid said, with a slight tilt of her head.

In glancing between mother and daughter, he found similarities in the sweep of their neck, the tilt of their eyes and the shape of their hands. He did not dare look at his father who must see it as well. Astrid's deception was about to tumble to the ground, and he had no idea how he would keep Maer safe then.

'My wife does have the habit of sitting in on my councils,' Thorfi said with an indulgent smile. 'It is good to see that you finally feel well enough to be up, my dear, but this is men's business, and your daughter is unaccustomed to such things. Cold-blooded murder, my dear.'

Astrid gave a serene smile and continued as if his father hadn't spoken. 'Much better now. And I believe it is the business of the kingdom, husband.'

His father mumbled something indistinct.

'I thought we were deciding the fate of your son,' Drengr said. 'Will he obey his king and do as he is told, or not? Will he confess to what he has done?'

'As I sent him on that quest that we spoke about, Thorfi, and which you promised to keep a secret, shouldn't you have informed me of his return?' Queen Astrid said. 'I expected he would visit me first, but I was wrong. This is the first I've heard of him murdering Beorn. I'd understood something else happened.'

'I believe my emissary brought you something while I attended to another matter,' Karn said, seeking to take charge of the proceedings. He was through being a counter in Queen Astrid's game of tafl, and he certainly was not going to allow Maer to be used. Drengr would do all in his power to ensure that she did not emerge alive if he thought she was the true daughter of Agthir.

'Your emissary?'

'Maer of Islay.'

'King Thorfi,' Maer said in a ringing voice as she stepped forward. The torchlight caught the pendant and threw flashes of colour over his father's face. 'Before you continue with this, there is something you must know. Drengr is lying.'

'Lying? How so?'

'Beorn is dead, that is much true, but he was not killed in cold blood but rather in a battle. An axe felled him. But more than that, your son was not the cause of the battle, but Beorn had challenged the lord of the land rather than respecting the rules.'

'How do you know this?' his father asked, seemingly transfixed by the pendant.

'I watched from the roof of my adopted uncle's hall. It was not Karn who administered the fatal blow but one of

Beorn's own men. Karn attempted to save lives and indeed that man pledged his loyalty to Karn.'

'She lies!' the man shouted out.

'What reason does this woman have to lie?' Astrid asked.

'Ask her who her adopted uncle is!'

'My adopted uncle is Halfr Hammdrson. He has arranged for the return of the arm ring as he sustained injuries in the battle.'

'And you are?'

'I told you who she was—Maer of Islay,' Karn said, before Maer did something.

Maer smiled. 'It does your son credit that he seeks to defend me, don't you think? I'm Maer of Islay because how can I be anyone else?'

'What do you wear about your neck?'

'It is a pendant given to Karn's mother. She was fond of it, I believe, and thought it brought her luck in battle.'

'I know what it is. Did my son give it to you because of your prowess in battle?'

'Karn gave it to me after the battle. That much is true.' Maer stood with her head held high. 'When my adopted uncle Halfr Hammerson saw it, he knew that this arm ring should be returned so that it could be placed on the arm of Karn Thorfison, the next king of Agthir in due course.'

'And why did he think that?' Drengr asked with a sneer.

'Because my uncle saw the courage and deep principles of the woman he'd once loved in Karn. Karn's mother might have proclaimed the pendant lucky, but she made her own luck, no more so than when she chose Thorfi to be her husband.'

His father put a hand over his mouth. A tear ran down his cheek. 'Even after all these years, I miss her. She'd know what to do. She always proclaimed the best luck she ever had was when she called for help holding that pendant and I rescued her. It is why I won her.'

'I did not know that story,' Maer said. 'I'll treasure the pendant all the more.'

'Sentimental old fool,' Drengr roared, shaking his head. 'This woman is trying to play on your memories. Ignore her. Do the right thing for your kingdom. Sentence Karn to death.'

His father sat upright. 'You give bad counsel, Drengr. You attempted to alienate me from my son, my best beloved's only child. Take him away. See how he likes being made a *dauthamathr.*'

'I… I…did what is best for the kingdom,' Drengr stammered.

'What is the best for the kingdom, or what is best for you?' Thorfi roared. 'I remain the king here.'

Sweat poured from Drengr. 'Yes, yes, of course.'

Drengr fell on his knees and began to beg and plead.

At his father's gesture, two of his father's guards took Drengr's arms. Another took out a sword.

'No, let him face trial for his crimes, including encouraging Beorn the Crook-nose to think you wanted your son's head,' Maer shouted. 'Justice must be seen to be done.'

'You give wise counsel, my dear.' Karn's father sighed. 'You remind me so much of my late wife.'

'I wear her pendant with pride,' Maer said. 'Both to honour the woman and to honour the man who gave it to me.'

'You've made me recall the promise I gave my late wife as she lay dying that I would tell our son to only bestow that pendant on a woman who was worthy of holding his heart.' His father tucked his chin into his neck. 'I regret I didn't tell him so. I couldn't bear to look at it and instead gave it to the man I entrusted with Karn's education, telling him to give it to him when the time was right.'

'I like to think I am worthy of his regard,' Maer said.

'Is there any hope that my son might have grown in wisdom? Is he going to allow you to slip through his fingers?'

Maer merely smiled. 'You will have to ask him.'

'You see, husband, Karn is doing what you asked of him—finding a bride who can help him rule this country. It is time you declared the decree of wolf's head lifted from him and his followers.'

'If you will allow me a breath with Maer alone,' Karn said, grabbing her arm. 'I will not have Maer being forced to do anything.'

'What are you doing?' Maer asked, turning to him with the annoyance showing in her face. 'Everything is going well.'

'Trying to save your life. For once, do as I ask.'

Maer counted very slowly and allowed Karn to lead her away from the hall to a secluded spot. All she knew was that she'd just saved his life. And she'd done so without revealing her parentage. There was indeed no reason for King Thorfi to know. She was more than her heritage; she was her own person.

'What do you think you are playing at? Bringing that arm ring in like that?'

She blinked twice. Karn must see what she had done and why she had done it. 'Trying to save your misbegotten hide. You have the arm ring. You become king.'

'That is what you call it? I had a plan to save you.'

'It didn't seem that way to me. You were about to be tried for murder along with my uncle's men. Shall I go back inside and tell your father that I made a mistake?'

'No! I made one.' He held out his arms. 'You mean everything to me, Maer. I should have said this before. I don't care what your name is or where you were born. What I do care about is you and only you. I should never have left you. I do believe in you. And nobody but you could have done what you just did.'

'You care about me?' she asked, a glimmer of hope burgeoning inside her.

'I should never have walked away from you. I should never have left you to face your mother on your own. I'm so sorry that she didn't recognise you. Can you forgive me for not being there with you? It is her loss, not yours.'

She put a hand against his cheek. 'She declared herself my mother to me and was ready to ruin her entire life for me. I found another way. I was once that little girl who ran from Agthir, but I grew up into the woman I am today. I want to be Maer of Islay with all my heart.'

'Does that mean that you want to return to Islay?'

'Is there another offer?'

'Yes.' He pressed his forehead against hers. 'You and me. No one else. Together. Married.'

'Married?'

'Not because my father wants it or your mother or even Helga going on about how you might be pregnant, but because I want to spend the rest of my life with you.'

He put his hands on her shoulders. Her entire body tingled. 'You want to spend the rest of your life with me?'

'If you will have me.'

'If I will have you?'

He put two fingers over her mouth. 'I want you to know something before we go back in there, before you make the decision.'

'Which is?'

'You can leave and return to your home. I'm not sure I can. I must stay and fight.'

'Fight for what?'

'For the people of Agthir. Too often they have been ignored, and…'

'Not the sort of marriage proposal I've ever dreamt of accepting.' Her heart squeezed, She wanted more than a marriage founded on duty. If she accepted on those terms, there would always be a shadow between them. 'Ask me properly and for the right reasons, or not at all.'

He chewed the knuckle of his left hand, watching her with his brilliant eyes, eyes she knew she could study for a lifetime and still fail to name all the shades, and willed him to understand what she was asking for. 'I will abide by your choice whatever that choice is.'

'Will your father?'

'My father will come around, whatever you decide.' Karn ran his hands through his hair. 'He did not seek my death. Others did. I never needed to prove my worth to him. I needed to prove it to myself.'

She reached up and touched his mouth. 'Brave words.'

'I love you, Maer. My home is where you are and nowhere else.'

She froze. 'You love me?'

'You were the girl who carried Tippi in my first battle. I always wanted to know what happened to you. When I asked, I was told I was mistaken and that the only girl was Ingebord the Golden Hair.' He captured a lock of her hair. 'But your hair was never golden.'

She looked at him in astonishment. He'd remembered her. He'd looked for her. 'I kicked you in the shin.'

He gave one of his smiles, the sort which warmed her

down to her toes. 'I bet you fell a little in love with me that day.'

'You can be very arrogant. I rarely thought of you afterwards,' she said allowing her love to show on her face.

'Rarely?'

'Maybe on occasion,' she said, enjoying being able to tease him a little again, secure in the knowledge that he did love her.

'I know,' he said against her mouth. 'It is why you love me now.'

She pretended to think about it. 'You might have a point. We should marry and make our home together.'

His mouth lowered, and his tongue tangled with hers, showing her how much he did love her.

'Were you really trying to save my life?' he asked a little while later.

Maer laid her head against his chest. 'You should not throw it away for foolish things. I had everything under control until you decided to mess it all up.'

He pulled her close so that his mouth hovered over hers again. 'You are far from a foolish thing. You're the most important thing in my life.'

She put her hand against his cheek. 'I wish I could claim that I fell in love with you on the day we met all those years ago, but I can't. That was far too many years ago. But when I had to rescue you, I knew you weren't my enemy.'

'You did more than rescue me. You gave me a new life.'

She smoothed the hair back from his temple. 'I've no wish to keep any secrets from you.'

The doors to the feasting hall slammed open, and Thorfi staggered out, leaning heavily on her mother's arm.

'Are you two finished?' he growled. 'Or am I going to have to issue another decree?'

Karn tightened his grip on Maer's waist and took a deep breath. The anger which once would have been there had vanished. His father was being himself, and Karn refused to allow anything to intrude on his happiness. It was never his father's choice but his as to how he'd respond to him. Enemies could become friends, even when they were one's parent.

'We're just getting started, sir,' he called out.

Maer dug her elbow into his ribs. 'Karn!'

He dropped a kiss on Maer's forehead. 'Simply being honest, my dear. I want to spend the rest of my life with you.'

'Just as well I accepted your proposal with all my heart.' She smiled up at him. 'Because I want to spend the rest of my life with you as well.'

'Congratulate me, Father,' Karn said after he'd thoroughly kissed her. 'I've found the proper wife just as you required. The one who will suit not only Agthir but also me.'

'I do believe you're right, son. Who needs the daughter of Astrid when you have a woman like Maer of Islay, a woman Karn's late mother would have thoroughly approved of?'

Maer smiled up at him. 'Who indeed?'

Astrid cleared her throat. 'You know, Thorfi, I have always wanted another daughter, and how clever of Karn to provide me with precisely the sort that I have always longed for.'

Thorfi patted her hand. 'You and me both, my dear, you and me both.'

'Shall we tell him?' Karn murmured against Maer's ear.

Maer shook her head. 'Sometimes it is best to allow the past to stay in the past.'

He raised their joined hands and kissed them. 'I bow to your superior wisdom. Always.'

# *Epilogue*

*Eighteen months later*

Maer shaded her eyes and balanced her baby on her hip. She'd seen the sails from her doorway. Karn's ship had arrived back from Islay sooner than she expected. She hoped that it meant her mother and Svanna's stay in Islay had gone well, rather than some massive fight which necessitated her mother returning.

Before it had properly docked, Karn leapt off the boat, strode over to her and enveloped them both in an enormous hug.

'I do believe you may have missed me,' she said when she could catch her breath.

'I do believe I have, and I intend to show you precisely how much, later,' he rumbled in her ear. 'I made them go at double-quick time to get back to you and our little one.'

'How are my mother and sister? Are they enjoying their stay in Islay?' she asked. 'Or have they returned with you?'

'Returned? They enjoy being away from the sadness which was my father's funeral.'

Thorfi had seemed to get a fresh lease on life after the marriage but had sadly succumbed to a chest infection early in the year. Maer allowed her mother and Svanna to nurse him as she didn't want to intrude. However, on the last day when his breathing had become laboured, he demanded she attend him and insisted everyone, including her mother, clear the room.

When all had gone, he beckoned to her and, grabbing her hand, in a hoarse whisper asked if she would tell him the truth to one last question. *Was she Astrid's actual daughter?*

She tightened her fingers about his and told him the truth.

His lips curved upwards, and he thanked her for solving the mystery which had plagued him in recent months, but he was pleased Karn had chosen her for his wife because her character reminded him so much of Karn's late mother, a woman he hoped to meet again in Valhall.

They sat there for a long time while he whispered of Karn's mother and how pleased she would have been in her son. He thanked her for opening his eyes to Karn's true worth. She told him that she was grateful for his being Karn's father.

His voice trailed off, and his breathing altered again. She ran to get her mother, but by the time they returned, he'd gone.

Maer forced her mind back to the present. 'How long do they intend on staying on Islay?'

'Svanna wants to stay for a few more weeks. The island life suits her and has put roses back in her cheeks,' Karn said, taking baby Thorfi from her and putting him on his shoulders. 'Your mother and Halfr...'

'Are they back together, properly?'

Karn's eyes bulged. 'How did you know that they would want that after all this time?'

'The way he helped you by giving you that whistle,' Maer said with a smile. 'He wanted you to succeed and knew it would be a sign to my mother that he'd forgiven her. Does that mean she wishes to stay with him forever?'

'You are very clever, Maer. Yes, she does. They were walking around, holding hands and exchanging kisses. Your mother seemed far younger and softer. I am very happy for them. It also means that we can rule Agthir without her interference.'

'Their former relationship is why I suggested the journey to Islay. Two can play at match-matching, Karn.'

'I don't care who caused you to enter my life, but I'm very glad you are at my side, helping me. You are the person who makes my hall a home.'

Maer leant her head against his chest and looked about the busy harbour and market. Agthir was becoming prosperous once again under their rule, which gave her great pleasure, but what gave her the most satisfaction was having Karn's arm about her and knowing that they had both found their safe harbour with each other. 'I agree.'

* * * * *

*If you enjoyed this story, then you're going to love Michelle Styles's latest historical romances*

Tempted by Her Forbidden Warrior
A Viking Heir to Bind Them

*And why not pick up her Vows and Vikings miniseries*

A Deal with Her Rebel Viking
Betrothed to the Enemy Viking
To Wed a Viking Warrior